Praise fo

Thank You, Mr. Nixon

"A collection to treasure. . . . [Jen] creates a panoramic universe of deftly sketched tales both comic and tragic. Her prose sparkles with clarity and moves with deceptive simplicity toward profound conclusions."   —*The Boston Globe*

"A jewel box of creativity and a joy to uncover. . . . These stories offer valuable insight into our world, which feels increasingly divided in countless ways. Surely everyone—us and them, whoever they are—would benefit if together we read what Jen has to say."   —*Minneapolis Star Tribune*

"Witty, engaging and profound, the stories in Gish Jen's new collection beautifully illuminate the evolution of American-Chinese relationships over the past fifty years. An indispensable contemporary voice."
                              —Claire Messud, author of *The Burning Girl*

"One of our finest practitioners of the short story form. . . . Wry and wise, these bighearted stories of immigration, identity, and exile linger."   —*Esquire*

"Sometimes heartbreaking and often funny. . . . Jen captures the pull, mystery, and myriad contradictions of China as it marches through the last decades of the twentieth century and bursts into the twenty-first."   —*The Christian Science Monitor*

"Gish Jen's masterly short stories are as inimitable for their voice as they are for their substance. They speak, with brio and canny wit . . . yet stirring below this brightness are the dark currents of Chinese history. . . . If this suggests anything like political or polemical fiction, it is overridingly something else: Gish Jen's ironical and feelingful and remarkable art. Or call it an art beyond art. It is life itself."
—Cynthia Ozick, author of *Antiquities*

"Be prepared to be awed and enthralled by one of our best writers! Fiercely funny and unrelentingly honest, Gish Jen's new collection places a finger on the pulse of many lives caught between the indifferent movement of history and the profound desires of individuals." —Yiyun Li, author of *Must I Go*

"My kingdom for a writer as savvy, empathetic, and hilarious as Gish Jen. . . . A literary trapeze artist, [Jen] leaps and twirls from first person to second to third, weaving in emails and letters with brio. . . . The moral authority of leading authors, such as Jen, is essential, leading us forward as we plunge deeper in a darkening century." —Oprah Daily

"Fantastic. . . . An original, mind-blowing exploration of U.S.-China relations/dynamics. . . . The collection makes you laugh, gasp, wonder, and sometimes gives you pause. In those little moments when you pause to think, you are actually witnessing the astonishing transformations that have been reshaping the world and era we live in." —*The Millions*

"Humorous and touching, in these stories Gish Jen brings her wide cast of characters off the pages and into our lives."
—Nancy Pearl, host of *Book Lust with Nancy Pearl*

Gish Jen

Thank You, Mr. Nixon

Gish Jen is the author of one previous book of stories, five novels, and two works of nonfiction. Her honors include fellowships from the Guggenheim Foundation, the Radcliffe Institute for Advanced Study, and the Fulbright Foundation, as well as the Lannan Literary Award for fiction and the Mildred and Harold Strauss Living award from the American Academy of Arts and Letters. Her stories have been chosen for *The Best American Short Stories* five times, including *The Best American Short Stories of the Century*; she has also delivered the William E. Massey, Sr., Lectures in American Studies at Harvard University. She and her husband split their time between Cambridge, Massachusetts, and Vermont.

gishjen.com

Thank You, Mr. Nixon

Stories

GISH JEN

VINTAGE CONTEMPORARIES
VINTAGE BOOKS
A DIVISION OF PENGUIN RANDOM HOUSE LLC
NEW YORK

FIRST VINTAGE CONTEMPORARIES EDITION 2022

The Library of Congress has cataloged
the Knopf edition as follows:
Names: Jen, Gish, author.
Title: Thank you, Mr. Nixon : stories / Gish Jen.
Description: First edition. | New York : Alfred A. Knopf, 2022.
Identifiers: LCCN 2021027612 (print) | LCCN 2021027613 (ebook)
Subjects: LCGFT: Short stories.
Classification: LCC PS3560.E474 T47 2022 (print) |
LCC PS3560.E474 (ebook) | DDC 813/.54—dc23
LC record available at https://lccn.loc.gov/2021027612
LC ebook record available at https://lccn.loc.gov/2021027613

Vintage Contemporaries Trade Paperback ISBN: 978-0-593-31409-8
eBook ISBN: 978-0-593-31990-1

Book design by Soonyoung Kwon

vintagebooks.com

Printed in the United States of America
1st Printing

To the memory of my parents

千里之行，始于足下 (qiānlǐ zhī xíng, shǐyú zúxià).

A long journey begins with a step.

—CHINESE SAYING

Contents

Thank You, Mr. Nixon

Thank You, Mr. Nixon

Mr. Richard Nixon
Ninth Ring Road
Pit 1A

Dear Mr. Nixon,

I don't know if you will remember me, especially now that I am
in heaven and you are in hell. I was one of the little girls you
talked to when you came in 1972. Do you remember? Not the
one in the famous picture. I was the other one. We were in a
park in Hangzhou. That was your other stop besides Beijing and
Shanghai, a famous place with a beautiful lake called West Lake.
It was February, and you mostly had your hands in your pockets.
Maybe your fingers were cold. First you talked to the girl whose
mother was right behind her. Of course, she smiled just the way
she was supposed to, and someone took that picture. Then you
talked to a little boy who was dressed in a new coat but who was
actually supposed to be in the background; that's why he did not
know which hand to reach out when you wanted to shake hands.
Everyone laughed, but some people worried because they did not

think you would talk to the boy. That was not the plan. And I was very embarrassed, but you did not seem to notice, just as you did not seem surprised that it just so happened that the two girls you happened to run into in the park were wearing such beautiful coats—so new and perfect, kind of an orange-pink color. Nor were you surprised that, when you asked where my mother was, I said, In the city. Shouldn't you have wondered what I could mean, since we were in Hangzhou, and Hangzhou was a city? In fact, my mother was living in Shanghai then, because she had been assigned to a unit there. But probably you had no idea people were assigned anywhere. Anyway, my red scarf was a real red scarf; that really was what we wore if we were Little Red Guards, and I really was a Little Red Guard. But that was not my real coat. Actually, my mother had to piece it together out of two other coats. Because she sewed for a factory, though, it came out just as if it were made in a factory.

Really, the whole China you saw was a tailor-made China— a Potemkin China, you might say, not that anyone would have said that then. That is only how we talk in heaven, where we know all kinds of things. For example, we know that today there still are a lot of things you cannot say in China. But back then there were even more. And while today you have to guess what you can't say, back then they would just tell you. No one was allowed to shout *Down with the American imperialists* to your face. On the radio and on TV, too, the phrase *American imperialists* just suddenly disappeared, as if everyone forgot it all at once. Which no one thought was particularly strange. We all knew how to forget, after all. We were good at it—experts, you might say. And if there was a face we had mastered, it was a stone face, for things changed all the time. One day Comrade Lin Biao was a hero, for example. The next day we forgot he was ever there.

The streets were cleaned up before you came, with certain slogans removed and new ones put up. The shelves of the stores were filled, and people were made to stay at school and work late, so that the streets would not be so crowded. Did you notice how few people there were around? Maybe you thought that was normal. But it was not normal, just like the number of fish in West Lake was not normal. Did you think there were always so many beautiful carp, waiting to be fed? Those of us students who were supposed to be background students in the park were told what to understand. What if the American journalists asked things like *Do you have enough to eat and drink?* or *Do you like America?* our teacher asked us. *Do you understand them?* Of course, that was a stupid question because anyone who answered yes would not have been picked to be a background student to begin with. But no one said it was stupid. Instead we promised that even if the translator spoke perfect Mandarin, we would not understand him. We were not supposed to understand anything about a man going to the moon either, which was easy since most of us did not actually know the American imperialists had put a man on the moon until we were told we didn't know anything about it. As for whether we were supposed to volunteer, *We had gangs of Red Guards breaking into our homes and destroying everything,* much less, *They took people out into the yard and beat them to death,* or *The young people were sent down into the countryside to be reeducated but also just try to stop them, they were so out of control,* you may guess whether we were supposed to say these things or not.

No—we were smart. And having been told to be *neither humble nor arrogant, neither cold nor hot,* we were exactly that, though I was so happy in my new coat, it was hard not to be warm with happiness. Indeed, I thought it the most beautiful coat in the world until I saw your wife's red coat. Can I call her Pat, now that we are all dead? She did not wear her red coat to the park. That was a disappointment. At the park she wore a fur coat, maybe because it was so cold. But I saw the red coat later, and anyway we students all knew about the red coat. We had heard about the red coat. It was already a famous coat. Of course, we understood, too, very well, that we did not love it. Though China had become a sea of dark blue and gray and black, with just a little color allowed for us children, for everyone else a red coat was bourgeois, after all. It was antirevolutionary. It was corrupt and corrupting. Couldn't we feel its pull? That was because it was venal. Imperialist. American. Beautiful.

No, we did not love it. We did not think how suitable it was that a beautiful coat came from a country whose name in Chinese literally meant "beautiful." China might be *Zhongguo,* the Middle Country, but America was *Meiguo*—the Beautiful Country.

A beautiful country full of beautiful coats. What could that be but evil?

The history books say that China opened when you shook hands with Chairman Mao. But I think it began with that coat. Because if on the outside we were *neither humble nor arrogant, neither cold nor hot,* on the inside we were torn. We loved our country, but it was not red flags we wanted. It was red coats.

Thank you, Mr. Nixon, for bringing that coat.

Here in heaven, we know much more about your situation than we did back then. It is terrible that people in your country called you Tricky Dick. That is so much more personal than plain *capitalist running dog* or *petty bourgeois individualist.* And it is terrible that they made so much fun of you because of your sweat. Is that why you wore makeup when you were in China? Up here in heaven there is an American interpreter who says he accompanied you on your visit, and that he once saw a glob of pancake makeup hanging down from a hair in your nose. Of course, if American people did not like for their leaders to sweat so much, that is something Chinese people can understand. Really, it is just lucky that we are not as sweaty as you; also that we do not have hair in our noses. And maybe you knew that pictures were going to be taken of you all day, historic pictures, and maybe you did not want for your nose to shine for everyone to see forever. So you put on some makeup. From our point of view, that was okay. As for how upset the American people became when they found out not long after your visit that you had asked some people to break into a hotel room and steal some papers, that we did not understand. Certainly, it was not so good.

But from the Chinese point of view, it wasn't that bad. Think about how many people Chairman Mao killed, after all. Of course, between Vietnam and Cambodia, you had some blood under your fingernails, too. But Chairman Mao! Even here in heaven, no one can say how many people he killed, between his crazy ideas and his purges—whether it was 45 million or just 25 million. Scholars are still bashing clouds over this; maybe they just miss arguing. But let's just say that no one claims Mao killed, say, 4 or 5 million. Because we need to be careful: if the angels laugh too hard, they can fall off a cloud and crack a halo. Our sweet Chairman Mao was unfazed even by the thought of nuclear war. *If worst came to worst and half of mankind died,* he said, *the other half would remain while imperialism would be razed to the ground.* And then? *And then the whole world would become socialist,* he said. I guess he was what today we might call an out-of-the-box thinker. Of course, some people said he gave China back our pride, and that is true, too.

Anyway, you can see why I myself am not sure you should be in hell, much less in the ninth ring. And in the first pit! Didn't you lose your job when you were alive? Wasn't that punishment enough? And mister, but it scared the Russians, to see China and America make friends! That was something only a redbaiter like you could have pulled off.

My family did not have a TV, but there was one in the village leader's house. It was black and white, naturally, so we all knew

even before he set it up that we were not going to be able to see
Pat's red coat—or my pink coat, either, if the program included
Hangzhou and I was in the program. Still, he put the TV on a
beautiful lace doily on top of a piece of plastic on top of a wooden
table, and attached three extension cords one to the next so he
could make the TV work. Also, he hung my coat up on a chair
beside the TV, so we could all see what a beautiful color it was.
That village leader was actually a kind of artist. He could paint
anything and always encouraged me to paint, too, even if my
father did not like it. But, whatever. As there were no chairs, and
the ground was cold, we all squatted to watch the program.

From the beginning to the end, we watched. I was not in it.
Still, my father thanked the village leader with some cigarettes and
said that he would tell my mother how much the whole village
admired the coat. As for myself, I helped put the TV away and
never forgot the village leader's kindness. It was very sad when
he was criticized a year later. My father participated in the group
criticism and was angry that I refused. But I could not participate.
It was just lucky that when I pretended to be sick, people
pretended to believe me. My father gave my beautiful coat to the
new village leader's wife for her daughter, just to be sure.

For months after you went back to America, I drew pictures
of people in red coats. People I knew, people I didn't know; I even
drew animals in red coats. When people asked me about them, I
said they were Red Guards. But of course, the Red Guards wore
red armbands, not red coats; these were all ghosts of your wife,
Pat. My mother, who would have come back to live with us if the
new village leader hadn't blocked it, told me to stop. But one day
I saw her looking at her reflection in the window, and she had her
fingers in her hair. And now that she is here in heaven and can
have whatever hairstyle she likes, I see she is wearing it to look like
Pat's.

Back then, you know, I used to hum the American songs they

played during your visit. "The Star Spangled Banner." "Turkey in the Straw." "America the Beautiful." And I wasn't the only one. I had many friends who hummed the songs. We loved them all. But the song we loved most was "Home, Home on the Range." No one knew all the English words, but we understood that it was about home—we understood that "home, home" meant *jia, jia*. We understood its heart. Home was where my mother wanted to live again. Home was where I wanted her to be. And I guess you could say it was one more thing that confused us, that heart. How could this be an American imperialist song?

The more we thought about it, the more we felt you were the best enemy we had ever had, Mr. Nixon.

Maybe it is no surprise that when China opened its door to the West, my family jumped into the capitalist sea right away. My father kept his job in the No. 6 chemical factory for a while, but my mother retired immediately and moved back home, where we started a small coat business. As we did not yet dare design our own coats, I copied famous designs from abroad, starting with your wife's coat. Of course, we had to make the coats in dark blue and black and gray because those were the colors we had. Still, the design was beautiful, and my mother was good at sewing, and we soon realized that if we made the coats big enough for the foreign tourists who were starting to come to visit, we could sell them in the street markets. And sure enough, the foreigners liked them, especially if we tailored them to fit perfectly and added whatever pockets or plackets or cuffs the foreigners liked. We did this overnight, too, which impressed them. And then it turned out my mother's friends in Shanghai could sell coats in the street markets there, and quickly learned to do the same thing—to customize the coats overnight or even on the spot. And everyone was happy.

Our little company was successful. But after a while the foreigners began to bring our coats back to their countries to sell, and that made people dissatisfied. Because it turned out people in

America did not like coats that said "Made in China," for example. A nice man explained that to us, his name was Arnie Hsu—an Overseas Chinese man who had come to visit his teacher brother. Actually, his teacher brother had only just come with him to help him buy a coat. But he could also translate when Mr. Arnie said that the problem was something called "prejudice." If you took a coat and said it was "Made in Italy," he said, American people would like it very much. But not "China." They did not like "Made in China." Because of this "prejudice."

So why don't we change the label to say "Made in Italy"? my father said.

An excellent question, Mr. Arnie said. We couldn't because if the American authorities found out, they would be mad and confiscate everything. So that was a problem. However, after we talked a little more, he thought of a way around the problem. He said that he had heard some factories had closed down in Italy. So if we bought a factory and did just a few things there, like sew on the buttons or put in the lining, maybe we could label the coats "Made in Italy." And then American people would buy them.

Buy a factory? In China we did not have such ideas. How could we buy a factory? And where was Italy? And how could their factories be closed? Even Mr. Arnie's teacher brother was surprised by the idea.

But Mr. Arnie was smart. He said he knew some people who knew all about this kind of thing. A family by the name of Koo; they lived in Hong Kong. He said he would ask them.

And sure enough, he asked them, and it worked. In fact, Mr. Arnie made such a good arrangement, the Italian people were angry at us, even though actually, we were happy to employ them. And actually, we really liked them. We liked their food, never mind if they copied their noodles from Chinese people. We liked the way they thought about family. We liked that they called each other "Auntie" and "Uncle" just the way we did.

But they did not like us. They did not like the Chinese food trucks that appeared at our factories. They did not like the way we worked on Sundays. And on our side, though we liked them generally, we did not like their long lunches and their long vacations. We Chinese people did what it took to get the job done, after all. We felt they were more interested in play than in work. With the result that even now there are Italian people who will not hang out on the same cloud as us. If they see us sitting together, they will move away. And quietly, quietly, they will call us monkeys—very quietly, of course, because this is heaven and no one wants to be kicked out. We try to tell them, *We never meant to take over your factories.* And that is true. We cannot speak for the Chinese people who came after us. In fact, we do not even know them, a lot of them came from Wenzhou. But speaking for ourselves, we were just trying to solve a problem. If the American people had accepted coats that said "Made in China," we would probably never think to look at a map to find out where Italy was—that is the truth.

But it is also true that my father is not here with us now because he just wanted to sell as many coats as possible. No one wants to pay for coats made one at a time, he said. He believed that the right way to make a coat was to make all the sleeves at once, and then all the lapels. He believed that the right way to cut cloth was the way that left the least waste, not the way that made the coat fall this way or that. He said no one was ever going to cut a coat on the bias in any factory he owned, and that he had learned about the market from the new village leader's wife, who had a book about it. The difference between Chinese people and Italian people is that Italian people don't want to listen, he said. They don't want the world to change. But according to my father, the world had changed, like it or not. Price, he said, was king.

Maybe you can see how he ended up in hell with you, Mr. Nixon.

Up here in heaven, I do not have to do anything. But still, I like to draw coats. I guess that is just how we human beings are, we like to keep busy. I don't know why your wife, Pat, hasn't come to heaven. Maybe she is around here somewhere and I just haven't seen her. I will keep an eye out.

In the meantime, now that I have met some saints, I know that you are not one. Indeed, I realize you are nothing like a saint at all. At the same time, you brought so many coats into our lives! Red coats, gold coats, orange coats, plum coats. Short coats, long coats, belted coats, quilted coats. You brought fur-trimmed coats and leather-trimmed coats, double-breasted coats and single-breasted coats, zip-up coats, and three-in-one coats. You brought coats people can wear in the snow and coats people can wear in the pouring rain. Even now I change my coat every day, and while I do not always wear a red coat, I never wear a dark blue coat, or a gray coat, or a black coat. I wore enough of those down on earth. Also, I use my English name. Do you know what that is? Tricia.

This is a heaven I never could have imagined. And so I thank you, Mr. Nixon. It is true that if I look down at China now and see the lights and the malls, I can still hear what people used to say about the Western way of life—that it is venal, that it is imperialist, that it is bourgeois, that it is evil. You let a big genie out of a bottle—a gaudy, awful genie, some would say. Maybe it has ruined what was left of Chinese culture. People say that, and it is possible. Still, I am glad that you came. Coats, coats, coats, coats! I thank you with all my heart, Mr. Nixon, and am sorry for what happened to you. If you ever draw up a petition to be moved to a cooler pit, I will sign it.

Eternally yours,
Tricia Sang

It's the Great Wall!

It was the trip of a lifetime.

"It's like going to Narnia. Oz. The Shire. The moon," mused Gideon.

"It is not the moon," said Grace sternly. But she knew what he meant. China had been no-go for so long that it was difficult not to think of it as a movie backdrop for tragedy and perfidy but as a place about which enticing travel books were written. It gave you whiplash to go from famines and terror to *The top of everyone's must-see list is of course the Forbidden City!* and *Though the Great Wall can be seen from outer space, nothing compares to seeing it in person.* But the bamboo curtain had parted. Not all that wide, really, but wide enough for tour buses to get through.

"I don't do tours," Gideon went on, trimming his black beard over the bathroom sink. "Nor do I do tour buses." Gideon, in truth, barely did other tourists.

But China was China, meaning that you could go on a tour or you could stay home. And yes, this was how the government was going to keep an eye on you. As for whether the operative word was actually "spy"—yes again.

"You don't have to go," said Grace. "You can stay home and

take care of Amaryllis." Amaryllis was their four-year-old. And how much better his taking care of her would be, really, than leaving her with Gideon's parents. For Amaryllis was independent; Amaryllis ate well; Amaryllis was exceptionally mature for a four-year-old. And if Gideon went with Grace, they would only be gone for twelve days. But Amaryllis had a notable interest in body paint, with a secondary interest in walls—in transformational use of color generally—and Gideon's mother had just bought a white couch. As for what kind of grandmother bought a white couch, never mind. Gideon took the path of greatest complaint.

"I'm dying to go," he insisted.

"Everyone is going to be speaking Chinese," Grace warned; Gideon hated events where everyone was speaking Chinese. But Grace's mother had picked out an Overseas Chinese tour. Everyone would be speaking Chinese.

"You don't want me to come. You think I'll be intrusive and opinionated and talk too much," said Gideon.

"Don't be silly."

"What if we go on a regular tour? You know, not a bargain tour but a tour tour."

"This is what my mom picked."

Still Gideon pressed on. "Don't you mind being classified as a kind of Chinese?" he asked. "As if you're not a real American? Stand up for yourself! Have some self-respect! You're not an Overseas Chinese! Plus everything will be better, you know it. The rooms, the food, everything. And we can afford it. We'll treat your mom."

As for the small fact of Gideon's gallantry resting conveniently on the raise that she, Grace Chen de Castro, project manager of the month, had just earned, she decided not to mention it.

"This trip is about my mother," she said. "It's about her family, who I've never even met and who she hasn't seen for almost forty years. There may be watershed."

"Watershed" was what they called crying in front of Amaryllis sometimes, especially when it seemed to go on ad infinitum. As for the causes of the potential watershed in this case—well, might that be the Cultural Revolution and, before that, the 1949 Revolution? Might it be the scattering of the family for decades and the losing of everything they had, including, for some, limbs and minds and lives? Sometimes Grace thought her parents would not have divorced had her father's family not decamped for Taiwan where, yes, life had been a struggle but a struggle of a different order. It gave him a relative sanguinity about life—whereas back on the Mainland, her mother's father had not only been killed by Red Guards but thrown into a river and left to float out to sea.

"Exactly. It's about her. It's about her trauma," said Gideon—cleaning up after himself, for once, without being prompted. "Why should she be treated like a second-class citizen on top of everything else?"

He made his case directly to Opal of the Perfect Posture, as he called her, for whom the words "second class" were predictably decisive. There was nothing she hated more than to be looked down on. They would go on the regular American tour.

As there was no direct flight to Beijing, they stopped first in Hong Kong, where they rode a big tramway and drank mango milkshakes and ate at a floating restaurant. Gideon and Grace knew they shouldn't be shocked by the crowding and the stall shops, by the tiny fluorescent-lit apartments you could see into at night, by the laundry hanging everywhere. They knew what that said about how sheltered they were, how first world, how American. They knew that Hong Kong was a rich city by

Asian standards. But still—even as they marveled at its steep mountains plunging, gorgelike, to its deep-dredged harbor, even as they gaped at the big ships plowing right through its heart, even as they smiled and nodded at the night ferry, with its worn reversible benches and spunky back and forth—they were shocked.

At the train station the next day, they saw people carrying everything—from pigs to TVs to pallets of bricks—on bamboo poles set across their shoulders. It was a hundred degrees out; there were no trees. There were no bushes. The sun bore down like a giant hot press in some infernal factory. Meanwhile their train compartment featured fans and lace curtains and soothing Chinese Muzak. A potted plant sat on a window tabletop; its polished leaves shone. There were shiny wooden armrests, too.

"The seats swivel," marveled Gideon. Grace clasped his hand. At home they mostly forgot they were different races, but here it was hard to forget. Not that he was of the colonial class, quite the contrary—his family was Caribbean Sephardic Jewish with maybe some Moorish something, which was to say he was no Brit; his parents' synagogue had had sand floors to muffle the sounds of their worship. But he was white, with a dark beard and wild-man hair if he missed his haircut by even a week, while Grace was, like most of the people around them, a smooth human with smooth hair. She could go an extra six months between haircuts, no problem.

"We are an interracial couple," said Gideon wryly.

"We are," agreed Grace.

"Did you see people looking at your wedding ring?"

She had. "Checking to see if we're married."

"As if you could be a concubine."

"I think the present-day term is *mistress*."

"Isn't that a step down?"

"You're right. A concubine was at least for keeps."

They shook their heads even as they gazed at their hands in a way they never had before. How odd that that his forearm hair extended right over the top of his hands, in a kind of feral triangle. Her arms, in contrast, seemed at one with the armrests.

Once out of the city, though, they forgot about their differences all over again. The terraced mountains, after all, the rice paddies, the water buffaloes. The dirt roads and farmers and bicycles. Grace had never thought much about the word "timeless," but there could be no other word for this—for the orange-brown soil, for the milk-gold water, for the lychee and banana trees, for the bamboo-walled huts—all of them part and parcel of something so large and deep and slow that Grace and Gideon and Opal found themselves moved to an unaccustomed peace. When they did talk, it was about things they had never talked about in America—things like how Opal's father had often wished to be a boy with a flute. How he would have liked to play as he rode on a water buffalo's back, herding it in for the night. Instead he'd been the sort of finance whiz the Red Guards had targeted first thing. Opal's mother, too, had died without Opal ever seeing her again, but at least it had been of natural causes, and not until last year. And at least Opal's sisters had been able to cremate her.

"You know why no one eats water buffalo?" Opal asked now. "It is because the water buffalo works so hard. When it dies, people feel they should not eat it anymore."

"That's beautiful," said Grace.

"Hope we'll be treated with as much respect," said Gideon, adding, "I'll have to tell Amaryllis when she's older—to make sure no one eats us, that is. Maybe I'll put it in our will."

They were quiet again. It was only after a long while that Opal pointed out a metal something under a tree.

"The farmers like to make a big pot of tea, put there for anyone to drink," she said.

She explained, too, after another silence, about rice—about how because rice grows in water but weeds don't, the farmers can use paddy water to keep the weeds down, and about how here in the South, the farmers were able to grow two crops a year. This was the start of the summer crop. That's why there were farmers hunched over the mud in some paddies, transplanting seedlings. Other paddies stood empty, already planted and flooded. Populated with fish, too, Opal said—carp that would eat the insects in the water, grow as the rice grew, and be harvested alongside the rice in the fall.

"Great system," said Gideon.

"I didn't know you knew that," said Grace.

"A lot of things you don't know," said Opal.

Then everyone fell quiet again—fallen already, Grace thought, under the China spell.

The city broke it. At the Guangzhou train station, there were so many people pressing in to gawk at them, they had to walk single file, holding on to the backs of one another's shirts like Amaryllis's preschool on a field trip. The minivan toward which Grace, Gideon, and Opal were pointed was the first of the three white vans assigned to their group; they spotted it gratefully. Even in the van, though, they were thronged. Though minivans in general did not attract much attention, caravans of them apparently signaled foreigners; people hung from their balconies to get a glimpse of the Caucasians in their tour group—three of whom, their fellow tour members were all suddenly aware, had bright-colored hair. Tom and Tory were an enormous blond couple from Cincinnati, and their group also included a befreckled woman with a waist-long red braid. Attracting interest as well, although a bit less keen, was Gideon's beard.

"What are they yelling?" he asked.

" 'Foreigners,' " said Opal, drawing her pink-lipsticked mouth tight.

Grace had never thought her mother diplomatic. But while many people were not shouting, some looked as though they might well be spewing something like *foreign ghosts* or *capitalist running dogs.*

"Am I the only one who always thought the Chinese were quiet?" Enormous Tom—apparently a former football player—looked genuinely puzzled.

Meanwhile, the people yelled so loudly, Grace could hardly hear him.

In the minibus, the windows had been opened because the air conditioning barely worked and because the temperature seemed to be, as it had been in Hong Kong, a hundred degrees. But now the tour group closed the windows. The redhead—her name was Charlotte—twisted her hair into a bun as she leaned away from the window glass.

"I see I will need a hat," she said.

Her face was colorful, too—bright pink from the heat—and in her hair shone a forest-green barrette. She fanned herself with one of the paper fans they had been given and drank some of the soda. Though there had been enticing ices and hunks of watermelon for sale in the train station, they had each been presented with a bottle of Pearl River orange soda by the tour organizers. This was warm and sticky sweet, with some sort of brown-black sediment at the bottom.

"Probably the soda is expensive," sighed Opal.

"More suitable for guests, you mean," said Gideon.

"Yes." Opal gazed out the window.

They drank.

There were bicycles and carts everywhere as well as buses, trams, trucks, and what appeared to be old Russian cars. All honked incessantly. On the smaller streets, people squatted

outside their homes, chopping and smoking. They were surrounded by large shallow baskets of vegetables and what Opal
said were pigeons drying; above them, faded laundry hung
everywhere. At one corner, there was a crowd: a minivan like
theirs had, it seemed, clipped a bicyclist. Happily, the man was
okay, but—his bicycle having been one of the many they'd seen
heaped surreally high with goods, like something in a circus
act—there were now rattan chairs scattered everywhere. People
sat on these as if at a show, watching the driver and bicyclist
argue and shout. Of course, the tour group was itching to get
out and watch, too; they were dying to walk the streets and witness everything close up. But when, at a rest stop, they were
finally allowed to climb out, they were mobbed so aggressively
that even Gideon got back into the van as soon as he could. The
van driver slid the door shut with difficulty, elbowing the mob
back.

"I wish they wouldn't try and touch my beard," Gideon said
plaintively when the door was finally closed. "Because my beard
is on my face."

He made a funny look; Grace laughed.

"And goddamn, I'm hot."

Grace wiped his face and neck with a Wet-Nap and promised that when they got to Beijing, he could spend as much time
in the bath as he liked. (In Hong Kong they had identified cold
baths as the way to deal with the heat.) She fanned him, too,
as he leaned his head against the window; he had a monster
headache.

"Send me home. I am going to die here. I am," he moaned.
"I am never going to see Amaryllis again."

"Don't be silly. Of course, you're going to see her." Grace hit
him playfully with the fan.

"He is overheated," observed Opal laconically.

"He is," said Grace, opening the fan back up. She liked the

subtle snap each fold made as it opened; what a clever inven-
tion, the accordion-folded fan.

The van turned at last onto what seemed to be a kind of
highway. It was dusk.

The Beijing airstrip was made of squares of concrete, like an
oversize sidewalk. Grace could feel the *thump thump thump* of
its seams as they landed and taxied. The airport was underlit;
the hotel was underlit. This might be the full-price tour, but
even so the carpeting was thin. The furniture appeared to be not
only from before the Second World War but quite possibly from
before the First; there was no elevator. The beds were character
building. The mosquito netting was crucial.

"Is that a mosquito coil I see before me?" said Gideon.

He had revived.

It seemed blessedly cooler here than in Guangzhou, both
outside and in. Still, the woman stationed at the end of their
hallway, dressed in loose gray trousers and an untucked white
shirt—the apparent Mainland uniform—had trained an electric
fan directly on herself. She pinned them with an unflinching
look, as if practicing to be a security camera.

"What is the difference between a concierge and a hall monitor?" whispered Gideon.

"What."

"One tells you where you should go, and the other just
thinks it."

There were no locks on the doors.

Breakfast in the morning was rice gruel with pickled things
and peanuts plus a Western option, meaning hard-boiled or
scrambled eggs, and toast with jam. The foil-wrapped butter
pats were fanned out on a platter as if to display them. Overhead there were chandeliers, but by their low-wattage light,

the carefully set-out coffee cups seemed half full of something more like bouillon than coffee. Happily, Grace had packed some instant coffee powder. She was outdone, though, by Tom and Tory, the blond Cincinnatians, who—owners of a coffee shop back home—had brought some ground coffee beans and a French press.

"Please have some." Tom generously offered "a cuppa" for anyone who'd like it, holding out what appeared to be a tiny cup in his enormous hand. When no one accepted, he looked a bit crestfallen until Gideon changed his mind.

"Thanks. I bet it'll help with the jet lag," he said.

Grace had some, too. "Better than the instant," she conceded. "Thanks." She offered Tom and Tory some Pepto Bismol tablets in exchange—which might not actually head off traveler's stomach, she said, but which many people did say were worth a try, even if they sometimes turned your tongue black.

"No thanks," said Tory.

With most of their fellow tourists in couples, Grace and Gideon were glad to see several other singles like Opal, although the women (they were all women) mostly seemed travel veterans of a certain type: pointedly participatory people who knew how to define themselves before they were defined.

"You brought your mother? That is so sweet." Charlotte the redhead, for example, their favorite already, was a musician from Boston who had come as a birthday present to herself. She was less pink today and more freckled; her hair was again in a bun. She carried a cloth bag embroidered with instruments. "I wish I'd done more of that when I could," she said.

Her roommate Diane, whom she'd only just met, was a retired jeweler. "No sooner did I decide to see the world when just like that! This whole part opened up," she exulted. Her hair was platinum; she wore diamond earrings and an enormous sapphire ring. "You should see the Taj Mahal. And the Pyramids! But this—this is going to be fabulous. I cannot wait to see the Great Wall."

Grace exchanged a quick glance with Gideon, who nodded his agreement. It was good they had paid extra for Opal to have a single.

Meanwhile Tory shared how she always had a thing for China.

"The emperors, the palaces, the eunuchs—I don't know. I took a course in college, and I was what you call hooked," she said. "It was the pictures. I'd never seen anything like them." A striking woman in a peach polo shirt and bright blue mascara, she opened her eyes wide as if recalling her moment of revelation. "And then, I mean, that picture of the Nixons."

"The one in *Life* magazine," supplied Tom. "At the Great Wall." He was wearing the same polo shirt as his wife, only in a much larger size and in dark brown; it was as if her shirt was from the spring line of some manufacturer, and his from the fall.

"We had to come after that. We were what you call compelled," said Tory.

"And now it's like her dream come true, only hotter," said Tom. Having managed to snag two fans, he was fanning himself with both hands as he shook his head. His huge neck rose from his collar like a tree trunk from a ring of leaf mold.

Most people wore vacation shirts with some form of khaki—shorts, skirts, skorts. Having been advised by the pretrip literature to dress conservatively, Opal wore a beige cotton piqué dress; Grace, a denim skirt and a short-sleeve, button-down blouse. She tried not to ask Gideon why he was wearing a Grateful Dead T-shirt and cut-offs. The real question, after all, was, Should she have let him talk her mother out of the Overseas Chinese tour? For she couldn't help but ask herself that as Opal gamely fielded question after question over breakfast. Yes, people might like the rice gruel if they tried it. No, they didn't call it rice gruel in Chinese. Yes, different Chinese people spoke different dialects. Yes, she spoke Mandarin as well as Shanghainese. No, you couldn't understand the other dialects necessarily. Yes, chopsticks took some getting used to. Though, yes, millions of children did use them, and yes, she could teach them to use chopsticks, too. No, she didn't know why they were given Kleenex instead of napkins. But yes, she was born in China, where yes, she still had family, some of whom, yes, were "struggled against," as they said, during the Cultural Revolution. She did not mention her father.

"What does that mean, 'struggled against'?" Formidable man though he was, Tom tilted his face up like a kitten.

"It meant you were a class enemy," supplied a man with tortoiseshell glasses—a professor, Grace guessed from his amiably authoritative air. Balding though he was, he ran his hand through what was left of his hair as if to reassure himself it was still there. "It meant you represented the Four Olds—Old Customs, Old Culture, Old Habits, and Old Ideas—which Mao had licensed the Red Guards to eliminate. Just about anyone who was not a peasant or a factory worker could be tarred and dragged through the streets; you could have signs hung on you and things thrown at you. You could be frog-marched onto a stage so that everyone you knew could denounce you. You could be gagged, beaten, and tortured. Many people threw themselves off buildings to escape; others were pushed." He paused.

"Interesting," said Diane.

The professor fanned himself and went on. "It ended a few years ago, thankfully. But the goal of the Red Guards was, like the goal of Communism more generally, to destroy traditional culture, and sure enough traditional culture seems to have been by and large destroyed. What's left of it is in Hong Kong and

Taiwan, although it's been Anglicized in the former and Nipponized in the latter."

"True," said Opal. Grace would have sworn Opal did not know what "Nipponized" meant. Still, she carried on—not wanting to be worked over by the table but not wanting to cede the role of China expert to a white man either, Grace guessed. "The Japanese ruled Taiwan for fifty years," she said. "And the British have controlled Hong Kong over three times as long."

"Your English is so good," said someone.

"I've lived in America for almost forty years," said Opal.

"So you're fluent," said someone else.

"I still make some mistakes." Opal smiled graciously.

"And your daughter is fluent, too," said yet another person.

"We practice every day," Opal said evenly.

By this point Gideon was openly guffawing; the professor looked down into this food. Grace watched her mother, who showed nothing.

The tour director was a rosy-cheeked young woman with pigtails, black glasses, and the poignantly stoical look of a young person who had been ordered to stand still; she could have been a trombonist in a military youth band. Her name, she announced unsmilingly, was Comrade something. Sum, maybe? She told them again. Then she told them a third time.

"Ah! Comrade Sun," said the professor.

"Comrade Sun!" repeated others. "Her name is Comrade Sun!"

"That's what they call each other, 'Comrade,'" supplied someone.

"Should we call each other 'Comrade,' too?" asked someone else.

It soon became clear that though Comrade Sun theoretically spoke English, she did not speak it clearly enough to be understood. Who first suggested that Opal translate in that case? It was hard to say. The idea, though, was quickly taken up.

"Her English is so good! You should hear her!"

"She's fluent! Completely fluent!"

"She should translate! She should translate!"

Comrade Sun did not acknowledge these comments. However, she looked as if she'd just flunked an exam. The tour members listened extra carefully to her next few statements, as if wanting to give her a second chance. Had Comrade Sun perhaps just gotten off to a rough start?

She had not.

For a moment, the group was all as frozen as she. When finally the professor said, "This is ridiculous," and even the sweetest of the women tour members began to frown, however, Opal stood, smoothed her dress, and, moving to the front of the room, began translating.

"Comrade Sun says we will have breakfast every day at seven and should be on the bus at the front of the hotel at eight sharp," she said crisply.

The relief was palpable.

"Thank god, there's at least one Chinese who speaks English!" said someone.

Comrade Sun adjusted her glasses. And later, as they filed out of the dining room, she touched Opal's arm. Was that a form of thanks? Who knew? Opal gave a quick nod in response as if to say, *I knew something had to happen but that you couldn't ask for help.* Would she have also added if she could have, *And I knew I had no choice?* It wasn't clear. When they boarded the bus, though, Opal sat up front so everyone could see and hear her. Comrade Sun sat facing her on a jump seat, splaying her legs like a man.

. . .

People might be mostly interested in imperial China, but the first stop was a commune.

"Vegetables before dessert," said Gideon.

"Why are we headed east? I thought we were going to the Evergreen People's Commune," said the professor. "The one Pat Nixon went to. That's what's on the schedule."

But they were not going there. As for why, when Opal conveyed the professor's question, Comrade Sun gazed out the windshield as if watching for approaching bugs. There was nothing to translate.

The commune tour guide, Comrade Tu—a no-nonsense man missing an index finger—kept Opal busier.

"He says there are approximately 170,000 households in communes nationwide, with 2,000 to 20,000 households in each commune, or 10,000 to 80,000 people." Opal stood at the front of a conference room, beside Comrade Tu. A blackboard behind them read WELLCOME! in blue chalk.

"Does that mean there are a million people in communes?" asked the professor.

"I don't know. You have to multiply yourself. Comrade Tu says each commune is organized into ten to thirty—"

"Bli-gaade," said Comrade Tu.

And to help her out, Comrade Sun echoed, "Bli-gaade."

"I think they are saying *brigade*," said the professor.

"Brigade," said Opal then. "Ten to thirty brigades."

Was a brigade a military unit? Never mind. The two comrades and Opal labored on, informing them all that each brigade had 1,000 to 2,000 people, which was 200 to 400 households, and that each brigade was 10 to 20 teams, with each team made up of 100 to 200 people, or 20 to 40 households.

"Really they should just call it a village," said the professor.

Comrade Tu replied, through Opal, that villages were feudal. As for whether Opal had gotten that word right—there were several back-and-forths about it—and what "feudal" meant exactly, who knew. Opal went on to struggle through terms like "bumper crop," "intensive crop management," "wheat scientists," "two-wheel tractors," and "intercropping." People fanned themselves hard and looked distinctly relieved when, finally finished with the introduction, they were given wide-brimmed straw hats in preparation for touring the fields. As the pre-trip checklist had included a checkbox for headgear, the tour members had come equipped with tennis visors, baseball hats, bucket hats, and sun hats, all of which they now obligingly exchanged for the straw hats. And so Opal did as well, though she had never worn such a thing in her life.

"Straw hats are for peasants," she said, sitting on the edge of her bed later that night. Her back ramrod straight as always, she spoke very quietly, in case the hall monitor was listening. "We go everywhere by car. No one have to wear anything." Had someone given Opal such a hat in her youth, it seemed, the assistant chauffeur would have carried it for her. Or else perhaps her maid or assistant maid.

But now, at the commune, awkwardly gripping her folded fan in three fingers of her right hand, she used her other two fingers to tie the hat's cotton cord under her chin.

The group admired the acres and acres of wheat and vegetables and ducks and pigs. They were impressed by the millions of bugs being raised to eat aphids, and thrilled to hear what an extensive and effective irrigation system the Chinese had in place. And the pig management! Raised on the by-products of a milk-drying plant and a grain-milling facility, the pigs supplied both meat to the farmers and manure fertilizer for the crops. Comrade Tu was at pains to explain how the commune used scientific farming methods to supplement traditional farming ways. But as he delved into the details, the tour group's attention wandered away from the advances in hybridization and chemical fertilizers, over to the many Chinese students out in the field. Standing around adjusting their hats, too, they looked about as useful as the tour group.

"Are they like the intellectuals sent down to the countryside to learn how the proletariat lived?" asked the professor. "The ones forced to do manual labor, wasting their lives and education?"

Opal translated.

The answer came back: "Comrade Tu says yes and no."

"Ah. So Americans are not the only people who prevaricate."

Opal turned back toward the guides at that—refusing to translate this comment out of nicety, it seemed.

Or was it something else?

"The first question was bad enough," Grace explained to Gideon later on, in their room. "My mom says Comrade Sun writes a report every night. And since my mom is doing the translating, she knows she'll be in it."

"And let me guess. She does not want a bad report."

"Yes."

"Because she wants to see her family."

"Yes."

"She doesn't want anything to go wrong."

Grace nodded.

The commune kindergarten visit, meanwhile, was charming. ("Don't you just wish you could take one of them home," said someone. "I mean, they are what you call adorable.") And the peeks into the commune's factories and repair shops, too, were impressive and fascinating. In a health clinic, they received an acupuncture demonstration just like the one that had famously made Pat Nixon cover her eyes. Then came a tour of a farmer's house. Was this a typical house? They guessed not.

Yet all agreed it was lovely—a simple, neat, freestanding hut. Though there was only one bedroom for a family of four, there seemed to be extra sleeping space in the living room—or so they gathered from a kind of bamboo stretcher they saw leaning against a wall. The hut's owner confirmed through Opal that the stretcher could be easily suspended across two benches. She also explained that though she had relatives nearby, they did not eat together.

"So where do they eat?" asked Gideon.

Through Opal the woman said, "In a dining hall with other comrades."

"Does that mean one hundred percent of Chinese families got split up? Even if you didn't go to the U.S. and stayed in China, your family got split up anyway?" Gideon asked.

Opal ignored him.

"And was that a public bathroom we saw?" asked the professor.

It was. The woman, though, seemed more interested in talking about how her family had a small plot of land on which they could grow their own vegetables. She described the cabbage they grew, the green onions, the carrots and turnips. She hoped to have chickens or a pig someday.

"From this natural enthusiasm for ownership, you realize, grows capitalism," remarked the professor.

Opal did not translate that, either.

It was all propaganda, but at least it was interesting propaganda, Gideon said later in their room. And weirdly private propaganda: at one point, when Gideon tried to take a picture, Comrade Sun put her hand over his lens.

"What kind of propaganda is kept secret?" he asked, sitting with Grace and Opal.

"Maybe she's just been told not to let us take pictures of anything," guessed Grace.

"Quite possibly," said Opal.

But at the time, she said nothing as Gideon put his camera away. Here it was, halfway through the first day of the tour, and already, Grace could see, her mother was exhausted.

Comrade Sun ate lunch separately from them, behind a bamboo screen. Though the official tour lunch had five courses, she and another tour guide shared just one. Still, she looked happy. Gone was her military parade demeanor; she and the other guide giggled and whispered like schoolgirls. Meanwhile on the other side of the dining room, another tour group was also having lunch—an Overseas Chinese tour group, it seemed. There was a lot of Chinese being spoken, just as Grace had predicted, although enough English that she wondered not only if Opal would be having more fun with that group than theirs, but if she and Gideon would, too. Was there even a table full of people their age? One of them, spotting her, crossed the room.

"Grace? Is that you? Didn't you go to Mamaroneck High?"

"David!" The last time she saw him he had just gotten a dog-walking job and was getting pulled every which way by a labradoodle. They had not really been friends. In fact, though he lived in the next town, they had studiously ignored each other, too embarrassed to acknowledge that being the only Asian American in their grade in their respective towns was any kind of link. But now she was delighted to exchange a few words with him. It was like finding a bit of sea glass in your pocket from a long-ago walk on a beach—an unexpected bit of another reality. They talked about stupid things—what they would do for a Coke float. How he'd brilliantly brought a Walkman. Whether anyone in China had heard of *Star Trek,* or even of movie theaters.

Back at their group, meanwhile, Tory was instructing Tom, "Don't ask her anything else." She stilled his fan with her hand to get his attention. "He got hit in the head a few too many times," she told Gideon as she did this. "Now get him near a fact, and he's like a dog after a bone. He can't stop himself."

Still Tom resumed both his fanning and questioning. "Why didn't we see any rice paddies on the commune?"

Opal answered that rice was grown in the South, and that the North grew wheat.

"These are *mantou*," she explained, holding up one of the wheat buns that had come with lunch. "*Mantou* is what the northerners eat. Also noodles."

Tom frowned. "So am I the only one who thought the Chinese ate rice?"

"Tom. Honey," said Tory.

But Gideon concurred. "I always thought the Chinese ate rice, too," he said. Even as Grace elbowed him, he went on, "I mean, have you ever gone in a Chinese restaurant and been given a wheat bun?"

"The Chinese in the South eat rice," said Opal firmly. "In the North, maybe they import rice from the South. But mostly they grow wheat. And because of that they give us *mantou* for lunch today."

"Does they mean that they have a South like we have a South?" asked Tom.

"South means south of the Yangtze River," supplied the professor. "The Yangtze is their Mason-Dixon line."

"Ah," said Tom. "I have another question."

"Well, don't ask," said Tory.

Charlotte agreed gently. "I think we should let poor Opal have some lunch."

Of course, Grace realized, her mother was not going to eat much anyway; the food was too greasy for all of them but especially for her. Even if she took Pepto Bismol as a prophylactic, it was bound to upset her stomach. She was sensitive that way.

Still, Opal gamely lifted some food to her lips now, and blew on it, and took a small bite.

Despite their collective jet lag, the group was impressed by their afternoon excursion to an ivory-carving factory. How could anyone carve ten concentric balls out of a single piece of ivory, one ball inside another and all of them free moving, much less forty-five balls? And yet, hunched over his tools in a concrete room with poor light, a worker had done just that. He reported, with Opal's help, that it had taken him seven months—not smiling as he said this, though he did smile when she translated his words, as if pleased and astonished to hear them in English.

"There's something so extreme about it," said Charlotte as they left. "It's like all that talk about killing aphids at the commune. And, I don't know. I've heard Chinese musicians can be kind of extreme, too."

The professor looked consternated as well. "I thought the Chinese believed in moderation. Isn't that what Confucius taught?"

"He did," said Opal. "But this is a poor country. People have to eke everything they can out of whatever they have."

"You mean, whether it is a block of ivory or their capacity for practice?" said Charlotte.

"Yes."

"So they preach moderation when in fact they are completely and utterly immoderate?" asked the professor.

"The way that Americans preach justice?" said Opal lightly; she turned away.

"Touché," said Gideon.

But Opal turned her back on him, too. She had had enough of everyone, it seemed.

It was a long afternoon.

Later, though, from the safety of their hotel balcony, Grace and Gideon and Opal were at least able to witness their first rush hour, with its broad river of bicyclists, without being mobbed.

"This has got to be the most physically fit population on earth," Gideon said, and Grace agreed. The grace with which even the elderly swung up onto their seats, their legs clearing their back wheels with ease! And yet more impressive was a certain dancelike synchrony. There was no choreography, of course; nor was there a ballet master. Still, people biked as if there were—they flowed. It was a beautiful thing, Grace said, evocative of the peace of the countryside.

But Opal had a different reaction.

"When I grow up, China did not have so many bicycles," she complained.

On the corner by their hotel there were three old men with birdcages. The bamboo cages hung up in a tree; the old men sat below them in undershirts, fanning themselves and chatting. Now, *that* she recognized, Opal said, pointing down at them with her own fan. That was China. This bicycling China was— what? A usurper. A fake. She had never been on a bike, she claimed. In fact, one of the reasons she and Grace's father had gotten divorced was that he had fallen so hard for the American fitness craze. All he had wanted was to lift dumbbells, she said. Then, folding her fan, she stood and left. Not in a huff, exactly, but with her lips drawn in something very like disgust.

"The translating," Grace said. "The translating is getting to her."

"It would drive me crazy, too," said Gideon.

"And the jet lag. I'm going to take a nap."

"Me, too," he said. But as Grace went after her mother, he stayed watching the bicyclists from the balcony. He leaned on his elbows; he got out his camera and took pictures.

.   .   .

"How do you think Amaryllis is doing?" wondered Grace.

This was the first time Gideon and Grace had been away from their child since she was born. She was old enough and hadn't even cried when they said goodbye, but still they worried.

"Let's call her tonight," said Gideon.

"Great idea."

They had told his parents that they probably couldn't call, that they had heard it was expensive and complicated and often plain impossible. And that, it seemed, was right. Sometimes you could call from a hotel, but more often you had to go to a post office and wait on a line, and then you might or might not get through. Opal thought they were crazy to try, and sure enough, it was three hours before they heard a ringtone, even with her help. But finally, astonishingly, there was the click of the phone being picked up and the same hello Gideon's mother would have given a pollster. Then she exclaimed, "Gideon? Grace? Is that you? Are you in China? Oh, Dad is going to be so upset he missed you!" She tried to get off the phone right away ("This must be so expensive!") but quickly reported that all was well, though did Amaryllis really normally have chocolate syrup on her hot dogs, as she claimed?

"No!" they shouted. And then, "Amaryllis! It's Mom and Dad!"

"Hi," she said. The connection was terrible; they could barely hear her, especially as, both trying to listen at the same time, Grace and Gideon had to hold the handset midway between their ears.

"We miss you!" they said.

"Are you in China?"

"Yes!"

Amaryllis didn't say anything; they were afraid she had hung up.

"Do you know where China is?" asked Grace.

"You have to take an airplane."

"Exactly!" said Gideon. "We're on the other side of the world! Is it morning where you are?"

"Yes."

"Here it is night!"

Silence.

"Are you eating your vegetables?" asked Grace.

"No."

"Are you listening to your grandma?"

"No."

"Did you tell her you're allowed to put chocolate syrup on your hot dogs?"

Silence. Then, "No."

"I think yes. And did you put an X on the calendar?" They had made a special calendar, so she could understand how long they'd be gone. When she had X'ed out all the squares, they told her, they would come home.

"Yes," she said.

"Good!"

"I put an X on every square," she said. "Now you can come home." Then there was watershed. "I want you to come home!" she bawled. "I want you to come home! And I mean now! Now! I mean now!"

Grace and Gideon tried not to think how much it was costing to calm her down. But when finally they got off the phone, Grace cried, too—cried and cried, she wasn't sure why. Back in their room, she took a cold bath, thinking that might help, and it did. But when she dried off, she was still not herself.

"Think how many times your mother must have wanted to go home," said Gideon sympathetically. "Is that it?"

"Maybe."

"It must have been hard," he pressed.

And suddenly she remembered why she had married him—all that keeping at things, all that getting to the bottom of things. All that insistence on finding the words for things.

"I guess I am," she said, after a moment. "I guess I am thinking about it."

"Your mother's mother must have really missed her."

"It must have been terrible never to see her again as long as she lived. To wonder how she turned out but not to really know."

"And to never get to meet her husband or children."

"All of whom probably spoke English, she must have realized."

"To miss all of it."

"And not to have this daughter there for her old age, either."

"And for her daughter, too—to have no mother."

"To be missing a limb, in a way."

"To be missing more than a limb."

"It must have been hard."

They watched the fan turn this way and then, after a pause, back. The mosquito coil flared, then died, then flared again as they sprinkled each other with talcum powder, which really did help with the stickiness even if it clumped up. Then they lay awake in the dark and listened to the Chinese street noise. Their bodies were still on American time—on Amaryllis time, as Grace thought of it. Amaryllis would just be waking up now—untwisting her pajama top and kicking her covers to the floor.

The next day was the Forbidden City. Those red walls! Those golden roofs! That white marble axis! The parade of gargantuan pavilions was staggering. And the layout—this had to be the largest rectangle on earth. One hundred eighty acres. Nine hundred eighty buildings. The scale of it was hard to comprehend. Of course, it took a million workers to build. And even so—how had the Chinese gotten it done in fourteen years?

Gideon winked. "They must have had a project manager like you."

Grace laughed.

So overwhelming were the sights that the tour group had a day off from being gawked at. People did point and stare, but by and large they were distracted by the vast stone courtyards and commanding stone lions and enormous bronze cauldrons. And for Opal, too, it was a day off. As everyone could understand the local guide's English, it was not Opal but the arithmeticians in the group who were kept busy. If the perimeter walls were 7.9 meters high, how high was that in feet? And if they were even wider at the base than they were at the top—8.62 meters— what was that? And if the moats were 52 meters wide—?

Where had their guide gotten her British accent? Never mind. She recited, "The Forbidden City was built in 1420, during the Ming Dynasty. It has been the home for twenty-four emperors. Because that was the feudal time, the common man was not allowed to come in. That is why it is called the Forbidden City. In feudal times, people say it has 9,999.5 rooms—just one-half room less than the Jade Emperor's palace in heaven. But more recently modern science found out it actually has but 8,707 rooms."

"Wow. How would they have ever figured out a thing like that without modern science?" said Gideon.

"It has four gates, the main entrance is called the Meridian Gate. The Meridian Gate has five holes."

" 'Holes'?" said Gideon.

"I think she means openings," said Grace.

"Behind the Meridian Gate lie five marble arch bridges which are leading to the Gate of Supreme Harmony. The Meridian Gate was the place for the emperor to issue the imperial edict. Here he granted spring pancake at the beginning of spring. He also granted bean paste cake on Dragon Boat Festival, and rice cake with bean paste on Double Ninth Day."

"Food, food, food," said Gideon.

"In Ming Dynasty, if the minister had violated the dignity of the imperial family, he would suffer the punishment of spanking buttocks in front of the Meridian Gate. Initially this punishment was quite symbolic. However, it was developed to beat someone to death or, as the saying said, 'Push out to the Meridian Gate to be beheaded.' Today, thanks to our late great leader, Chairman Mao, this backward practice has been discontinued."

"Well, whew, though wasn't your grandfather effectively killed by Mao?" said Gideon.

The group toured the Hall of Supreme Harmony, the Hall of Central Harmony, the Hall of Preserved Harmony, the Palace of Heavenly Purity, the Hall of Celestial and Terrestrial Union, and the Palace of Earthly Tranquility.

"Power, straight up," said Gideon.

And indeed, the tour guide seemed at once proud of and disgusted by the sights. *Feudal, backward, proletariat,* she said. *Landlords, oppression, revolution.* And *Liberation, Liberation, Liberation,* especially *after Liberation.* But shouldn't the phrase be "after *the* Liberation"? Grace thought.

Opal, meanwhile, listened intently to everything, her guidebook in her hand. Stopping here and there to examine something more closely, she seemed distinctly happy not to have to stick right by Comrade Sun's side. Nor did she seem particularly close to Comrade Sun in the afternoon, when they toured the Summer Palace, with its glorious classical gardens and beautiful lake. Like everyone else, she enjoyed the two boats on the itinerary—one a dinghy in which they could row themselves around, and the other the palatial marble pleasure boat that the

Empress Dowager built, people said, with funds earmarked for a navy—one of the disastrous decisions that led to China's century of humiliation. But when Grace got out a notebook to take notes, and Comrade Sun started to stop her, Opal looked over.

"What are you writing?" said Comrade Sun.

"Nothing," said Grace.

"Put it away."

"Why should she?" said Gideon.

"She'll put it away," said Opal, patting Comrade Sun on the arm. "Don't worry." She smiled.

And at that, Comrade Sun hesitated but then turned away so calmly that Grace asked her mother about it that night.

"Are you friends with Comrade Sun?" she asked.

"Shh." Opal nodded toward the hallway.

"I'm being quiet," said Grace.

"Not quiet enough."

Gideon opened the door, leaned out theatrically, and gave them a thumbs-up.

"Are you some kind of friends?" asked Grace again.

"We are not friends."

"Then how come she just turned the other way when you said that about my notebook?"

"Because that is how Chinese people behave."

"What do you mean?"

"We have some *guanxi*, that's all," said Opal. "Some relationship."

"You mean you scratched her back, so she'll scratch yours," inserted Gideon.

"No," said Opal. "It is more, I see she is having some trouble and try to help, and in her heart she appreciates that." She paused. "This is Comrade Sun's first tour. If people complain, she will have a lot of trouble. But actually, she did not even ask to give this tour. Actually, her big-shot father arranged it."

"Even though her English isn't great," said Grace.

"Yes. As she knows. But she has no choice. As I understand."

"Which no one else on the tour would probably get," said Grace. "Which people on the tour would probably just complain about."

"I understand them, too," said Opal. "They paid a lot of money."

"So I guess it's pretty lucky she has a Chinese speaker on the tour," said Grace. "Comrade Sun, I mean."

"That is what she says," said Opal thoughtfully. "She says she is just lucky I am not one hundred percent American."

"But you are," Grace objected. "You are one hundred percent American."

Opal closed her eyes. "I don't know," she said.

Before Opal could see her family, there were the Ming Tombs. Or rather, the Ming Tomb, singular, as only one of the thirteen royal tombs scattered throughout the hills had been excavated. What's more, there was almost nothing of that tomb's contents to see because, as Comrade Sun quietly told Opal, during the Cultural Revolution Red Guards had not only ransacked the museum but exhumed the remains of the emperor and empress, that they might be posthumously denounced and burned. Still, the parade of stone animals along the Sacred Way was impressive. And that, of course, was just the precursor to the Great Wall.

The Great Wall, the Great Wall! For all the buildup to their big stop, no one was disappointed, not even Tory. The mountains from which the wall rose like the ridge of a lizard's back were so dramatic to begin with, so intimidatingly steep and rugged that, though vegetation could grow on them—as evidenced by some sporadic green—not even the Chinese were trying to farm their slopes. And the scale of the thing! The local tour guide explained how the wall actually included many sections, with some connecting up to the main wall but some not. The sections varied widely in height and width, but the entire thing with all of its branches was believed, she said, to measure over twenty thousand kilometers.

"How many miles is that?" asked Tory.

"Twelve thousand," answered Tom.

"Twelve thousand miles," echoed Tory then, her eyes wide.

"It is simply mind-boggling," said the professor. He adjusted his sunglasses as if to get a better look.

The wall went all the way from the Yellow Sea in the east to Xinjiang province in the west and, the guide explained, was more than just a wall, really. Really it was a series of connected watchtowers—as many as twenty-five thousand of them—with associated barracks, armories, and stables. And yes, it was very old. Though the part they were visiting dated, like the Forbidden City, from the Ming Dynasty, Emperor Qin Shi Huang started the wall in 220 BC.

"What year was the Forbidden City built again?" said Tory.

"1406," said Tom, "when that Ming emperor moved the capital to Beijing, remember?"

"And here we thought that was old," said Charlotte.

"It's practically new construction," said Gideon.

Everyone laughed—including Opal, Grace noticed.

Of course, the guide told them, many of the older parts of the wall had disintegrated, as they were made from rammed earth.

"Meaning mud, basically, right?" said Diane.

Later sections, on the other hand, used stone or brick and included parapets on either side, with an enormous elevated roadway between them. The parapets provided protection for archers and other soldiers, and the roadway allowed troops to move back and forth, not only on horseback but in carts and chariots.

"In other words, they should really have called it the Great Highway," said Gideon.

"And all this to keep the barbarians out," said the professor.

As for just why the North was so full of uncivilized marauders, no one seemed to know. But the wall was meant to hold off the Xiongnu and the Jurchens and the Mongols, among other tribes, not that it always worked. The Mongols did get through, and so did the Manchus who, marching through a major pass with the help of a turncoat general, toppled the Ming Dynasty.

"I take it back. Forget the Great Highway, it should really be called the Great Try," said Gideon.

By the end of the day, it wasn't only Tom and Tory who dragged their feet, wanting to buy one more red bean ice, it wasn't only they who begged for one more chance to sit on the warm stones, taking in this epic folly. Everyone begged—Opal and Gideon and Grace, too. When they got back to the hotel, though, Opal grew pensive. They were traveling the next day to Shanghai.

If for others the Great Wall had been Mecca, for Grace it was Shanghai. She knew that the Shanghai her mother had grown up in—the 1930s Shanghai of cars and dances and magnums of champagne—was gone. And so too, thankfully, was the Shanghai that came next, the Shanghai of the vicious Japanese occupiers ruling the streets with their bayonets. But she knew, too, that when Opal came to America for graduate school, she had never imagined she was saying goodbye to it all—that its time was up and that she would get stuck in the land of meatloaf and turkey. How strange to hear from a distance first about the 1949 Revolution, and then the Great Leap Forward, and then the Great

Famine, and then the Cultural Revolution; it was like one earth-quake followed by another and another and another. She had gleaned a little about the upheavals through a letter here and there—the precious few that reached her. But mostly she had learned about them through American reporters, some of whom reported things so preposterous she had thought that surely they or she—someone—had misunderstood something; there had to be a mistake. Sadly, the Communists themselves were conceivable: bands of Communists had been raiding the countryside for years before Opal left. But the Red Guards! No foreign barbarians could match these homegrown marauders. The stories were hard to believe—not only of people being humiliated and terrorized in every way but of people being turned in by their own children. Who were these animals that had broken into Opal's father's study and ripped up his priceless paintings? What were they, that they had thrown her father into the river and left him to drown, that they had bound the hands of her mother and sisters, and forced them to watch as his body floated out to sea? And could all this really have been happening while Opal was trying to figure out what a Jell-O salad was? Life wasn't easy for her and her then-husband, Ronnie, all alone in the weird place that was America; they lived for a while near a football stadium, one of the weirdest places of all. Yet it was, in comparison, nothing.

Grace knew all this.

And now as Opal stood in the lobby of their Shanghai hotel—an improbably grand if half boarded-up art deco lobby with a gilt sunburst clock, and exuberant old grillwork—Grace tried to square the decades of trauma with the cluster of women huddled around her mother. Somehow, because their history was so epic, she had expected that her aunts would be larger. But though one stood a half head taller than the others, two were actually smaller than Opal, who even with her perfect posture was all of five feet tall. Sensible shoes, dark pants, white shirts, glasses, dyed black hair; Opal's hair seemed, in contrast, gaily streaked with gray, as if to fit in with her striped theme. Indeed, in a pink-and-white-seersucker dress, she evoked nothing so much as a candy striper. But otherwise the aunties were variations on the theme that was Grace's mother. Not only did they have Opal's posture, they had Opal's thin-lipped mouth and Opal's wide-set eyes. And they were crying Opal's cry—a hiccupy sob—in an oddly contrapuntal way. Theirs was, somehow, a quartet of happy lament, at once eerie, joyful, heartbreaking, and heartwarming. Then the crying turned to babble as Grace was grabbed roughly, and associated, she gathered, with Gideon.

"Daughter," said one of the short aunts.

She spoke English!

"Yes," said Opal. "This is my daughter, her name is Grace. And this is my son-in-law."

"My name is Gideon," said Gideon.

"Oh! So tall!" said the aunts—or so Grace gathered from the way they craned their necks.

Gideon, who was five foot seven, grinned. "And I have a beard," he said, bunching it and pulling it forward as if offering to let them touch it. But they laughed and shrank back.

"Beard," said the English-speaking auntie. She was auntie number two. Opal herself was number one, and the other two aunties were numbers three and four, with number four— the baby—being the tall one. Though Opal was the oldest, she looked younger than her sisters—plumper and healthier, with better teeth and brighter eyes. And her sisters' hair was, it seemed, dulled by their hair dye; it looked to Grace like doll's hair.

"You mother is very fat," said second auntie.

"Ah," said Grace.

"Because she lives in America, you see."

"Ah."

"There is so much food there."

"There is." Grace wondered if she should explain that there was so much, some people had to go on diets.

But no. Now came so much more chatter she was not sure it would ever tail off—many presents, too. Her mother's eyes brimmed with tears even when she was laughing. Then finally the sisters all relocated to Opal's hotel room. It was not clear that outsiders were allowed upstairs. As the hall monitor seemed to be on a break, though, they were able to talk awhile before she returned. Was the hall monitor now deliberately pacing back and forth down at their end of the corridor, though? They listened, decided they were okay, and then—as Opal teared up again—changed their mind. Gideon scouted and when the hall monitor disappeared around the corner, gave a signal. The aunts then escaped with surprising stealth—a practiced stealth, it almost seemed, as if they had executed this maneuver before.

As for what they had been talking about, Opal, surrounded by presents, was too upset to explain.

"A lot of things," she said. "Too many things."

She closed her eyes; she needed a bath. Grace drew the water for her. The Victorian tub had a rolled edge and rubber stopper but sat on a wooden base—its claw feet having no doubt been melted down for some backyard steel furnace during the Great Leap Forward. She left Opal alone.

The tour group visited the Bund in the morning, strolling along the waterfront and marveling at the European buildings. Could this be China? They took pictures of the Shanghai Custom House Building, of the Hong Kong and Shanghai Bank, and of the copper-roofed Peace Hotel. The way the Huangpu River wound past the colonial buildings reminded them of the way Victoria Harbor wound past the skyscrapers of Hong Kong, except that Hong Kong had had skyscrapers on both sides of the waterway. Shanghai, its poor cousin, boasted big buildings on one side but only rice paddies on the other.

They all enjoyed the walk. But then right after lunch and before a shopping excursion—including a stop, if they liked, at a custom-order coat place—the aunties suddenly appeared. At that moment, too, to Grace's surprise, a minivan pulled up outside the restaurant. Were she and Opal and Gideon really being allowed to break from the group? And to go on an independent excursion? How was that possible? Who had arranged it?

"Was it Comrade—?" Gideon started to ask, but Grace kicked him.

"Just get in," Opal said.

Grace did not dare ask where they were going, but she noticed that even her aunties were quiet and attentive. They were not babbling or crying. They were sitting on the edges of their seats, monitoring every turn, as if afraid of being abducted.

Finally they were ushered into a nondescript institutional building. A few windows, then a huge hall with high ceilings, from which hung bare fluorescent tube lights and a smattering of fitfully turning fat-bladed ceiling fans. Under these towered row after row after row of what could almost have been the nightmare bookstacks of some student's anxiety dream, except that their endless shelves were not lined with books. Rather they were lined, from floor to ceiling, with what looked like large rectangular metal mailboxes.

Grace looked inquiringly at Opal.

"My mother," she explained.

They were not mailboxes. They were boxes of ashes.

Opal's mother's box was number 18,669. Grace's aunties

were at great pains to say how lucky they were that their mother's receptacle was at eye level, rather than up near the ceiling or down by the floor, and that it included a pull-down brass ring into which flowers could be placed. They had brought a cone of white chrysanthemums for Opal to insert; Opal nodded, lifting her arm. She placed the flowers in the ring. She bent her head and closed her eyes. But then she melted into her sisters' arms, weeping as Grace had never before seen her mother weep.

Watershed.

Grace would have glared at Gideon had he said anything and had she been able to take her eyes off her mother. But he did not and she could not. It was as if Opal's very bones had turned into tears—as if she had turned into a river of grief such as might never return to human form. And she was wailing—or, no, not wailing. Keening? Making wave after wave of a sound Grace had not known her mother could make, if her mother was even making it; it was hard to tell if it was coming from Opal or her sisters. Grace did not know what to do until its pitch dropped, and it subsided to something more like sobbing.

"Mom?" she said then, helplessly. "Are you okay, Mom?"

Opal put a hand out to reassure her.

But her hand was wet and hot, and she did not look like herself. It wasn't just that her face was pink and swollen, or that she could not stand up straight. She looked like a usurper, a person pretending to be Opal. The old Opal had of course known that her mother had died peacefully—thankfully—unlike her father. Of heart problems, in her sleep, the old Opal would have answered, if asked. The old Opal would have said that her mother was lucky. But this Opal understood what the old Opal had previously only known. This Opal understood that for years and years and years, she, her mother's daughter, had been unable to go home. And standing here now, in this room, with her sisters, this Opal understood she never could.

. . .

When Grace and Gideon called home again that night, Gideon's mother reported that Amaryllis had ruined the couch.

"Don't worry, we'll take care of it," said Gideon. "We're coming home soon."

And to Amaryllis, Grace said the same thing. "We're coming home soon."

"I want you to come home now!" Amaryllis was crying the way she had on the last call. "I mean now! Now! Now!"

"Now, now." Gideon cracked his knuckles. "Be a big girl."

But Grace said, "I want to come home, too. I want to come home, too." And, "We're coming as soon as we can. I promise. We're coming home now." She was shouting into the phone.

In the morning Gideon ribbed Grace for packing so quickly.

"Packing time is not flying time," he said gently. "You're not going to get us home any faster."

Still she raced. She was glad that they made their flight without incident. She was glad that they took off on time. She was glad that they were projected to land early. In the meantime, she could not nap. She could not read. She could not watch a movie. She just wanted to be home.

It wasn't until dinner was being served that she finally relaxed enough to ask her mother if she had done a favor for Comrade Sun knowing she might need a favor in return.

"Not so simple," Opal answered, prying the tinfoil lid off her rectangular dinner container; like Grace, she had gotten the noodles. She left off her efforts for a moment so the lid could cool, then pried some more, though the gray-brown noodles, once revealed, looked more like plastic than like food. "In many ways, China is completely changed," she went on. "But in one way, China is the same. I understood her heart. She understood mine." She pulled her chopsticks from their paper sheath. "That's what I told my mother in heaven."

Grace stopped. "Your mother in heaven?" She had never before heard Opal say anything about talking to anyone in heaven. "And what did your mother say?" she asked, unsheathing her own chopsticks.

"She said, the people understand you, they are your home now."

Grace nodded and picked up a droopy bit of carrot.

"That's beautiful," she said. "Although what about the people who don't understand you? Did you ask your mother about them?"

"Yes."

"And what did she say?"

Opal stared at her dinner a moment. "She said, you will translate for them all the rest of your life." Then she put down her chopsticks and closed her eyes.

Duncan in China

Duncan Hsu, foreign expert. That was his name in China. In America, it had been Duncan Hsu, dropout. He had dropped out of a military academy, a med school, a computer-programming night class, a soap opera of a relationship, and even, recently, a career-exploration minicourse, as a result of which he was now twenty-seven, with many people not speaking to him—for example, his mother and, so far as he could tell, his father. Duncan's father, Ed, was a master of the art of speechifying without speaking, unlike Duncan's mother, Marge, who called every day, lest Duncan forget she was not speaking to him. She called lest he imagine he had become the sort of son about whom she could boast, or lest he overlook how well his younger brother, Arnie, was doing. Arnie was headed for the apex of the Chinese bourgeois experience.

Duncan, on the other hand, tortured himself with the idea that there had to be more to his heritage. He went to China because, having seen Song Dynasty porcelains in museums, he wanted to know more about that China—the China of the scholar-officials, the China of ineffable nobility and restraint. Duncan was no artist—art school being the one kind of school he had never thought to drop out of—but those porcelains could make him cry, what with their grace and purity and delicate crackle glazes, what with their wholeness and confidence and supremely untortured air. They made him feel what life could be and what his life was. They were uplifting; they were depressing. That was beauty for you. Duncan had not been an Asian anything major, but in his frequent periods of incipient employment, he had read about the tremendous integrity of the Song scholar-officials and had speculated that some of their noble code had survived in the spirit of the Long March. Should there not be, somewhere, a vestige of it left still? Maybe even in his own family? He had had scholars in his family, after all; they had not always been attitudinal geniuses of his brother's ilk. Some of them had run schools. Some had studied abroad. One of his father's brothers had been a kind of horticulturist-folklorist-herbalist; he had studied English and married a violinist-entomologist. Their son, Duncan's cousin, was still alive and living in China. Perhaps Duncan would have a chance to meet him. Or perhaps Duncan would fall in love. Later, Duncan would remember that even before he left the United States, even before he met the perhaps beautiful, perhaps noble, completely maddening Louise, he had considered the possibility of love. For wasn't that what happened to people in foreign lands? He'd learned that from the movies. Anything was possible. So argued one voice in his head, even as another said, Folly.

Folly. Almost as soon as Duncan reached Shandong, he knew that he had come for naught, that the China of the early 1980s had more to do with eating melon seeds around a coal heater the size of a bread box than with Song Dynasty porcelain. He gave up his goal easily, more easily than he would have thought possible, a man without dismay, and all on account of the cold.

At home he had railed against degree programs, movies, voting procedures, sports equipment. He had reviled the local Motor Vehicle Department; he had denounced mindlessness, fecklessness, spinelessness. But in China so many things were poorly run and poorly designed that there was no point in railing against them. And who could fault the people for a certain scrappy element? Certainly not in the winter. Duncan had read table loads of books about China before he left, but none had prepared him for the plunge in mental functioning that he experienced; it was as if his thought-bearing fluids had gone viscous. There were two kinds of rooms for him now—barely heated and unheated. There were two kinds of days—slightly warmer and no warmer. When Duncan had a chance to catch a reflection of himself, he was amazed to see how much less baby-faced he looked here than he had at home. His face was no gaunter and still featured dimples, but it was chapped and reddened in a cowboy-on-the-prairie kind of way, rather than smooth and shiny enough to be featured in a soap ad. This brought him a certain contentment. More generally, though, he was contented when he was warm enough and discontented when he was not. Whereas at home he had been impatient with people who thought of nothing but their comfort, now he thought of nothing but his comfort.

Already, in short, Duncan was becoming like Professor Mo, the head of the English-language program at the coal-mining institute to which Duncan had been assigned. Professor Mo always made sure that Duncan the foreign expert was seated next to whatever meager heat source might be available, if only so that he, as protector and guide of the foreign expert, might also sit next to the meager heat source.

"I'll order up some beer for you," he would say when he himself was thirsty. Or else, "The shark's fin soup in this restaurant's said to be marvelous. Shall I order some up?" And his arm would be in the air before Duncan had a chance to object.

Professor Mo was a haggard man in his fifties, who in his idealistic youth had forsworn his inheritance, hoping to join the revolution. Was that not noble? And yet during the Cultural Revolution, he had been struggled against just the same. Since then, he had been reinstituted as a valued member of society because he spoke English. Now he laughed a shrill laugh. Had the Red Guards paraded him on a leash and taunted him? Had they incarcerated him and forced his family to abandon him? Thanks to the restoration of a fraction of his family's fortune, he inhabited one of the largest apartments in town these days; and it was his distinct pleasure to give grades to former Red Guards. Moreover, at a time when other professors were still wearing Mao jackets, Mo let his heavy quilt coat fall open so that everyone might glimpse the double-breasted suits he wore underneath. These were, in truth, more than a little seedy—relics of his years of study abroad, during which he had also picked up his strangely inflected English, along with an amazing variety of mannerisms that served to obfuscate any real sense of his being. A habit of draping one arm over the back of his chair, for example, in an exaggerated, man-of-the-world pose. A loop-de-loop manner of talking with his hands, and a way of letting his cigarette dangle so loosely from his lips that it resembled a sort of burning dribble.

"You must assign more homework," he told Duncan one day, his cigarette hanging so precipitously that Duncan worried it would fall into his lap. "Otherwise the students will loaf about and make trouble."

"I assign four hours a day," ventured Duncan. "They're in class from nine o'clock to four. That seems like it ought to be enough."

"Not enough," said Professor Mo. "And no more songs. You are not engaged in a popularity contest."

"But they like songs," Duncan protested. "They specifically asked for songs." Duncan recalled the day that the class monitor, William—the students had all chosen English names for the year—had made the request on behalf of his classmates. William was a square-headed, square-bodied man, so strong that he had dug himself out from under a building after the earthquake in Tangshan. Yet in presenting the class request to Duncan, he had blushed red as a pomegranate, feeling the difficulty of his task.

"You are not engaged in a popularity contest," repeated Professor Mo.

Duncan knew what the real problem was. The real problem was that Mo, endeavoring to do as little work as possible, had elected, as his semester offering, to give a practice session every day from four to five. Whereas before Duncan arrived, Mo, as the only English speaker at the school, could count on a full class for whatever he taught, though, now he was finding that almost no one came. The students complained that the practice session was a waste of time, and one had only to peek in the door and behold Mo pontificating at the front of the room to understand why. To begin with, though the classroom was of average size, Mo had a microphone on his desk. This was hooked up to two speakers, each on a desk of its own, flanking him. Mo took long drags of his cigarette, his chin jutting up into the air, then swooped down importantly into the mike. "Well," he drawled. "That's a matter of opinion." Pause. "One might say." The students—there were three of them—looked bored. Mo's classroom, like Duncan's, had been outfitted with an elaborate trellis of overhead wires, from which brown extension cords hung down, one beside each desk, so that the students could plug in their all-important tape recorders. Duncan's own class was punctuated by the constant sound of cassette tapes running out and being flipped; at times he had wondered if there was anything the students, in their avidity, would not tape. Now he had his answer. None of the students was operating a machine.

Bearing all this in mind, Duncan endeavored to deal with his supervisor in a diplomatic and sagacious manner, such as befit a foreign expert.

"Perhaps you could take over the song instruction," he suggested, though he doubted that Professor Mo could sing. "We could coordinate other parts of the curriculum as well. I could assign the practice session as part of their homework. Make it required." Duncan tried to broach these ideas as delicately as he could.

"What a nice idea," said Mo in reply. "How very kind of you."

Then he laughed, showing his nicotine-stained teeth. He looped his arm over the back of his chair with an elaborate motion as he recrossed his legs.

Thus did the enmity begin. Over the next few weeks, Mo did not make a comment to Duncan that did not include the word "kind." If you would be so *kind,* he said. Just a *kindly* reminder. How very *kind* of you.

The curriculum coordination Duncan had proposed did not take place, though Mo did sit in on several of Duncan's classes, presumably to make sure Duncan wasn't teaching any songs. Mo set up camp in the back of the room, drinking tea and smoking cigarettes. He read the newspaper, turning the pages so loudly that the students complained he was ruining their tapes.

"The students feel he is, well, a bit strange," allowed William one afternoon, after relaying to Duncan what he called the "difficulty."

"Like Jiang Qing, only man," said another student. The reference was to Mao's widow, an effigy of whom Duncan had recently seen, with a noose around her neck, in a park. As for the speaker, that, of course, was Louise—Louise, who from the first day had seemed to burst from the dingy rows of the classroom like a streak of pure color. Duncan had noticed that she changed her hairstyle almost every day. Yet she did not seem vain, perhaps because she was not a beautiful woman. She was, rather, inexplicably beautiful—a woman whose pedestrian eyes, long nose, and bowed mouth were eclipsed by the extraordinary radiance of her face.

"Seems like Professor Mo would like Gang of Four to be Gang of Five," she said.

William laughed but then looked away pointedly, so that when Duncan asked if Louise had seen the park effigy, she answered, blushing deeply, "I see nothing."

"Of course," said Duncan tactfully. "Excuse me."

It took three days for Duncan to "raise his opinion," as his students would say. But finally he said, "If you would *kindly* desist from reading the newspaper in my class, I would appreciate it." He braced for Mo's reaction. Mo, though, simply smiled with a kind of satisfaction, tapped some ashes onto the floor, and said, "I guessed from the start you had something inside your coat."

"What do you mean?"

"What an interesting question." Mo rehung his cigarette in his mouth. "A Chinese man, you know, would go home, figure out what my meaning is."

"I see," said Duncan, though he did not see.

"Are you Chinese?"

"Yes," said Duncan. "I mean, I don't know. I guess no." He felt, for the first time since he had come to China, too hot.

"In that case, I explain to you."

Duncan watched the ash flare. He studied his superior's

hands, which were nicotine-stained, but also surprisingly delicate and fine. "My meaning is, I guessed from the start you are inside here"—Mo indicated the inside of his lapel—"a sarcastic brute."

"Ah," said Duncan.

"Do you understand me now?"

"Yes and no," said Duncan.

Mo smoked.

Finally, finally it was getting to be spring. That meant first of all that instead of winter cabbage, day in and day out, now there were other vegetables to eat—first big scallions, then spinach and leeks, then small scallions. The trees grew green fingers, beginning with the willows, bringing shade. Quilts were hung out to air. Students went for walks. Often Duncan would glimpse Louise's small, slim figure out with one classmate or another; she seemed to pick a different classmate every day. People began to play basketball on the packed dirt court outside Duncan's window. As often as he could, Duncan joined them. This brought him real pleasure, especially the couple of times Louise managed to goad some of the other women into playing with the guys. How startlingly quick and savvy she was! Agile as a greyhound, she was able to find her merry way around players far bigger and younger than she, including Duncan. Every day he hoped she would be moved to play again.

In the meantime, a fish truck came. For an hour, a man with red gloves stood astride a mountain of ice and shoveled fish out into the baskets borne by the joyful crowd. Fish and fish parts rained through the air as if it were New Year's; the silver scales threw out points of light. People feasted. Duncan began to shed layers of clothes. By now he was beginning to feel more at home speaking Chinese and could at least answer the kinds of questions people typically asked him—had he eaten yet, and did he like salty food or sweet, and was a place clean or dirty. He could buy stamps at the post office; he could bargain over what little there was for sale. Also, he had begun to feel more at home in his apartment, which featured a concrete floor and a hodge-podge of furniture, ranging from an enormous art deco ward-robe with veined mirrors to a blue metal bedstand, stenciled with panda bears and bamboo. There was a coal stove, which had not quite warmed the room in the winter but did now, and, to go with it, a maid, Comrade Su, whose job it was to keep after the soot that settled everywhere.

The furniture and stove and maid were not Duncan's only luxuries. As the first foreign expert this coal-mining institute had ever had, he also enjoyed the use of a sit-down toilet—not unknown in the rich South, but of note here in the North—and, most impressively of all, a bathtub complete with hot and cold running water. Never mind that the hot water emanated from a tank on the roof, under which Comrade Su would make a fire half an hour before Duncan's appointed bath time. The tub with its faucets was nonetheless a fabled fixture on campus, a subject of much rumor and, for visitors, a must-see.

Duncan had more visitors now. When he posted a sign-up sheet for individual conversational practice, almost all his stu-dents came, bearing stories. Many of these involved the Cultural Revolution, during which some of them had been struggled against; others had been Red Guards. How could they sit next to one another in class? Yet they did. They were civil; they lent each other blank cassettes. Those who had been made to dig ditches had not forgotten it. They told Duncan of rape and tor-ture, of seeing loved ones blinded, smeared in shit, drowned, driven to suicide. No, there was no forgetting. How could they forget any of it? The former Red Guards, on the other hand, professed to have forgotten much. They vaguely recalled riding the trains around the country—being out on a lark, seeing new places. None of them admitted to participating in anything ugly; indeed, at least one of them seemed quite genuinely more interested in magic tricks and Chinese chess than in ongoing revolution. Still, Duncan was amazed and touched by the fantastic restraint that held his classroom together. Wasn't this related to what he had come to China to see? He had not expected that it would be so tinged with sad realism, though—all anyone wanted anymore, the students said, was to be left alone. Nor had he expected it to verge so on the surreal. He had thought, naïvely, that it would have more to do with the old noble code of the scholar-officials. A truly antique idea, such as one found preserved via porcelains in museums.

Or was it?

Louise's turn for conversational practice came on the same afternoon as a basketball tournament. The *thud thud thud* of the ball was so loud, Duncan could hardly hear her speak. From time to time, too, the basketball would hit his window grating with a disconcertingly resounding bang. Yet in a way, Duncan was grateful for the commotion, which helped him relax. His heart had pounded so hard at the prospect of a half hour alone with Louise that before she came, he had emptied the pencils from his shirt pocket, for fear that they would rattle.

Louise, in contrast, was unfazed.

"How about we play basketball instead of practice English?" she suggested brightly. As if anticipating that possibility, she had braided her hair and affixed it over the top of her head in a simple crown—the style she usually chose for athletics.

"Absolutely not," he said with mock seriousness.

"Must we have to practice English?"

"Do we have to practice English."

"Do we have to practice English?"

"Yes, we do," he said.

A basketball hit the window grate with a particularly loud bang.

"Such a peaceful room," she said, pursing her lips.

He laughed. "Would you like to see the bathtub?"

He showed her the tub with the faucets, then poured her a cup of tea and made her tell him something about herself. By then there were only twenty minutes left to her turn. Still, Duncan managed to learn that Louise was a former aristocrat whose grandparents had made a fortune abroad, but whose parents had elected to return to China, their homeland, during the War Against the Japanese. Also he gathered, with some shock, that she was quite a bit older than he—in her mid-thirties, maybe? That did not seem possible; she looked much younger. But she had married twice already and had lost both husbands—to illness, it seemed. Also, she had a nineteen-year-old daughter in Nanjing; Louise talked about her with the kind of fretful pride Duncan associated with the wives of astronauts on space missions. He learned that Louise was unusually acquainted with the world, having lived as a child in Germany and France; and, interestingly, that her family had not been struggled against during the Cultural Revolution. She did not volunteer why not. Just when Duncan was about to ask, a basketball crashed so hard against the window grate that the windowpane shook.

"Look—the metal is—how do you say?—bended," she said.

"Bent," he said. "The metal is bent."

A knock on the door; the next student, already. It was up to Duncan to imagine, later, how Louise had managed to protect her family—to imagine her calmly confronting an angry crowd, like Gary Cooper in *High Noon*. How easily he could see the mesmerized crowd melting magically away before her! Never mind that in picturing this, he knew himself to be shamelessly romanticizing her—inflating, no doubt, both her charm and her integrity. Try as he might, though, he could see nothing in her to disabuse him of his illusions. Just now she was a coal-mining expert—not something she would have chosen to be. Still she had spoken without resentment of her assignment. She had spoken of rebuilding the country as if it were her own family fallen on hard times.

"How can China go forward?" she had asked, leaning forward. She steadied her chin in her hand like an egg in an eggcup. "I try to study hard so that I can help to build up the country, make China strong."

Duncan's last student for the day, Reginald, maintained that there were more and more people in China these days who said one thing even as they did another, and thought a third thing still—the inevitable result of a repressive regime. And Duncan could see that this was probably true, perhaps even of some of his students. Coal mining in China was horrifically dangerous; these students were supposed to go abroad and bring back safer techniques. But would they indeed come back? Duncan had to believe that they would—or at least that his favorites would. He trusted Louise, and William, and Alan, and Rhonda, and Reginald. But was that just because he liked them? As the weeks went on, Duncan spent more and more time with his students. He made dumplings with them. He watched TV with them, helping them translate programs about Buckingham Palace. He discussed world affairs with them. He visited their dorms.

But best of all, he went on excursions with them, in the ancient green car he shared with the school leaders. This was the Warsaw, a Polish vehicle whose tires were so bald, they felt silken, and whose windshield, which predated curved glass, had a metal seam up the middle. The seats had been lovingly reupholstered with floral-print towels; the steering wheel had been covered with red velvet; and the innards of the machine had likewise been ingeniously coddled. The driver once proudly showed Duncan how he had painstakingly fashioned his own replacement springs from heavy-gauge wire.

If only Duncan enjoyed as much control over the inhabitants of the car! Not that Professor Mo proved his inescapable guide on every trip. But Mo took Duncan to task for choosing William instead of himself for an excursion to Confucius's gravesite at Qufu. And regarding Duncan's plan to take Louise with him to climb the great sacred mountain, Tai Shan—did he really think it appropriate to take a woman, alone, with him anywhere?

"I put her name down on the schedule for a turn but meant for her to bring a partner," sighed Duncan—who in truth had half-dreamed some oversight might occur. "Besides, there would have, of course, been the driver."

"May I name myself to be that partner?" said Mo.

"Oh no, no, you are far too busy with important matters," protested Duncan.

"In other words," said Mo, "you would prefer not to have a lightbulb."

Duncan started a little. "Lightbulb" was the same term his father used to use for a chaperone. "You're welcome to come, Professor Mo, but I understand it's quite a climb. I'm not sure I'll make it myself. Haven't you had an operation on your lung? Certainly there will be other opportunities."

Professor Mo studied him openly, smoking. He was wearing a three-piece suit today, the vest of which sported several moth holes. "Of course, you are single man," he said.

"I have a girlfriend," lied Duncan, even as Louise's visage floated before him, complete with cupped chin.

"Perhaps I will accompany you to the mountain base," said Professor Mo. "And then, of course, there is the other excursion."

"What other excursion?"

"To see your relatives."

"Has that been approved?" Duncan had succeeded in contacting his cousin's family by mail a few months before, but he had been seeking permission from the provincial and school officials for a visit ever since. Mo nodded.

"And they have permission, too?"

"Their unit wants them to travel down from Harbin to Beijing, to meet you. That way you will not see their living conditions."

"How typical—wonderful!" said Duncan. "Thank you for your help in arranging this. It was kind of you." He blurted out this last without sarcasm.

"I have not been to Beijing in some years," observed Professor Mo. "It will be pleasant to visit, especially in the spring." He snuffed out his cigarette, then hooked his thumbs in his vest.

The trip to Tai Shan started off most magically. Professor Mo settled into a marble-floored hotel to recuperate from the drive, which had consisted almost entirely of roads under repair; this left Duncan and Louise and William free to make the climb alone. They stopped in at the enormous temple at the bottom, then began to wend their way uphill. Lilacs bloomed; vendors under pine-bough shelters sold turnips, walnuts, ices, tea. Everywhere there were goats and chickens, sheep and black pigs. Louise and William, equipped with canteens and shoulder bags, proved lively and informative guides. This was the most sacred of the five sacred Chinese mountains, they explained. They translated the stone steles left by the countless dignitaries and emperors who had journeyed to the mountain over its three-thousand-year history, as well as the most famous of the thousands of inscriptions covering the rock walls. They quoted the poet Li Bai, arguing about how to convey the meaning and beauty of his lines. They pointed out a stand of two-thousand-year-old cypress trees, dating back to the Han Dynasty; they identified temples, gates, and ruins. Tai Shan, it seemed, was a Taoist mountain, formed from the head of Pangu, the creator of the world. But, well, they explained, people asked things of the Buddha there anyway because that was how China was. People were Taoist, Buddhist, and Confucian all at the same time, and the mountains were, too.

Then the gentle incline abruptly turned into an ascent unlike any Duncan had ever made before. He had expected woods, streams, pine-needle-strewn paths. Mud. Bugs. Fungi. Instead, he was confronted with a formidable series of rough stone steps, ascending straight up a sheer mountain face. If this was, as some believed, the stairway to heaven, it appeared designed to prevent overcrowding in paradise: the route was relentless, with no shade whatsoever. Indeed, the sun felt surprisingly low to the earth—close and intense, as if, whatever season it was elsewhere, here it was high summer. Louise and William were prepared for this, having brought a hat and a pair of sunglasses, respectively. Both pressed Duncan to borrow their gear. He refused.

A drought was on; every creek, every waterfall was dry. Hands on his complaining thighs, Duncan stopped frequently to catch his breath; also to marvel, panting, at the thousands of little old ladies—the *lao taitai*—who labored alongside him. These were tiny women, dressed in shapeless blue or gray smocks and black cotton pants. Their gray hair was hidden under black kerchiefs or netted in squarish buns, sometimes with flowers or branches stuck in them. Some wore earrings. A few had fantastic, baroque fingernails such as Duncan had thought were no longer permitted. Didn't everyone in China have to work now? And how was it that so many of the women had bound feet? Duncan associated bound feet with cracked, sepia-toned photographs from the nineteenth century. He beheld the women with amazement; they had to be in their seventies or eighties. Of course, they were peasants. And change came slowly in the countryside. But how could they climb this mountain at all, much less on those feet? And why weren't there any men? The women moved slowly, slowly—fanatically—some of them crawling on their hands and knees. They had come, William said, with the idea of climbing all day and all night, so that at the top of the mountain, at dawn, as the sun leaped into the sky—and it really did leap, people said—they might look into their hearts, purifying themselves. Then they could make a request of Buddha.

"This is old China," said William. "The government tried to get rid of this kind of superstition. But the old people are hard to change their minds."

"It is hard to change the minds of the old," corrected Duncan automatically.

"It is hard to change the minds of the old," repeated William. "It is hard to change the minds of the old."

"The trouble is they are—how do you say? Have no hope," said Louise.

"Desperate," said Duncan. "The trouble is that they have no hope. They are desperate."

"The trouble is that they have no hope. They are despate."

"Des-per-ate," said Duncan. "Des-per-ate."

A few of the *lao taitai* had younger women with them—presumably their daughters—to support them or fan them or shade them with an umbrella; but even the younger women had wizened faces that looked to have been weathered by the centuries. They all stopped frequently to snack on a kind of flat cornmeal cake they had brought, or to kowtow and make offerings in the many little rock caves and wooden temples on the way up. Ducking his head into one of the temples, Duncan was appalled to find that it housed a bonfire so fierce that he did not dare step inside the building.

"That temple is going to burn down," said Duncan. "It's crazy. And look at all that dry scrub nearby. It's dangerous."

"They burn paper money, send up to heaven," explained William placidly. "It is an offering for good fortune."

There were three gates on the way up—the First Heavenly Gate, the Middle Heavenly Gate, and the South Heavenly Gate. At the First Heavenly Gate, Duncan was sweating, looking at his watch, making calculations. By the Middle Heavenly Gate, though, he was thinking less of himself and more of the *lao luitai,* many of whom were kowtowing on the stairs. He wondered how many deaths there were every year on the mountain.

William bought bamboo walking sticks for them all; Louise opened the collar of her peach-colored polyblend shirt. What an unutterably beautiful part of the anatomy the neck was! Especially the base, with its perfectly matched meeting of graceful, strong bones and impossibly vulnerable flesh. Duncan felt a distinct spring of desire. His ex-girlfriend, Alice, used to say that he was perverse in his ardor—that nothing stirred him like the wholly inappropriate situation, and that this was, in keeping with his entire life, a form of escape. Was that true? Was he attracted to Louise exactly because she was ten years older than he? All Duncan knew was that his desire to touch her there, on her handsome clavicles, so overwhelmed him that he had to put his hands in his pockets whenever they stopped. Louise's neck, he noticed, was flushed a roseate color that Alice—a catalog copywriter—would have called "lovemaker's pink."

Louise herself, meanwhile, was growing more gregarious and inquisitive as the climb went on, as if in unbuttoning her top button she had unbuttoned in other ways as well.

"Are you tired?" she asked Duncan repeatedly, almost tenderly. "Go slowly," she enjoined him. "Take it easy."

She began to quiz him about his health. Perhaps she was interested in health in general, because of what had happened to her two husbands. Perhaps she was brushing up on her health-related English. Perhaps he only imagined that she looked at him more and more searchingly as she progressed from questions about his exercise habits—did he get enough exercise, and what kind of exercise did he get, and did he have partners for the forms of exercise that required them—to questions about his nutrition. What did he eat for breakfast? For lunch? For dinner? And did he cook for himself, or was there someone who cooked for him? Louise smiled when he told her that his girlfriend used to cook for him sometimes, and that he sometimes used to cook for her.

"Of course! Nice boy like you has girlfriend," she said.

"Had a girlfriend," said Duncan. Was there a way of saying this without it seeming like a correction? His teacherly air seemed to nose up into the conversation, not unlike a part of his anatomy he was trying to keep under control.

"Had a girlfriend," said Louise, still smiling. "Nice boy like you had a girlfriend."

"Meaning, I don't have one anymore."

"Ah," she said. "I catch your meaning."

"I catch your meaning" was a favorite phrase of the students, which Duncan had worked all semester to try to eliminate. But now he just sighed and offered no correction. Instead, he said, "We broke up."

"Broke?"

"I don't have a girlfriend anymore."

"Now he has no any girlfriend," put in William, in an explanatory tone.

No any was another phrase Duncan had focused on for months. He felt a rise of irritation. "Now he has no girlfriend," he corrected.

"Who?" said Louise.

"I," said Duncan. "Now I have no girlfriend."

"Broken heart?" she asked, head atilt, chin cupped in hand.

"Broken heart," he affirmed, with a feeling of simultaneous connection and defeat. In fact, he had broken the relationship off, and the heartache, to his surprise, had proven mostly Alice's. But how to explain that? Here he was, the foreign expert, and yet he felt as helpless in his communication as a student.

Louise looked at him sympathetically. Duncan noticed that she had not tied the ribbons of her straw hat, but rather had tucked them, eccentrically, behind her ears, so that they mingled with various loose strands of her hair, which was gathered today in a low ponytail.

"We are—how do you say?—comrades," she said then, firmly—at which point, William, in distraction or discretion, turned his head as she quickly, consolingly squeezed Duncan's hand.

Did William see that squeeze? It was hard to tell, what with his sunglasses. Quite possibly the good soul was too preoccupied with the role of guide to think of much besides how best to provide for his teacher's comfort.

"May I offer you a cup of tea?" he asked. "Would you care for a piece of sorghum candy?"

They climbed on. Now, walking stick in hand, William led their party. This meant that Louise followed a bit behind him, and that Duncan, happily, followed a few paces behind her. For a while, he watched the swing of her ponytail—how part of it caught inside her collar and part swung loose, fanning itself over the cloth of her shirt. But slowly, inevitably, his interest drifted downward. He was not the kind of man who spent his time looking down women's blouses. Who could climb steps behind a female form for hour upon hour, though, and not notice the tightening and loosening of her gray slacks across her buttocks, the working of her pant legs in and out of her crotch? He contemplated the creasing of the cloth, the strain of a certain seam. He watched a sweat diamond grow. What had she meant when she said they were comrades? Finally tiring, she began to rest one hand behind her back, delineating the extraordinarily graceful line of her waist. She leaned on her walking stick, readjusted her canteen, her shoulder bag. She even flapped the hem of her shirt a little, to cool herself—an unconscious act, he assumed; what an intimacy it seemed, to be privy to a moment when she had forgotten herself. Alice had never forgotten herself. Alice had been utterly witty and composed, except when she was not.

It seemed an intimacy, too, the several times Louise and Duncan stopped, to be flushed and panting together.

"Stop, William," they called at one point. But he did not hear them and plowed steadily ahead.

"He is a water buffalo," said Louise, looking up.

"Look back," said Duncan. "Look how far we've come."

She turned. "Oh," she said. "It makes me dizzy." She bowed her head. A stray breeze came up; her hat tumbled down a few steps, landing at the knees of a struggling *lao taitai*. Duncan retrieved it, considering his little gallantry with some irony. What did it say about him that he chose to help lithe Louise instead of the old woman? He was glad this old woman at least had not one, but two younger women with her.

"Are you all right?" he asked Louise, and almost placed her hat on her head. She looked so uncomfortable, though, that he handed it to her instead.

Did she regret squeezing his hand as she had?

"I am in excellent health," she answered, replacing her hat ribbons behind her ears. "How about you?"

"I, too, am in excellent health."

"Good." Smiling her pursed smile, she squeezed his hand again. "Have you had any big sickness?" she asked as she resumed climbing.

The crowds of *lao taitai* continued their inexorable way up the mountain. The steps were steeper now and so crudely made that Duncan found himself concentrating less on Louise's posterior and more on his footing—so much so that when William suddenly appeared, Duncan startled.

"We are almost at the top," said William. "I come back down to make report."

The few scattered bushes at the top of the mountain were abloom with rocks. Those were prayers, William explained. The *lao taitai* threw the rocks into the bushes; if the rocks stuck, it meant the prayers would be answered. Besides the rock bushes, there was bedrock—no trees—and a hostel, into which William checked himself, Duncan, and Louise. The hostel was at once a basic affair and a luxury difficult to enjoy. How could Duncan sleep in a warm, soft bed, after all, when those pilgrims who were not still climbing all night were going to be sleeping on the ground? Duncan asked if he couldn't give his room up to some of the old women, but William's answer was a laugh.

"You are foreign expert," he said. "The hotel will make report about you. Can they write you slept outside on the ground? Impossible!"

Still Duncan mulled over matters of birth and happenstance as he tried to elbow his way to a dinner of bean sprouts and steamed rolls in the smoke-filled dining room. The *lao taitai* were proving surprisingly aggressive. They grabbed food right out of his hands; they demanded that he give up his seat that they might sit down. So pushy were they about the latter especially that Duncan found himself, to his surprise, shaking his head no. Hadn't he just been thinking about giving his hostel room up to the *lao taitai*? Yet now he would not give his seat up to them. Indeed, he shook his head almost as adamantly as did William and Louise.

Once he left the dining hall and realized how precipitously the temperature had dropped, though, he felt a renewed sympathy for the *lao taitai*. How many of the old women had brought jackets with them? Blankets? None, apparently. Yet now that the sun had set, it was cold enough to set a person's teeth on edge, and a formidable wind had risen, too, with great broadsiding gusts. What with the drought, the hotel was out of water, but Duncan and his students each had a full canteen; in his private room, Duncan slipped into sleep provisioned. Still, his sleep was fitful at best as he dreamed of dropping things, some of them quietly, some with a loud clang. Another loud clang—no, a loud clanging. A bell; voices; people running up and down the hall.

Now he was awake. Shouting, swearing, banging. He thought the voices were saying *zhao huole*—"fire"—and when he peered out the clear streak in his whitewashed window, sure enough, there it was—a broad sulfur-yellow glow, gently curved at the bottom, like a picture of the surface of the sun from a text on the solar system. Those bonfires in the temple . . . He dressed, shaking. Outside his door, he waited for Louise and William. The courtyard was in a flurry. Only the moon was itself, overhead as always, implacable and still, its brilliant light a reassuringly hard white—the proper color of night lighting. Duncan clutched his water canteen, feeling the dig of its webbed strap in his shoulder, the cool of its metal belly against his hand.

He could hear his mother's voice—*What do you mean, you died in China?*—and didn't know what to say.

The fire burned through the night. William kept saying that there was no danger, that the top of the mountain was solid rock, but Duncan couldn't help but worry that they would all be asphyxiated by the smoke. It mostly blew away from them. Sometimes, though, it blew their way, burning their throats and eyes. It was thick enough to obscure the moon—and the people, too, so that they instinctively began to wail in the billowing blackness like riders on a roller coaster, plummeting downhill. The wind, the wind. Even more than of the fire, they all seemed at the mercy of the wind. Another gust; the *lao taitai* wailed again. Duncan envied them their keening release as, flanked by Louise and William, he watched the fire silently, from a perch on a large rock. In America, there might be a rescue attempt, with helicopters. In America, there might be a fire-fighting attempt, too, unless the fire had been deemed part of the mountain's natural cycle, essential to the survival of, say, a certain charcoal-eating beetle. Here there was no attempt. Even if fire trucks could make it safely up the road to the Middle Heavenly Gate, which they conceivably could— Duncan having learned that there was indeed a road that far—what could they do? There were no streams to pump from, and anyway, the Middle Heavenly Gate was so far from the top. No, there was only the fire, still burning, and the wind, still howling. They sat.

Louise sat closer to Duncan than did William, but even William sat close enough that Duncan could feel the warmth of his body and appreciate the shelter he provided from that wind. William wore his canteen hanging straight down from his neck; Duncan wore his the same way. As for Louise—how hard it was not to put his arm around hatless Louise, whose canteen lay on the ground, and who was shivering. He had started to, at one point, but she had seemed to stiffen and move away. Was that because of William? And why should they care, if they were going to die? He should sweep her up in his arms and take her into his room. They should throw off their shackles and live these last few moments in freedom. As the night wore on, he resolved over and over to do it—to live. He recalled scenes from *Last Tango in Paris* and *Swept Away*; he wondered what movies Louise had seen. Not these, he knew. Still, he pictured scenes in which she lay on a beach or arched back against a garden wall. He pictured her pelvic bones, as beautiful as her clavicles; he envisioned the adjacent vulnerable flesh. Her hair spread around her, unbraided, undone; she offered him her hard-nippled breasts. He imagined sucking, biting, sweating—imagined her impatient, then languid, then impatient once more.

But when he looked over at the woman at his side, these visions seemed tawdry and insufficient, the stuff of a schoolboy's wet dreams. For Louise seemed to believe either that they were going to live, or else that she should die according to the code by which she had lived. Not that she said so. She simply sat in silence, staring at the fire, thinking thoughts Duncan could not fathom. She was, he knew, a physical woman, a woman unafraid of sweat—a woman who had fallen in love and married twice. A woman ardent in all things. And she liked him. When he had drunk the last of his canteen, she instantly took it from him, leaped to the ground, and replenished it from her own. Was there something maternal in that? He protested, hoping not; she clasped his hand for a third time. But mostly she waited to know what was to come and, with something like nobility, chose to do nothing.

. . .

Still the fire burned. But the hostel did not burn; no one was asphyxiated; and slowly, finally, the fire began to peter out. A scrub fire, that was what Duncan learned to call it later. A scrub fire—blown out, perhaps, by the very wind that had fanned it. The yellow that was the mountainside gradually faded to a wheaten color—the color of dry grass—just as the sky lightened, so that it seemed as if the fire had risen up and been absorbed into the atmosphere—as if there were no real division between heaven and earth. How movingly magnificent the heave of clearing land, as it came into view, an expanse of purple crags and mist-sunk valleys—an unpeopled sweep, the manifest province of clouds and gods. It did seem the province of gods. Then the moment the *lao taitai* had come for was upon them. The wind seemed to die down as the sun came up—jumping little jumps, just as it was supposed to, a leap leap leap into the sky; and for a long moment, there was holiness on the mountain. In the pure calm, Duncan felt a twinge of envy for the *lao taitai*, who did not seem desperate at all now, but at peace—full of an old, large faith that would never live for him. It was he who was desperate— godless, modern man, whose most stirring visions came from sex scenes in movies. He looked on the blackened mountain, visible now with the risen sun. Then he closed his eyes with the other pilgrims and found, to his surprise, that he had much in his heart. For what was he but a free man who had rejected much and embraced little? He was a free man who had never truly loved—a free man who believed nothing in particular, who did nothing in particular. He was a free man who had not even embraced his freedom.

He was a long time opening his eyes.

When finally he did, he found that many of the *lao taitai* had gone to breakfast, and that William had gone for a walk, but that Louise remained beside him.

"Did you ask Buddha for something?" she asked.

He hesitated. "I asked Buddha that I might find love." In fact, he had not asked for anything, exactly; but he realized now, accepted now, that he was speaking in a kind of translation. One had to be willing to do that, to begin with, if one were to tangle with the world.

"I asked Buddha to introduce you to someone special," she said.

"Do I not know someone special?"

She stood up. Her feet angled downward on the sloping rock as, arms spread, she sprang to the ground, graceful as Peter Pan. For all the trials of the long night, her blouse looked entirely fresh and unwrinkled.

"You know no one," she said mysteriously. "Wait and see." Then, adjusting her canteen around her neck, she added, "Be careful about William."

Louise did not come to class the next day, and the day after that, she was reported gone altogether. Gone home, people said. Applied for home leave and got it. They seemed mostly amazed that Louise had managed to get her unit to agree to let her travel on such short notice. Must have some string somewhere, they said, giving Duncan a funny look. William especially seemed to steer clear of Duncan. Only with great effort did Duncan manage to corner him and ask what was going on, to which William answered that it was better to avoid standing in a stable for fear of smelling of shit.

"You are a foreigner," he said. "Better not to be involved."

"Did you make a report?" asked Duncan.

"I am class monitor."

"What did you say? In your report."

William looked away. " 'Honesty is best policy.' Isn't that what you teach us? I am not clever man, know all kinds of back door. I am simple man. But I am honest, all my life, since I was born."

"You are a spy." Duncan regretted his words as soon as he said them.

"I am no spy," William said. "I am just honest." And again, "I am class monitor."

The weather turned almost as hot and dry as it had been on Tai Shan. Comrade Su reported that her husband had begun sleeping on the floor, now that it was too hot for them both to sleep with their child on the bed; on the streets, women carrying their vegetables in plastic net bags hugged the walls as they walked, trying to stay in the shade. The wind blew up such enormous clouds of dust, Duncan's ears were gritty with it; he was forced to keep his apartment windows shut, as if it were winter. The campus electricity went out regularly. No one played basketball. No one came to visit. Duncan kept to himself. Though Louise, worryingly, did not reappear, he said nothing. From time to time he thought about the climb up Tai Shan, and about the fire, and about the holy moment at dawn, and about how changed he had felt by it all—how full of possibility, as if he were on the brink of living a new life. But now he did not feel changed at all—not unless he were to count, say, finding himself more prickly about his authority. When a student questioned his grading on an exam, he found himself answering more curtly than necessary. He also noticed that he gave more dictations, strolling up and down the aisles of the classroom like an old-fashioned drillmaster.

When it came time to make his trip to Beijing, he was glad to be getting away.

. . .

From the moment they boarded the train, Professor Mo proved an insufferable companion.

"So the star has faded," he said, tea in one hand, cigarette in the other. "Once a beloved teacher, not so beloved now."

"I was never trying to be popular," said Duncan.

"That's good. For who stands by you now?" Mo laughed, drinking his tea, in a gulp, down to a bed of leaves. "No one stands by anyone. That was the lesson I learned in years past, and it's still true."

"Thank you for sharing your wisdom."

"How kind of me."

"How impossibly kind." Duncan gazed out the window at the flickering fields. His own tea remained untouched on the doilied flip-up table before him. "Do you know where Louise went?" he asked finally.

"She was summoned home for immoral behavior," said Mo, lighting a cigarette with an old silver lighter. "I wrote the report."

"What did you write?" asked Duncan. "How would you even know what to write? You were in the hotel. She did nothing even slightly immoral."

"Either I knew or I guessed," said Mo. "Either it was indeed quite true or else quite false. Either William made a report or he didn't. I will tell you, though. Louise is a clever girl, from a rich family. I knew her father. He made a fortune smuggling drill bits—German drill bits, the best in the world, made of a special steel. From whom were they coming? To whom were they going? Why did they have to go from Manchuria to Beijing to Shanghai to Hanoi to Chongqing? He chose not to know. Those drill bits were worth ten times their weight in gold back then; do you know why? Because they were used for making machine guns. Of course, Louise was just a baby—maybe she was not even born. But it's a talented family. During the Cultural Revolution, they were not struggled against. How did that happen? You may be surprised. But you should not be surprised." Mo held his cigarette delicately, like a scientific specimen, pinched between his thumb and forefinger. "It's a talented family."

In Beijing, Duncan trudged from the Forbidden Palace to the Summer Garden to the Temple of Heaven. Carvings, marble. Dynasties, intrigue. Emperors, concubines. And history, great quantities of history, complete with historical implications. The history cheered him somewhat. Still, on the second day he claimed to be sick and stayed in the hotel, as he did on the third day. Professor Mo called a doctor, who diagnosed Duncan, via his pulse, as too yang. Duncan's body had too much heat, he said. Duncan needed cooling foods, like mung bean soup, or seaweed, or chrysanthemum tea. He also needed an herbal remedy. For this last, the doctor wrote out a prescription, which Mo dutifully went to fill.

And so it was that Duncan was blissfully alone when the front desk called to say that his cousin was in the lobby.

"Duncan?"

"Guotai?"

"Nice to meet you, nice to meet you!"

Guotai had the family dimples, which had always mortified Duncan, and also the square family jaw, of which Duncan had felt rather proud. Duncan guessed him some ten years older than himself, though; and where Duncan was of medium height and stocky, Guotai was tall for a Chinese man, and spindly. A bend in his torso gave him a hinged look in profile, as if he had been designed to fold up; he held the palms of his hands in the small of his back, seemingly to prevent this eventuality. He had very little hair, some of it black, some of it brown, some of it white; his skin was pitted; and he smiled a broad smile of rotten teeth as he described how he had ridden down hard-seat from Harbin to Beijing for this visit. Twelve hours, he said. His teeth were yellow or blue-gray and looked as if they had no enamel, yet they were hardly as alarming as his cough. Nothing serious, he insisted, hacking, though he also mentioned that he had not brought his wife because she thought she might have TB.

Duncan considered how close one should stand to someone whose wife thought she might have TB.

"And who is this?" Duncan indicated the child by his cousin's side.

"What you say?" demanded Guotai then in English. "What you say?"

The child—a large-headed boy of about nine—hung his head. He, too, had the family dimples and jaw; Duncan wondered for a moment what it would be like to have a son. Happily, the child looked healthier than his father, though just as skinny. He had close-shaved hair, large dull eyes, a scar across one cheek, and two missing teeth.

"What you say? Huh? No face. Come on now."

"Nice meet you."

Guotai smiled. "You see his English how good. What you say next?"

"I good boy. Never make trouble."

"I train him," boasted Guotai. "My father teach me. Now I give him lesson every day."

"Ah." Duncan recalled that before the revolution, Guotai's horticulturalist-folklorist-herbalist father had studied English abroad. "What's his name?"

"What your name?" repeated Guotai.

The child pulled at his shirt. A square of light from the window fell on the outstretched fabric; he gazed at it as if in a mirror.

"What your name!" said Guotai.

"Bingbing."

"You understand English, Bingbing?" asked Duncan.

Bingbing let go of his shirt. "If I go to America, I no trouble." He stuck his tongue out through the gap in his teeth.

"Stupid!" said Guotai. Then as the child recoiled: "My father, mother have big trouble, you know. We were struggle against. I raise this boy by sell matches on the street. We have no cooking oil. We have no place to live. We have no coat to wear. In springtime we ate tree leaves. Even today I have no job. My wife is sick now. How can we live?" He coughed and coughed.

"We'd better talk upstairs," said Duncan.

"He needs to see a doctor," Duncan told Professor Mo later. "I'm not saying he has TB. But just in case."

"That cough," said Professor Mo. "Terrible."

"Is that why you left right after I introduced you?"

"A cleverer reaction, perhaps, than inviting him to your room."

"He said he was fine."

"You will be lucky if he has TB. That way the government will tell him he cannot go to America. Otherwise you will be required to tell him yourself. After all, a man like that, who is going to give him a job? A man like that, how can you let him come live in your house?"

"I don't know what you mean," said Duncan—although in fact, for once, he did.

. . .

To begin with, there was the cough.

"I don't have TB," said Guotai, over and over—so insistently that Duncan had tried not to turn away every time Guotai began hacking.

Still, Guotai shook his head. "You don't believe me," he said. "You turn your face. You think I have TB. But why I should lie? A strong man like me."

Also, there were the stories. Duncan had thought he had heard every horror story the Cultural Revolution could produce from his students, and indeed, nothing Guotai had to say about what he and his family had been through—the famines, the shortages, the beatings, the prison camps—seemed entirely new. At the same time, because of the outcome, it was worse. Duncan's students had, after all, gone on to become part of a new elite. Guotai had emerged not even a bitter man, like Professor Mo, but a broken one. He had been reduced to begging. He had lived for many years on the street. Who knew what would have happened to him and his family if his wife had not been given that factory job? It was lucky her class background was not, as Guotai explained, quite as bad as his. Also, her father had not deserted the army, as had Guotai's.

"They ask my father go fight in Korea," said Guotai. "At first he say yes. He has no choice. But then time to kill somebody, and he cannot. Instead, he cry. He say he love peace so much, he name his son Guotai. That is me. My name means 'country peace.' He say he must go home, all his plants waiting. Of course, the army kill him for just go home like that. First they kill him, and then the government try to kill my mother. Until one day, she is dead. Then try to kill me."

"What do you mean, try to kill your mother?" asked Duncan.

"No food coupon, no place to live, no job," said Guotai.

"That's how they try. My mother die right after my father. But here I am today, still live."

Duncan smiled, feeling for a moment his cousin's triumph, even as he made some calculations and realized, with a start, that Guotai was not ten or so years older than he, as he'd thought, but about his age. That meant that the whole time he, Duncan, was eating hot dogs and learning to ride a bike, his cousin was living on the streets. While Duncan was reading *Oliver Twist*, Guotai really was begging for "some more." Duncan tried to imagine what his brother Arnie's reaction to their cousin would be. Would Arnie wonder what Duncan and he had done to be born to their father, and not to their father's brother? And how much had their father known about what had gone on? Guotai's coughing began again. Duncan concentrated on not turning his head. He tried, too, not to take note of the places his cousin spat, when he spat on the floor. When Guotai asked for food and gifts, Duncan tried to provide them without judgment.

Impossible to overlook, though, was the haranguing of the child. Bingbing, having never seen a bathroom before, peed into the floor grate. He also moved his bowels there, only to have his father hit him so hard, he fell against the bathtub.

"Stupid!" he told his son.

"It's all right," said Duncan, but still Guotai raised his hand to hit his son again. Was this how Bingbing had gotten that scar on his cheek?

"Stupid!"

"He didn't know," said Duncan.

"He should ask. Stupid!"

Bingbing sniveled. Duncan tried to suggest that Guotai might be gentler with the child.

"His mother spoil him," Guotai explained blithely. "I make sure he is afraid of someone."

"In America, we don't treat children that way," said Duncan, adding, "If you came to America, you would have to stop."

"If I come to—?"

Immediately, Duncan realized he had made a mistake. Still, he nodded.

"Who stop me?"

"The government."

"The government?" Guotai was so amazed that for a moment he could say nothing. "You mean American government worse than Chinese government?"

"In this way—you might think so. Yes."

"If I come to America, I stop," he said. "My English so good, I no trouble, you know. Bingbing, too. I am strong man, healthy."

But he did not stop that afternoon. When Duncan gave Bingbing an apple and Bingbing dropped it, Guotai hit him again.

"Stupid!"

"It's all right. I'll get him another one," said Duncan.

"He eat this one, okay."

"But it's dirty," said Duncan. The apple had fallen right into one of the islands of spittle Guotai had left on the floor.

"No dirty," said Guotai. Using a coffee cup as a basin, he rinsed the apple off with orange soda, then handed it back to his child. "He no trouble. When he go to America, you will see."

"You are going to have to leave them both here," said Professor Mo. "You are a foreign expert. You have things to do in America. If your cousin has TB, you have to tell him to go save himself. Every man for himself! In America, in China, it's the same. Every man for himself!"

"Would you like to join us for dinner?" asked Duncan politely. "We're going to the Duck House."

"Perhaps another time," said Mo.

"Ah," said Duncan.

"After all, my foreign expert is sick all day, cannot go sight-seeing. I have to buy medicine, I have to make report."

"I understand. There are so many important matters. It's a real problem."

"It is. But what can I do?" Mo flung his arm over the back of his chair even as he shook his head in resignation.

On the walk to the restaurant, Guotai brought up America so aggressively, Duncan felt as though he were in the dining hall at the top of Tai Shan again, being pushed by *luo taitai*. He wondered where Louise was, and whether she had returned to school. And why did she tuck her hat ribbons behind her ears? He wanted to ask her, and to tie the ribbons under her chin, and to show her how much less likely her hat was to blow off then. He imagined her laughing at these little attentions, he imagined himself drawing her face toward his, meeting in the lovely wedge of shade under her hat's wide brim.

"What was your mother like?" Duncan asked Guotai in the meantime, trying to move the conversation onto a different plane.

"My mother was good woman," said Guotai. "A—how do you call?—saint. All her life she suffer, and when she die, she say to me one thing."

"What was that?"

" 'Go to America.' She say, 'Promise me you go to America. Ask your cousin help you.' "

"She said that?"

"She did," insisted Guotai, coughing.

"But she didn't even know you had any cousins."

"Your father wrote letter. She knew."

"And wouldn't she have told you to ask my father to help you?" Now they were in front of the restaurant. "She wouldn't have told you to ask me. I was just a child. She would've told you to ask my father."

"She say that, too. She say, 'Ask your cousins. Ask your uncle.' She say, 'They will help you.'"

"She would have first said to ask your uncle, and then she would have said to ask your cousins, if she mentioned the cousins at all. And why would she have told you to ask her husband's brother? What about her own brothers and sisters? Wouldn't she have told you to ask them?"

"Why you ask me these questions? How you know what my mother say? It was long time ago." Guotai coughed.

Duncan turned his head.

"I do not have TB," said Guotai.

"What's that cough, then?"

"I have a cold."

"We had better get you some cold medicine."

Guotai put his hands to his back, mustering his pride. "I think Bingbing and me go back to Harbin now. We waste time here. Why should we go to America anyway, become rich American who never help anybody? Better go home see my wife before she die."

At this Duncan, softening, insisted Guotai and Bingbing at least stay for dinner.

"Smell the duck," he said. "Come on. Are you going to make me eat by myself? You can't get a train tonight anyway."

Guotai thanked Duncan several times as the meal progressed, in its elaborate way, through various duck parts, up to the duck skin. It was not a meal he was going to have a chance to eat ever again, he said, and he was glad Bingbing was having a chance to try it, too.

"He remember this when he is old man," said Guotai. "Both of us will remember for a long time."

Between thanks, though, he was surly. "You turn your head," he told Duncan, coughing. "I told you before, don't turn your head."

"Why would I have dinner with you at all if I thought you had TB?" said Duncan—reflecting that this was, in truth, a good question.

Guotai heaped his plate with stir-fried duck innards; Bingbing began to squirm.

"*I can't eat any more,*" he announced in Chinese. "*I'm full.*"

Duncan's Chinese having improved since he came to China, he understood this much.

"*Delicious special food like this, of course you have room for more,*" answered Guotai ferociously, also in Chinese. He seemed about to hit Bingbing but for once stopped himself. "*You know, children in America don't get hit. That's what your uncle says.*"

Bingbing's eyes widened.

"Some children do," said Duncan, in English. "But most don't."

"*You hear that?*" said Guotai.

"*But we are not going to America.*"

"*That is true, too,*" said Guotai. "*We have no one to help us because we are poor and I have a cold.*" He smiled his lusterless smile. "*However, we are having this nice dinner. Have a Coke.*" He pushed a bottle toward his son.

"*I want a beer,*" said Bingbing.

"*Then have a beer,*" said Guotai.

"He drinks beer?" said Duncan, amazed.

Guotai laughed, pouring the remains of a beer can into a mostly empty soda glass. "Of course he drinks beer. In Harbin, everyone drinks beer. The average is twelve bottles per person per day. We are so close to Russia, you see. They taught us everything we know. To the Russians, those drunks!" He lifted his own glass as Bingbing, with two hands, lifted his. "Bottoms up!"

Duncan watched, aghast, as Bingbing chugged his drink. The child's face was so small that the rim of the glass almost touched his eyebrows. "Can he really hold his liquor? At that age?"

"Of course!" Guotai pushed another glass across to his son. *"Show your uncle what you can do."*

Bingbing, elbows in the air, dutifully chugged a second beer. When he emerged from behind the glass, the gap in his teeth was filled with foam.

"If he drink enough, he will dance on the table," promised Guotai.

"That's more than enough," said Duncan. "Don't give him any more. Look at his face. Look at how red he is. Look at his eyes. He's drunk."

"More beer!" said Bingbing.

"No more beer," said Duncan. "You know, in America, children don't drink beer."

"He says in America, children don't drink beer," said Guotai.

"But we're in China. We're not going to America. More beer! More beer!"

"No more beer," said Duncan. "It's not good for you."

Guotai poured another glass.

"Stop," said Duncan. He grabbed his cousin's arm. "I said stop."

"What's the matter, are you afraid he will embarrass you? Just the way we will embarrass you if we go to America? Don't worry, nobody here will even care. This is China. He can dance on the table and nobody will say anything. Who wants to look for trouble? Better not to get involved, that's how Chinese people think. Sweep the snow from your own doorstep."

Bingbing, meanwhile, was indeed climbing up onto the table.

"Stop!" said Duncan. "Stop!"

But Bingbing was dancing on the white tablecloth. " 'We all live in the yellow submarine, yellow submarine, yellow submarine,' " he sang. " 'We all live . . .' "

"*Good dancing, good dancing!*" cried Guotai. "*Show him what his Chinese cousins are! Embarrass him to death! He's here to visit China—show him what our country is. In China, you can dance, you can starve. Still people act as if they do not even see you! Show him! You watch.*" Guotai turned to Duncan, his eyes glittering strangely. "This is China! Nobody will say anything! You watch!"

But he was wrong. In fact, a hostess was headed their way with a frown on her face when Bingbing passed out and fell into the soup.

On the train back to school, Duncan said nothing.

"I heard about your party," said Professor Mo.

Duncan looked out the window.

"What a distinguished family you have."

Duncan looked at the floor.

"If you start to cough, let me know right away."

"I called a doctor for my cousin before we left."

"How interesting. Also, no doubt, you gave him money."

"I'm going to adopt that child," announced Duncan, although in fact he had not decided what to do. In fact, he wasn't even sure a single man could legally adopt a child, much less from China, or that either Guotai or Bingbing would agree to such a move. Still, it was what he wished to do. Or more accu-rately: he wished to be the sort of person who would adopt a child like Bingbing. A wise person, who understood what he owed fate, and how to acknowledge that. A noble person, who in another time might have become a scholar-official. But was he that person? And if he was, why did he feel as though he needed to lie down and sleep for a long, long time?

"How interesting," said Mo again. "Has your cousin gra-ciously agreed to accept your kindness?"

Duncan did not answer.

"I'm so surprised." Mo made a loopy movement with his foot, happy and full of triumph. "Perhaps you should head back to America right after you're done teaching, instead of traveling around. So you can work on the adoption."

Duncan said nothing to this, either, not wanting to agree with Professor Mo, although in fact he was indeed thinking about cutting his stay short. There were too many truths here; he wanted to go home. This is what he knew: That the weather was extreme in China. That he missed pizza. That he envied his brother Arnie, with his sense of purpose in life. How shallow it was to believe in making money, and yet how it protected one against life itself—disorienting, disconcerting life. It was as use-ful as religion. Perhaps it was a religion, to which he, Duncan, should convert. For Louise had her code; the old women on Tai Shan had their belief; even Professor Mo had his vengeful calcu-lation. What did Duncan have with which to organize pointless, brutal life? He had rejected his old code of rejection, and rightly so; but now more than ever he could only cry to think of those Song Dynasty vases, all that certainty behind glass.

Perhaps he was just another idealist on a road to end badly, like his uncle or like Professor Mo.

So he thought before he arrived back at the coal-mining

institute. But then there, waiting at the door of his apartment, magical as a spot of moonlight in the middle of the day, were Louise and what appeared to be her younger self—an impossibly lovely girl, very like her mother, only in finer form. Louise's agility was, in her, grace; Louise's radiance was, in her, luminosity. Blue comes from indigo but is better than indigo, that's what the Chinese said. Louise's daughter had the sort of beauty around which hushes fell and plots rose. There was no real goodness in looks; Duncan knew that. And yet the gentle perfection of her cheekbones, of her eyebrows, of her eyes and mouth, of her utterly diaphanous complexion—how it moved him all the same. It gave one hope that from the messy world might occasionally arise clarity; that poise and harmony were part of the natural order of things. Duncan could only imagine how protective Louise had had to be of her daughter; how much trouble she might have already attracted. Was Duncan the man who could shelter her? And could he do this for Louise, for love—learn to love her daughter instead of her? Perhaps he was getting ahead of himself. And yet how he adored Louise already for wanting such a thing, if that's what she wanted. How he adored her for wanting more—he hoped she wanted more— than for him to sponsor her daughter to America.

"Hello," said Louise. She was wearing the same peach-colored blouse she had worn climbing Tai Shan. The top button was buttoned now, but the blouse still appeared as preternaturally fresh as ever.

"Hello," said Duncan. "How is your health?"

"I am in good health," she said. "And you?"

"I am healthy, too. And who is this?"

"I like to introduce to you the someone special," said Louise.

"I'd like to introduce to you someone special," corrected Duncan.

"No," said Louise. "The someone special. Remember? I promise you. On the mountain."

He started. "Ah. I do remember. This is your daughter?"

"My daughter, Lingli."

"Hello," said Duncan.

"Nice to meet you," said Lingli. Her voice was low but clear—a guileless, confident voice.

"She speaks English better than her mother," said Louise.

In other words, she can go to America, Duncan almost said. He wanted to ask, *And how did she learn it? Who taught her? Who pulled a string?* But he held his tongue.

Louise said, "I told her you are a good man."

"Ah," he joked. "You made a report."

"I don't catch your meaning."

Had she startled?

"You made a report," he repeated carefully. "About me."

"No report," said Louise. "What report?"

"I just meant about me, to your daughter. You made a report to your daughter."

"I thought you ask if I made a report to Professor Mo."

"Of course you didn't," he said. "Why would I ask that?"

"I bring you my daughter," said Louise. "All the way from Nanjing. Her name is Lingli."

"Yes, we've met."

Lingli looked at her mother with consternation; her delicate brow rumpled. A shadow cast a hard line across the exquisite undulation of her cheek.

More gently, he said, "You've come all the way from Nanjing. How was the train ride?"

Louise looked at Lingli. "You say."

"Very comfortable," said Lingli.

"It's a long ride all the same," he said.

"Do you have something more to say?" said Louise.

"It was not long at all," said Lingli. "It was very comfortable."

"Perhaps you'll both come in and rest?" said Duncan. And again: "You've come all the way from Nanjing."

Louise hesitated, touching her chin. Her head listed; her face reddened as though she were going to cry. "I've made a big mistake. How do you say? A terrible mistake. I've make a terrible mistake."

"Please," he said then. "No mistake."

"A mistake," she insisted. "My meaning is—"

"Please. I understand your meaning," he said. "No mistake. I'm sorry. I'm the one who's made mistakes. Please."

And with that, he unlocked his door, marveling at how it seemed, with no effort at all, to open wide. It was possible Louise had made many reports. It was possible that she came, after all, from a most talented family. It was possible she was sorry; it was possible she wasn't; it was possible she loved him herself; it was possible she didn't love him at all. It was possible that he would never love her daughter, or that her daughter would never love him. It was possible her daughter would make reports, too. It was possible he could never forgive himself if he sponsored Lingli to America and left poor Guotai and Bingbing behind. How tangled up everything was already. Still he could say this, that there was one thing he had, being an American— not so much an unshakable conviction as a habit of believing in the happiest possibility. Truly it was a form of blindness. He understood why denizens of the Old World laughed at people like him.

Yet he saw now, finally, that it was as incurably his as any faith. For how noble Louise's daughter seemed to him, how pure an expression of everything elegant and upright about China! And how easily, still, despite all he had been through, he could see the proper end to his hopelessly tortured story. He offered Lingli a seat. Heart throbbing, he offered to show her his bathtub. For there she was, his heart's leading lady. How vividly he could imagine the scenes and the credits; and, after the credits, the applause.

A Tea Tale

Case: Tom and Tory Shore own a successful independent coffee shop in a small Cincinnati suburb. Consistent with national trends, more people in their area are drinking tea.

Hoping to expand their tea offerings, they attend a late fall World Tea Expo. There they meet Song, owner of the Heavenly Cloud Tea Company, based in a remote part of Yunnan Province, in western China. Heavenly Cloud is a small tea company that produces black tea. As Tom and Tory don't know much about tea, Tom asks questions at different booths and learns that all teas are produced from the same bush but have different processing methods: White and green tea are not oxidized, oolong tea is partially oxidized, and black tea is fully oxidized. Discovering that over 80 percent of tea consumed in the United States is black tea, which stands up to being iced, as well as to the addition of milk, sugar, lemon, and honey, Tom and Tory eventually circle back to the Heavenly Cloud Tea Company, which is offering a Yunnan black tea known as Dianhong tea.

"You're writing a business case about us?" I asked.

"Everyone wants a piece of China," said Tom, adjusting his

reading glasses, a.k.a. my reading glasses. "And we have a valuable perspective." Glancing down at the keyboard, then up at a porthole of a screen, he seemed too big a guy to be squinting at a box of a computer that packed up into a Cordura bag like a picnic. But there he was, a former linebacker scrunched up like a horse jockey. "Plus, Billy wrote a case about the insurance business and made a lot of money."

"Ah," I said. "Mystery solved." Though the youngest of the three Shore brothers, Billy had always been the quarterback.

Tom typed on, pecking with two fingers.

They taste the tea and are instantly taken by the honey notes and smooth flavor. As coffee drinkers, Tom and Tory note that this tea is not bitter or astringent. They admire the light amber color of the infusion. It is like maple syrup, says Tom, who grew up spending summers in Vermont.

Song does not speak English, but he has brought a translator named Feng, who recently graduated from a regional college in Yunnan. It takes some effort, but the parties get to a point where they feel they understand each other.

"Some effort is right," I said, reading over the shoulder seam of Tom's Bengals T-shirt. "What we really needed was someone to translate for the translator."

"Like what's-her-name from our China tour," he said. "Oval."

"Opal."

"Opal. I must be getting Alzheimer's."

"You're not getting Alzheimer's."

As their conversation concludes, Song invites Tom and Tory to visit Yunnan.

Tom and Tory do some research on black teas, learning that most U.S. tea is sourced from India, Sri Lanka, and

Kenya. They view pictures of Yunnan Province, too, with its misty mountains, amazing architecture, and curious ethnic minority cultures and conclude that Dianhong tea may represent a new, wonderfully different option for their customers.

"They really were amazing pictures," I said.

"Who even knew that part of China existed?"

"I can't believe you asked if it was in Tibet."

"Well, when you marry a dumb jock, you get dumb jock questions," he said genially. "Plus, what's that you like to tell people? That I got hit in the head once too often?"

They write to Feng, saying they would indeed like to visit Yunnan. To their surprise, Feng responds ten days later with a formal invitation from Song. If Tom and Tory agree to pay for their own airfare, Song will make and pay for their land arrangements. In January, Tom and Tory depart for their trip. Two days and three connecting flights later, they arrive in Yunnan.

"Oh my god, now that was what you call exhausting," I said. "We couldn't have been more zonked if we'd walked."

Song, Feng, and a group of others who are hastily intro-duced greet Tom and Tory at the airport. They depart for the hotel and are told to meet in the lobby in fifteen minutes for the welcome banquet. Tom and Tory want to clean up and rest a bit, but Feng insists there's no time for that.

"They were pretty rude, really, when you come right down to it," I said.

Teaching point: While American businessmen might be acting on their own behalf, their Chinese counterparts are often part of a large network of people, including local officials, with whom the Chinese businessmen are completely preoccupied.

"Who told us that? I forget," said Tom.

"Me, too, but god, they were right. You think you're this important guest, but actually you're just a trophy." I did not add *as I understand* since, Miss Ohio though I once was, I was now what my mother used to call a barren woman. After all those years of trying not to get banged up—it was what you call ironic.

They are treated to an enormous banquet in a private room of a local restaurant, including exotic mushrooms they know to be expensive. Over the next four days, too, Tom and Tory are given the royal treatment. They depart after breakfast each day for tours of the tea fields and tea processing plants, as well as of rushing gorges, a stone forest, a monastery, and an unspoiled ancient town. They are serenaded by ethnic minorities in exotic costumes and also enjoy the unusually warm weather. When Tom asks if they always wear T-shirts in January, Feng says that, actually, they usually have to wear light jackets. Tom and Tory delight in their good luck.

"Do you really want to include that about the weather?" I asked.

"You must have forgotten what happened," he said.

Indeed, they are so taken by what they see that they decide not only to sell Dianhong tea in their shop, but to go whole hog and set themselves up as its U.S. distributors. It is the biggest financial risk they've ever taken, but they feel this is a once-in-a-lifetime opportunity. Song and Feng are thrilled. The day before Tom and Tory are scheduled to depart, they all meet to discuss their first order. Tom and Tory taste some samples and choose one with distinct honey notes, light color, and clean flavor. Through Feng, they agree to purchase two tons of this tea, using a standard international goods sales contract Feng calls "government approved."

As Song doesn't have two tons of tea in inventory, he promises that when the growing season begins in the spring, he will process the tea and send it to them. Tom and Tory agree. Since they need time to build a distribution chain anyway, this arrangement seems perfect.

The contract includes a number of provisions, including:

- *All disputes will be settled through friendly consultations. If no settlement can be reached, the case shall then be submitted to the Foreign Trade Arbitration Commission of the China Council for the Promotion of International Trade.*
- *Any decision rendered by the commission will be final and binding on both parties.*
- *The contract will be in Chinese and English. In case of any discrepancy, the Chinese version will prevail.*

Tom and Tory sign. They then take photos with Song with the local media present.

"I think you should add something about how focused they were on playing up our Americanness," I said. "Like, I had that Chinese dress, but they didn't want me to wear it, remember?"

"And our hair," recalled Tom. "They didn't want us to wear hats, so our hair would show. Maybe I should put that in."

"Put in how they positioned the lights, too. To make our

hair shine as bright as possible. And how they literally put us on a pedestal. It was like the Miss Ohio finals only we didn't have to suck our stomachs in."

Tom and Tory are told to remove their hats, so that their blond hair would show, and are encouraged in every way to appear as foreign as possible.

"I think I'll leave it at that," Tom said.

That evening Song, Feng, the local government representatives, and many others who are never introduced treat Tom and Tory to an elaborate closing banquet.

*Teaching point: Many people will be invited to the banquet as a way of showing respect for the American guests and of signaling the importance of the event.

Fish, rare mushrooms, wild vegetables, and even sea cucumber, a slimy delicacy Tom and Tory don't much care for, show up on the menu.

*Teaching point: It is best to try and eat what you can as people will discuss everything you push to the side of your plate.

Unlike previous dinners, where the food was placed on a lazy Susan in the middle of the table for all to share, this meal has waiter service. Apparently to exoticize the occasion, beautifully dressed waiters bring individual portions to each person.

"That was so funny, that showing off for the big shots meant serving Western style," I said.

"It was just another exotic thing. Like our hair and our clothes."

I laughed. "You mean our costumes."

The local spirit known as bai jiu *is served. After several "bottoms up," Tom and Tory feel more comfortable with Song, sharing stories about their life and families. Song responds by saying he has a wife and son but offers no other information.*

"They just don't talk about themselves the way we do," I said.

"Which might be their culture, but let's face it. It makes you feel like they're hiding something."

"Of course, you did ask a lot of questions. Maybe they weren't used to that."

"While all they wanted was to know what I ate, that I got to be so big."

"Big as an ox, wasn't that what they said?"

"They were crude and rude, those Chinese," he said. "Crude and rude."

*Teaching point: The Chinese will freely discuss things like salary and how much you paid for your house, yet they won't say much about themselves personally, which may feel strange but is actually just their culture.

At the meal, Song toasts to making Dianhong tea the most famous in the world—with everyone getting rich in the process. The mood is upbeat.

Tom and Tory return to Cincinnati thoroughly pleased. In May, Feng writes to say that the tea is being processed and that they should send the wire transfer to proceed. They make the wire to Song's bank, arrange to ship the tea from Shanghai, and rent warehouse space. The delivery goes without a hitch. Tom and Tory prepare to offer this "new and exotic" tea to their customers.

Unfortunately, though, when the tea arrives and they sample it, they find themselves frowning.

"Oh my god. Do you remember?" I said.

"Of course. That's why I'm writing the case."

"It was what you call a fiasco."

They do a side-by-side comparison of the tea shipment and the sample that Song had given them in January. There is a marked difference. The sample is smooth and sweet. The tea they received is flat and bitter. They put together a focus group to get some objective opinions. Without exception, the customers dislike the tea.

Tom kneaded his forehead at the memory. "What was it Duncan Hsu said?"

"He said it made Lipton's taste like the tea of emperors. But of course, that was partly just him and Lingli feeling offended we didn't ask them for advice beforehand, don't you think?"

"Nothing like a Chinese wife to make a guy a China expert." Tom smirked.

"And you know what everyone calls her," I said.

"No, what."

"Miss Fake."

"That's not nice."

"It's because no one's ever seen her with a hair out of place. Plus, she never gains weight."

Tom laughed. "Now there's a sin."

Outraged, Tom and Tory put a hold on selling the tea to the public. They arrange for a phone call. This is no easy matter, but they feel it will help underscore that the tea is unsalable. They explain why the customers don't like it and complain that the flavor doesn't match the sample.

With Song apparently beside her, Feng explains that tea is like wine, with each year's vintage being a little different.

*Weather and growing conditions have an impact on tea, she
says. This year's warm weather could well have affected the
tea's sweetness. Still, she maintains, they chose an estate tea,
meaning tea from a certain acreage, and this is that estate
tea. Heavenly Cloud Tea Company has conformed to the
contract by shipping 2 tons of Dianhong black tea. In closing, she emphasizes that tea is a natural product. Variation
is natural.*

"As if we didn't know that from coffee," I said.

"And as for whether they gave a rat's ass that we were out
the equivalent of a half a year's rent on our shop . . ."

"They didn't care any more about that than they cared how
tired we were when we landed."

"Total bullshit artists."

"The worst."

*Tom and Tory read up on dispute resolution in China.
They learn that it is important to select a lawyer with good
connections—with what the literature calls guanxi. But is
this really any more important than in the United States?
Figuring that business is business, they turn to an associate
in a law firm that does international work.*

"It's good you don't say it was your brother Randy," I said.
Tom shrugged.

*The lawyer, Randy, understands that Tom and Tory want to
make a claim for nonconforming goods but are barred from
suing in U.S. courts because they agreed to binding arbitration in China. He knows that arbitration is expensive and
guesses that there will be an element of subjectivity when it
comes to determining whether the tea is a conforming good.*

And he guesses, too, that Chinese arbitrators will be biased toward Chinese companies like Song's, given the government support for this contract.

Tom and Tory are furious. But Randy also thinks that the government is actually eager to build a tea business—as, it seems, is the Heavenly Cloud Tea Company. He therefore counsels Tom and Tory to demand damages but prepare themselves to take a loss in the hopes of building a long-term relationship.

"Something he could afford to recommend, of course, not being us," said Tom.

Is his approach correct? In whose favor is an arbitrator likely to decide?

"I don't know. Is there really any point in asking that?" I asked. "When anyone can guess a Chinese arbitrator was one hundred percent likely to find in favor of the Chinese company?" Tom backspaced.

Given that a Chinese arbitrator is almost guaranteed to find in favor of the Heavenly Cloud Tea Company, what are Tom and Tory's options going forward? Randy also counsels that in any future negotiations, they should be sure to seek a more airtight contract to begin with. Is he right? And if so, what might provide effective protection for Tom and Tory?

"How can a contract be airtight when the government writes the contract, the English version doesn't count, and they don't have a regular legal system?" I said.

Tom played with his mouse. "The summary teaching point should really be: Stay out of China."

"That'll make for a case that sells better than Billy's."

Tom straightened his tiger-striped mouse pad. His shirt and the mouse pad were like a set.

"I don't know," I went on. "Maybe we should consider what Randy says. I mean, would it make any sense at all to take the loss, build a relationship, and see what happens?"

"That's called throwing good money after bad," said Tom. "Plus what does Randy know, when he's never even been to China?"

"Well, it's what Lingli thinks, too, for what it's worth," I said.

"You talked to Miss Fake?"

"I got put on a slow shift with her at the co-op and couldn't help bringing up the whole mess. Since we were just, like, standing there."

"And?"

"And she said that while Song and Feng might really have been cheating us, it might also have been what you call an honest mistake. I mean, this is a tiny firm with no experience with foreigners, right? She said maybe there really is a lot of variation in tea. Which a Chinese buyer would have accepted."

"Even if it was undrinkable?"

"They might not have thought it undrinkable. Or maybe they would have blended it with better batches."

"The way Alejandro does with coffee."

"Adriano."

"I'm getting Alzheimer's."

"You're not getting Alzheimer's. Also she said Song and Feng might not have been able to split the loss with us even if they wanted to because of the government. And you know, all those pictures. The whole thing was so public. But Lingli thought that if we take a loss, Song and Feng might feel bad, and think us sincere and committed, and really try to make things work." I hesitated. "She also said she knows someone who knows someone, if we'd like to be introduced. I think her English name is Tricia?"

"Ha. And what kind of kickback would this Tricia need? Oh, I'm sorry. I meant commission."

"I don't know. But Lingli also said she would be willing to try to help, if we'd like. Though she's not Tricia, so."

"Meaning that we can possibly recoup some money if she and Tricia each get a cut?"

"I'm not sure. She says Tricia thinks Americans brought a lot of good ideas to China. Apparently she is very experienced with trade. And Lingli thinks we maybe could use some of this famous *guanxi.*"

"The original Chinese secret sauce."

I shrugged.

"Tory," he said then. "Did you see on TV what happened in that huge square we saw in front of the Forbidden Palace? The one full of kites? Remember?"

"Tiananmen Square? Where the protesters are?"

"Yeah, well, now it's full of tanks, too, and they're firing. On the students."

"I did see. And it's horrible, honey. It's barbaric. It's what you call beyond the pale. But what does it have to do with us?"

"You can't trust these people."

"That's the government," I argued. "That's not the people. The government is doing the shooting. The people are the ones being shot at."

"Don't you think the government was behind every one of those banquets?" said Tom. "The company was even called a 'township and village enterprise.' Song and Feng are probably party members."

"So a sunk cost is a sunk cost. Is that what you're saying?"

"I'm saying we should stick to coffee."

"Maybe we should open a coffee shop in China."

"What is it with you and China? The Chinese drink tea. Ask Lingli."

"Okay. The next time I see her, I'll ask her, Do the Chinese drink tea?"

"There's China the dream and China the reality, Tory." Tom powered off his computer.

"Aw, come on, honey," I said then. "Aren't I allowed to disagree? We don't have to take your brother's advice. Yours is the only opinion that counts. Sayonara, China! I'll never mention it again."

But he'd already taken off my reading glasses and stood up from his too-small computer, and he never did go back to the case.

Probably we could have updated it, though, when four years later, Duncan and Lingli opened a tea shop, complete with Dianhong tea, half a block from our coffee shop.

"Do you see what I mean?" said Tom then. "Can you trust them? Can you?"

"Don't you have to ask whether you can trust your brother, too?" I said. Because Randy, after all, was now Duncan and Lingli's lawyer.

But Tom only replied, "I'm telling you, they'll do anything."

"*They*? Who's *they*?" I asked.

At the same time, I did wonder if Duncan and Lingli really had to open up a shop so close to ours. Ours was a small downtown, it was true—all of six square blocks. There weren't a lot of options. Still.

As Tom and I now had an adopted Chinese toddler, and as I took her on an adventure every morning, I brought her to visit Duncan and Lingli's opening day open house. Mei was in her umbrella stroller, and I was secretly glad to find the shop empty as I began maneuvering through the front door—leaning into it with my shoulder, then propping it open with my foot. Even as I backed the stroller in, though, I could tell the store wasn't going to stay empty for long. There were enormous photos of Yunnan on one of its gold-washed walls—full-color blowups of the gorges, of the stone forest, of the ancient town, of the monastery. On the other wall there was a large Chinese curio cabinet full of tea canisters and clay pots and vases, and on the chairs there were red seat cushion covers that looked like real silk, with gold tassels hanging from their corners.

Duncan suddenly appeared behind Mei and me.

"Welcome!" he said, holding the door. "Come in! Come in!" If he felt guilty about opening so close to our store or taking over our tea connection, it wasn't obvious. His dimpled face was bright as a star, and he was wearing a Yunnanese ethnic minority costume that looked like pajamas on him: white tunic, white pants, blue and gold vest, and on his head, the crowning touch—a thickly padded multicolored headwrap that but for its pink and green pompoms could have been some sort of concussion cryotherapy.

"Congratulations!" I said. "This is just great! And what a great outfit! Is that from the Bai people?" I guessed that because his outfit was predominantly white; and *Bai,* we had learned in China, meant "white."

"Thank you! Yes! You're very kind!" he said. But then, with an embarrassed "You'll have to excuse me, you're our first guests and we're not quite set up," he disappeared.

"Can I offer you some free tea?" Lingli asked from behind the counter. Though in costume, too, she—unlike Duncan— was a breathtaking sight. Indeed, she looked so lovely that I couldn't help but think it too bad that being married and probably too old—it was so hard to tell with Asians, but I guessed late twenties?—she could never compete for Miss Ohio. Though what about Mrs. Ohio? Was she a U.S. citizen? With her rose petal complexion and her drop-dead gorgeous outfit—a flowing red-and-white affair, with camellias embroidered everywhere—she would be a hit with the judges, I knew. The white ribbon that hung down from her waist matched her pants, and on her head she wore a huge flaring white headdress, a bit like a Native American war bonnet, except with downy white things instead of eagle feathers.

"No, thank you," I said.

She said that her offer stood anytime. "A special for neighbors," she said. "Not just on opening day. Every day."

"Thanks," I said. And then, because I felt I had to, I added, "You're welcome to a free cuppa at our place anytime, too."

"Oh!" she said. "A chance to learn from a master about coffee."

I wasn't sure what to think about that. "Maybe someday we'll open a coffee shop in China," I joked.

"Great idea!" she said. "We can be partners! And who's this?" She leaned so far over the glass counter, she had to hold her war bonnet with her hand.

As Tom and I had been among the first to adopt from China, we were almost always asked either "Is she yours?" or "Where did you get her?" when people saw Mei. Lingli was the first to express simple delight in our cherubic daughter. "Her name is Mei," I said.

Mei bounced up and down in her stroller at the sound of her name. "Mei!" she shouted. "Mei!" Now that her feet reached the foot strap and she could use her legs, there was real propulsion to her bounce; I had to grip the handles of the stroller to stabilize it.

"How old is she?"

"How old are you?" I asked the top of Mei's head.

"Two and half!" Twisting around toward me, she put up two fingers in a V.

"Two and *a* half," I said.

"Two and half!" She giggled as if she knew perfectly well this was wrong.

"Very smart," said Lingli. "How come we never met before? Does your name mean 'beautiful'?"

Mei knew but didn't answer.

"Yes," I supplied.

"You can have all the free tea you want, too," Lingli told Mei. "We have a special in our store for all Chinese people. Especially beautiful girls whose name means 'beautiful.'"

I knelt beside Mei, one arm behind the stroller.

"Do you want a cookie?" asked Lingli.

Mei's mouth hung open. She nodded gravely—not the way grown-ups nod, with their mouth closed and their eyebrows down, but with her mouth still open and her eyebrows up.

"Here, I give you. That's an almond cookie—a kind of Chinese cookie. And I have a present for you." Lingli rummaged around behind the counter and produced a small stuffed animal. "Do you know what this is?"

"Bear!" said Mei.

"Yes. It is a special bear, a Chinese bear. Call panda bear. Can you say 'panda bear'?"

"Panda bear!"

"How about in Chinese? Can you say *xiongmao*?"

"*Xiongmao*."

"Very good! Your pronunciation is just like a Chinese girl. I give to you."

Mei reached up; Lingli reached down. The bear changed hands.

"Do you know what he eats?" asked Lingli.

Mei shook her head.

"He eats bamboo."

"Bamboo!"

"What do you say?" I interrupted from beside Mei. I wasn't sure why I didn't want to give Lingli a chance to teach Mei how to say "bamboo" in Chinese, but I didn't.

"Thank you!" said Mei, more to me than to Lingli. She clutched the panda with both hands.

"Very good," I said.

Lingli rarely smiled a big smile, but now she gave Mei a broad toothy grin. "Do you know how to say 'see you again' in Chinese?"

Mei shook her head emphatically.

"*Zai jian,*" said Lingli.

"*Zai jian!*" Mei shouted.

"Very good! *Zai jian!*"

"*Zai jian! Zai jian!*" Hugging the panda, Mei bounced hard in her stroller seat.

"Next time you come, you can have free cookie and free tea and free Chinese lesson, all together," said Lingli.

"*Zai jian!*"

We were all smiling when Mei and I left, especially Lingli, who now had a second visitor to chat up—Ned Ward, a longtime customer of ours, who had sat by our window reading the paper every morning for years. He looked dazzled even before Lingli offered him a free cup of tea. Then he straightened up and, grinning, tucked his shirt in a little before accepting the sample.

Back in our own shop, I thought about redecorating. We hadn't upgraded since we opened for business fifteen years ago. The chairs were the same banged-up bentwood chairs; the tablecloths were the same red-and-white-check easy-clean tablecloths. The staff, too, wore the same blue TOM & TORY'S COFFEE SHOP shirts they always had, complete with our steaming-coffee-cup logo on the back. We should at least paint, I decided. Maybe try a sky-blue background with sponged-on white clouds? Or was that what you would call a cliché? If we had not lost all that money on the China tea deal, we could afford to do more—but, well.

And now, just as we'd gotten back on our feet, here was Duncan and Lingli's shop.

"I don't know why, I didn't like the way she talked to Mei," I told Tom at home. Mei was busy grinding sidewalk chalk into pink and purple patties on the patio; from time to time she would water the chalk with a watering can. Then she would mush it around some more.

"You don't trust her," he said.

"We're the ones who walked away from the deal," I said. "We're the ones who refused her advice, and Randy's, too. You can't really call what happened their fault."

Still, as Mei stepped into her watered chalk and tracked it around, making footprints, I had to admit that I didn't want to teach Lingli about coffee. And I didn't want Lingli teaching Mei Chinese, either.

"It was cool that Mei could repeat the Chinese perfectly," I said. "She probably remembers the sounds from when she was a baby. And I'd love her to learn Chinese. It's what you call an opportunity. But I don't know. I didn't like the way Lingli gave Mei that panda bear."

"A panda bear is just a panda bear," said Tom. "And let me just say, we might have lost money on that tea, but we do have at least one successful import." Laughing as Mei wiped her chalky hands all over the patio chair cushions, he caught her up in his arms, buzz-kissed her, and made her squeal. "We'll just have to think of a blocking strategy."

"Stock up on almond cookies so she won't want theirs?" I said. "Get her a bigger, better panda bear? Is that what you're thinking?"

"Exactly." He accordioned some newspaper up into a fan and fanned himself.

I nodded. Still, I turned off the baby monitor and sat by Mei's crib that afternoon, watching her nap. If she wasn't cold, Mei sprawled when she slept, spreading herself out like a starfish— which might suggest it would be easy to pry the panda bear out of her fingers. But that would be what you call a fantasy. It was only by straightening one miniature finger at a time that I managed to work the panda away from her. Still I did, and when Mei woke up, still sweaty from her nap, I blew on her tummy to distract her. She giggled but then started looking around.

"Where's Panda?" she demanded immediately. "I want Panda!"

"How about a clean diaper first?" I said, launching her like a rocket out of her crib.

That made her giggle, too. But she would not lie down to be changed until she had her panda bear back.

"Panda! Panda!" she cried. "I want Panda!"

I produced the bear. And later, when she insisted, I allowed Panda to join us for dinner, too. We set up a seat for Panda. We tied a bib on Panda. We supplied Panda with a place mat and a spoon. As for what Panda wanted for dinner, that was of course ice cream. Then it wanted bamboo and, in a sippy cup, tea.

Lulu in Exile

Arnie Hsu the success, brother of Duncan Hsu the failure, had his own import-export business. This now involved not only a U.S. office and a Hong Kong office but a factory in Shanghai and a factory in Italy, as well as forty lucky employees, all of whom amassed frequent-flyer miles at an enviable rate as a result of their good attitude toward life. Arnie, who boasted the best attitude of everyone, wore Italian suits in colors named for vitamin-rich vegetables like eggplant and kale. Also, he wore wraparound sunglasses and had his car washed inside and out while he went shopping with his nubile girlfriend from Hong Kong, Lulu. Lulu did not have to have a good attitude, being less than half his age and full of entertainingly skewed views. For example, she could never get over how underdeveloped malls were in America. She believed Americans were not true shoppers, being too enamored of parks.

"Explain to me about trees," she once said to Duncan, showing him a tie she had bought for Arnie, but that Arnie had turned out to already own. "I know people in America like to walk around in the woods with the mosquitoes. But why do they like such things? How about you explain to me, okay?" Her tone turned wheedling as she made a pretty show of her dimples. "I give you this nice tie for a present."

Nobody loved Hong Kong like Lulu. First of all, as a vertical city, easily negotiated by chauffeured car and elevator, Hong Kong was perfect for high heels. Also, it was a city where girls were girls, where Lulu could top a lime-green bustier with a red velvet Mao jacket and laugh at American tourist girls in their flip-flops and sackcloth.

But now, thanks to history, here appeared her future: exile in natural-fiber land. Some people thought Hong Kong would be fine after the Handover, but the Hsus certainly didn't. You watch, we are all going to end up in a nice American suburb, they predicted—including Lulu in that "we," even though Arnie and Duncan's mother wondered if Lulu would make a good wife.

"All she knows is spend money," Marge complained to Duncan, never mind that she was theoretically not speaking to him. Recently, she had taken to cutting out articles about every sort of learning disability now known and sending them all to him, as if one of them must explain something. "Children need a real mother, tell them what to do. What is right attitude, what is wrong attitude, who their friends should be. Otherwise, what? Otherwise, nobody is going to graduate school, that's what."

"Otherwise, all the kids turn out like me."

"Exactly."

"So bad the mothers can't sleep at night, thinking it is their own fault."

"What do you mean, my fault?" Marge said. "You never listen to anything I say, you think you know everything already. That is your whole problem. If I tell you you are stupid, do you listen to me? Of course not. Instead you say, 'If I'm so stupid, how come blah blah blah blah.'"

"But it's true, Ma. If I'm so stupid . . ." Duncan tried to

remind his mother that he did have a wife and kids, and a tea shop that, if not a big deal company like Arnie's, did at least break even.

But Marge wasn't listening.

"Forget about true! That's your whole trouble, you want to tell me what is true. As if you are the mother! That's why I'm not speaking to you these days, because I am the mother. I am the one who says what is true, do you hear me?"

"Faintly," he said.

This may or may not have been why his mother really did stop speaking to him, and how it happened that she advanced her plot on Lulu strictly on her own. Arnie did not believe this, but it was true. It was strictly on her own that Marge called the fanciest store in town and ordered a red silk duster, a matching red silk jumpsuit, and a see-through red motorcycle jacket—all in size two.

"Try them on, try them on!" said Marge as Lulu opened the boxes. "You can wear the jumpsuit with the duster or with the jacket! Either way!"

Lulu hesitated. "But I am a size six."

"No, no, no, no," said Marge. "Only in your mind you are a size six. What I say is true. You are a size two. Size six is the size of a horse."

"I am not a horse!" wailed Lulu.

"Of course not," said Marge. "You are a size two."

Also, she cajoled Lulu into having lunch with her. "Arnie says you love chocolate mousse," she said. To which Lulu said, "No, no, no, no," only to have Marge order it anyway.

"Don't be polite," she said. And, "You haven't eaten one bite." And, "You don't like it? I order something else."

"No, no, no, no!"

But a banana split arrived, and after the banana split, a

strawberry shortcake, and after the strawberry shortcake, a
baked Alaska.

"I love you," Lulu told Arnie that night. "You are a great success.
But I wonder about our future."

"Oh, Lulu," said Arnie, with a misty look. "There's nothing
to wonder about. I've just been waiting for the right moment to
ask."

"That's not it."

"And the ring. You said yourself that you didn't know what
cut you liked best."

"Your mother had so much fun, she wants to take me shopping every week," said Lulu.

Arnie stopped short, puzzled.

"She says if we get married, she's going to take me shopping
every day."

"But, Lulu," said Arnie, after a moment, "you like to shop."

"And after shopping, lunch," said Lulu. "She says if we get
married, she's going to take me to lunch every single day."

"And that's too much to ask? To have lunch with my mother?
For me? For us? I thought we were in love."

"We were," said Lulu. But then she could say no more, as,
overcome by sobbing, she adjusted Arnie's tie for him, one last
sweet time.

Gratitude

For what did one raise these children? For what did one labor and heave and suffer reconstructive surgery; for what did one feed and clothe and coax and school, raising them from sitting to standing to making their own money, if not for their well-deserved gratitude? It was work, it was a lot of work, even with Filipino maids and international schools and pull at certain American universities, it was work! It was donations. It was atriums, reading rooms, auditoriums; it was handicap ramps and indoor trees and architects who had never been taught when to stop. Did not parents who had sacrificed, who had lunched, who had dealt with schematics and precedents and flow (how Tina detested flow), deserve a child who at least left her cell phone on? Was it too much to ask?

It was not too much to ask. And yet Tina's number-one daughter, Bobby Koo—age twenty-five, living far far from Hong Kong, in a New York apartment of her own in a building with a doorman, maybe not in a top top neighborhood, but still (thanks to guess who?) on a very nice block she could have not afforded by herself, even working on Wall Street as she did—did not feel she owed it to anyone to keep her cell phone on. Never mind that all sorts of lawyers and bankers and brokers lived in her building. Never mind that every day she had the chance to meet someone nice, maybe even very nice, right in the elevator. All the same Bobby was inexplicably unavailable—at first it was sometimes, then it was half the time, and now it was all the time. She had misplaced it, she had not recharged it, for all they knew she maybe even kept a second phone, with a secret number known to everyone except her helpless mother in Hong Kong. Was it possible? It was possible. And how was it that Bobby was always in a meeting when Tina called her office, but not when other people called? Tina had vowed a hundred times to test that robot secretary someday—to call pretending to be a client—but in the end she never had, wanting and not wanting to know. She was ambivalent. Though she did indeed now very definitely one hundred percent want to know how it was that Bobby's sisters called and reached her fine.

"Luck," said number three, in Cantonese. (This was Lulu the baby, back for good thank god from the U.S.)

"Karma," said number two, in English. (That was Betty the good girl—married, pregnant, everything right on schedule.)

But what was this "karma"? Tina knew and yet wondered. She herself had gone to the United States for her MBA and come back sounding okay, not like some people who took words to the United States and brought them back sounding strange. Would she have tried so hard to prepare the kids for the future if she knew they would sound like this? Ever since the Handover, she and Johnson were looking out for opportunity but looking out for danger, too; it was like having two heads. You needed an apartment in Shanghai to make money, and an apartment in Vancouver to get out, and you couldn't have too many passports, they were like bracelets. Degrees, too, especially from those top schools, for example, Harvard. But now, in English especially, her older daughters sounded strange, and somehow they also did in Shanghainese, and in Mandarin, and probably if Tina understood Cantonese, she would find them sounding strange in Cantonese as well.

"I want you to tell your sister something," Tina said now, in Shanghainese. Outside it rained in fine perfect hairs, as if the clouds just had to show they did not have to straighten their hair Korean style, they were already Korean style. "I want you to find something out."

But both girls were suddenly busy over there in the big chairs—Lulu in her own seat with her magazines, and Betty in Bobby's seat, playing with the new puppy she claimed made her feel less baby sick. One thing good about SARS was that everyone had had to stay home, so that even though things were better, the girls still stayed home quite a lot. They had a new habit. Although that dog—when Betty was not sleeping or throwing up, she carried it around everywhere, in a handbag; Johnson said he just hoped when the baby came, Betty was going to at least let the *amah* carry it. Though what if Betty then kept carrying the puppy? The puppy that was supposed to go *xuxu* on a paper mat but naturally preferred a certain silk rug. With its squiggly wiry fur and coarse doggy features, it wasn't even that cute, in Tina's opinion. Look at her girls—that cashmere skin! And that superstraight, yes, Korean-style hair, no more big curly perms, trying to look like an American movie star, why did Tina still do that? Habit. She did wish they would listen to her. But at least today they were ignoring her over by the picture window, in the blue light, the mountain and mist like a screen-saver behind them. How vibrant the girls were! She could hear Johnson as she thought that—*despite these factors, I consider this economy still vibrant.* Yet Tina thought "vibrant" the best word for them anyway.

Tina and Johnson had a water view for the dining room—
it was like eating on a ship. For sitting, though, they had
skylights—that was one thing nice about a mansion—as well as
Bobby's favorite, that picture window facing the mountain, which
she said came straight out of a Song Dynasty ink painting, that's
how big it was. Too big, even. So big you had to just bow to it in
a way, Bobby once said, and one day in Hawaii, Tina thought she
knew what Bobby meant. It was when Tina first saw the mountains being born, the molten lava stealing down to the sea—when
she first saw the lava char black on top, like a giant burnt alliga-
tor skin, molted off by its own burning guts. That halogen core
advancing, advancing, then crusting and darkening, only to be
streaked by new screaming bright stretch marks—everything
oozing, hissing, steaming, puddling down into the cold hard
ocean—wow. Tina's arms were so covered with goose bumps, she
had to get back in the car. She made Johnson get back in, too, and
she took her pictures with the window up, thinking, *What could
you do about a thing like that? Nothing!*

Still, you tried.

"Listen to me," she begged now. "Have pity on your mother.
What am I going to do? Tell me. What am I going to do?"

"Make offerings to the cell phone god?" said Betty, in
English.

Tina drew herself up on her high heels. "Is that how children talk in the U.S.?"

"They have notably ironical tendencies," said Betty.

"Wait until your baby is born, then you will have a child of
your own," predicted Tina. "And then, well—let me just give you
one piece of advice. Do not send it to the U.S. too early. We sent
you and Bobby too early, that was our mistake. 'Ironical.'" She
lifted her chin. "Who knows what "ironical" means. But ironical
children, I can write down for the dictionary what it means."

Betty let the puppy chew on her manicure.

" 'Ironical children: children whose parents do not help them. Let them find their own financing.' "

"I do apologize," said Betty then—thinking, no doubt, of the company she wanted to start with her husband Quentin. She took back her nails. "I admit the error of my ways."

Tina called the maid.

The next day, no answer again. Outside it rained sideways—typhoon season for real now, where did so much water come from? It was a level-two attack, meaning a loud *rat-at-at-at* on the skylights, you had to shout to hear anyone. Once again Betty admitted—in fact, both girls admitted—to having no trouble reaching Bobby; also to knowing something they could not tell anyone.

Proving, Tina told Johnson over dim sum, proving not only that Bobby had some secret communication system, but that the girls were all three of them against them. Against them! Their own daughters! She waved a cart on, then realized—the *gau choi gau*, the *char siu bau*—oh well. She liked to try everything, but Johnson said she took one bite and made him eat the rest, which was true. What happened to filial piety? she demanded.

Johnson looked up from his newspaper, popped a half dumpling in his mouth, and shrugged.

And would this be happening if they celebrated Chinese New Year? she asked. Recently she and Johnson had taken to going to Hawaii over New Year's like their friends, New Year's was just too much work. But sometimes she wondered if that upset their ancestors, even as she wondered, Did she really believe in ancestors?

Johnson looked up again. "New Year's is not a factor in this problem," he said in English. And then in Mandarin, "*Bie kai wan xiao*"—don't be ridiculous.

Except for certain expressions, Johnson and Tina generally spoke English, the first reason being that he could barely speak Mandarin—that accent!—and the second being that he had not learned any more Shanghainese than she had Cantonese. They were both stubborn that way. He hated the Shanghainese hiss—all that s-s-s—while who could stand that Cantonese *loh-sup-gaw*? So she said, though in fact she might have been less stubborn had she not been expected to understand that men were men for the first thirty years of their marriage. It was only just recently that she had decided, Enough! Just when he had decided the same thing, luckily. Too much work, those young girls, he said. Too much money. Hong Kong girls were spoiled and dramatic, Mainland girls expected you to help their whole family; you could not get them an apartment without finding the entire clan living there. He was done. Done! Tina and Johnson went out to dinner to celebrate, though she honestly didn't know if she believed him or not. Until after dinner, wow—after all these years—who was knocking on her door in his green dot boxers? The front slit already gapping. Betty called Tina a clone of Tina's mother, and Tina's marriage a clone of Tina's mother's marriage, too, completely Chinese. But in fact it could be more Chinese. Much more Chinese! Tina's parents had fought so much that even at her father's deathbed, her mother had read the newspaper. Even as his monitors went to zero, a straight line, nothing, she sat there, reading, reading. Later she claimed it wasn't a bad marriage, he just didn't appreciate her. And how she had wept over the coffin! Banged and banged and banged on it, distraught, just as if she'd loved him. Of course, there was nothing inside; the coffin was for show, he had been cremated. Still she banged, and also died right after him, all of a sudden— everyone said of grief.

Now, here Tina sat with Johnson, not only at their favorite dim sum place, but at their favorite table, by the window. Would she die of grief if he died? It was true, he agreed, putting down his paper, that the girls were against them, all three of them, it was a conspiracy. But then he picked up his cell phone and dialed, checking his messages. Tina watched the rain through the window. She admired the restaurant's fancy new reception desk; the owner must be making money. More carts. Everyone, everyone was speaking Cantonese. The cell phone window glowed blue in Johnson's hand, like a view into another world. It was hard to call him rude when half the restaurant was on the phone, Hong Kong people did that—came and sat all morning, playing cards and making phone calls. Still.

"Johnson," she said.

"Done!" He put his phone down and winked. Since giving up girls, he had gotten pudgier, his wink had too much to do with his cheek. "As we were saying?"

"I'm worried about Bobby," said Tina.

"Bobby." Johnson's frown was also somehow cheeksy—as if the plumping of his cheeks had somehow caused his forehead to buckle.

"Bobby," she repeated. "Our daughter."

Johnson folded his paper. He looked out at the rain. He looked at his watch—avoiding the subject, she knew for sure then, you did not have to be a psychiatrist to know he was avoiding something!

"Bobby Koo," she said yet again. "Number one."

"Bobby left her job," said Johnson.

"What?"

"Bobby left her job."

"Says who?"

"No one."

"Was it Betty? Betty told you."

"Let's just say I have some research opportunities."

"What research opportunities?"

He would not say. A cart stopped, then another one right behind it, with a broken wheel. He picked out chicken feet, duck's feet—he did love feet.

"Did she find something better?"

"No." He chewed. "She just left."

"Left for what?"

He shrugged.

"I am going to call her office," Tina said, and probably she really would have this time, except what was the point, if Bobby'd left? And at this hour the robot secretary was not going to be there, anyway.

Rain.

"I read Betty's e-mail, that's all," explained Johnson finally.

"How do you know her password?"

He shrugged.

"Do you know mine, too?"

He looked at his watch.

Of course, Johnson was not the only one who knew someone else's password, how else could you find out the answer if there was something you needed to know?

"You should thank me that I know so much," he said, gnawing and chewing.

She picked up her chopsticks. The drips on the window cast trickly shadows on her hands, on the tablecloth, on the dishes, everything.

"I just want Bobby to come home," she said. And finally, she couldn't help it—she cried.

Tina did not actually believe in psychiatrists, Chinese people in general did not believe in psychiatrists, even Chinese people who got their MBAs in the United States did not believe in psychiatrists. And yet she had recently gone to one, anyway. Her friend Titi said it was relaxing. She said a friend of hers having trouble with her children had gone to a psychiatrist and that the doctor had written a letter to the children that made them come home right away. Of course, after hearing that story, Tina wanted to switch psychiatrists, because hers just shook his head when she told him about the letter. Clearly the other psychiatrist was a better value. However, the other psychiatrist had left Hong Kong a long time ago—for Shenzhen, Titi said, where he now had a factory making some sort of meter—and Tina's psychiatrist at least listened to her, not like Johnson. The very first session her psychiatrist had said that he could understand why she wanted to cry, that a daughter who turned her cell phone off made a mother feel abandoned. It was one of the ironies of our communication age, he said, that people, being so much more able to keep in touch, were so much more apt to feel abandoned. Because what did it take to stay in touch these days? Nothing! How she had cried when he said that.

How could this be happening? Just yesterday Bobby was the smart daughter, the daughter who needed less and less help with every school. The daughter they considered practically (without telling her, of course) a son. Number one in her class in Hong Kong, got into Andover in the United States with only a little help, just to make sure. And once there, well, Tina did not have to boast, all of their friends knew it already: top 10 percent of her class, got into MIT all by herself. Interned on Wall Street, got into Harvard Business School, played soccer; she was all-around and pretty, too, with a high straight nose that had been the envy of her girlfriends in Hong Kong. She wasn't one of these girls where you knew why they had to be so smart and all-around besides. If Tina worried about anything, it was about Bobby's sisters, who were also okay, Tina told them every day how they just needed to find a good husband. And that had seemed to work. Betty was not jealous, despite having gone not to Andover like her sister, but to a very nice school in the United States, and not to MIT like her sister, but to a very nice college, also in the United States, and not as far from the airport as Johnson said, only four or five hours. Betty was not jealous because her husband Quentin had gone to MIT like Bobby and in fact knew Bobby there but would never, ever have asked her out. Bobby was so intense, he said. Meaning, he once explained to Betty, that it was always questions, questions, questions with Bobby. It was like she had a question problem.

As for number three, she was not jealous, either, being too pretty for her own good. Even in high school Lulu had been approached by The Gap to model blue jeans, an agency had pored through her school face book and called her up. Which small fact Lulu did not tell Tina, in fact she never told Tina she was going for a test shoot, Tina knew nothing about anything until a friend called from Shanghai, saying guess who she ran into in a Gap store there? Lulu! Lulu was going to be okay, you could see it, even if she did leave Arnie Hsu, who was very nice and very rich, just because he had a hole at the top of his hair like a golf hole. She didn't want a putting green, she said, and booked a flight home. Lulu was not like Bobby, who had started off majoring in applied math, but then switched to anthropology, as if she just had to show that she could get a Wall Street summer internship without advanced quantitative skills—which she did, thanks to guess who. And then she had to show that, even after having made comments about tribal rituals all summer, she would be able to return to the company when she graduated from college. As she did, of course, with a raise, besides.

Then B-school. But then more trouble. Johnson and Tina had both thought she should go to Kunshan next—close enough to Shanghai that she could have some fun, and talk about vibrant! What with Mainlanders and Taiwanese and Hong Kongers all there, and Chinese Americans, too, it was like a reunion. Families that had ended up with one branch in Canada, and another in Malaysia, and yet another in Australia now found themselves partners. Optoelectronics! Robots! Smart factories! Kunshan had everything. You had to be careful how you talked to those Communists, and those party secretaries always needed tea money, but it was worth it—especially after China joined the WTO, it was worth it. Kunshan was the new Hong Kong.

Bobby would have made millions.

But instead she stayed in New York and went to work for a nonprofit. A nonprofit! At first they thought maybe they had gotten the word wrong. How about going back to Wall Street? they said—once, twice, a million times. And finally, finally, she had gone. Now, though: could she really have quit?

Johnson and Tina called Bobby's office that night and did not even get the robot secretary they knew. Instead there was a new robot, who told them the same thing three times, as if they did not speak English: *I'm sorry, Bobby Koo no longer works at this office. I'm sorry, Bobby Koo no longer works at this office. I'm sorry . . .*

"Time to recruit Betty," said Johnson. "Sit down with her when she calls, and when Bobby answers the phone, quick, get on the line."

They tried this. But though Betty had been able to get through before, now she couldn't. Her emails, too, were bouncing right back. All of which was making her feel so exhausted, Betty said, she could hardly scroll down her message list. Sometimes her face had the blank look of someone putting on makeup—Tina thought maybe she was trying not to gloat. But today Betty just looked tired and worried. She put her sleeping puppy in its handbag and went through her messages again while Tina stood and watched.

"She's selling her apartment," said Betty finally.

"She's what?"

"You didn't hear it from me."

Tina stared at the computer screen. "Is there a . . ."

"The drummer," said Betty.

The drummer. Tina's feet ached.

The drummer, the drummer, the drummer. Tina could not sleep. The rain, she said, when Johnson complained. She wanted to call the police, but what police could they even call? When they did not even know where Bobby had gone.

"It's a problem," agreed Johnson, snoring.

They had met the drummer once. He wore a bandanna and stared at you with his wolf-blue eyes as if besides being against laundered shirts and shaving, he was against the overuse of eyelids. Normal things like holding the door open for people he ignored, but when he noticed a mosquito bite on Bobby's arm, he scratched it for her, his hairy knuckle working up and down.

Now suddenly Johnson sat up. "The realtor," he said.

But of course! They found the listing easily enough and reached the listing firm first try. Yes, yes, the seller was motivated, said the realtor, or at least so far as she knew; it wasn't her listing. And of course she had the means to reach the seller. However, contact information was, as they might imagine, confidential.

Tina listened in on the speakerphone, in the half dark.

"Then how about we make offer?" Johnson asked the phone. "See if she responds."

"Would you like to see the property first?"

"Not necessary. We just make offer."

"Is this a serious offer?" said the phone. "I can only present it to her if it is a good faith offer with an appropriate deposit, signaling an intention to buy the property. Should she accept."

"Why should we buy the apartment, we paid for that apartment!" exploded Johnson.

"I'm sorry?" said the phone.

Outside, more rain; somehow it always surprised Tina that the rain just kept on raining all night.

"And how about the price?" asked Johnson, after a moment. "Do you feel she is asking high or low?"

Later he shook and shook his head, finally as upset as Tina.

"Priced for quick sale!" For all his pudginess, Johnson looked drawn. "Okay, this is our strategy. We are going to make offer on the apartment."

"High or low?"

"Low then high," said Johnson. "As if we are making up our mind how high we can go. Except we are going to offer until she signs the P&S. Of course we will find someone else's name to use."

"And then?"

"And then we go to New York and see her at the closing."

"Ah! Great idea!"

"There is some chance she will send a proxy. But I know Bobby, more likely she will come herself."

They went back to bed. In the morning, lawyers, offers, faxes. Phone calls. No hard feelings about Lulu, said Arnie Hsu; of course, he could buy the apartment for them. And the next day, success. That just left the co-op board. How lucky that Arnie was on his way to New York and could meet with the board right away! What with no conditions and a cash offer, they could then go ahead and close. Johnson put his assistant to work on the letters of recommendation, even as Tina cried to see Bobby's handwriting at the bottom of the signed P&S. For an address, there was a post office box in New Jersey.

A state they had heard of, at least.

"Such a beautiful apartment, even before the renovation," said Tina.

"Sold it for nothing," said Johnson. "Didn't even push back."

The rain.

Right there in the sitting room, in what used to be Bobby's seat, sat Betty now, bigger and bigger every day. Soon they would know girl or boy. How happy! And yet all Tina could see was Bobby, smaller and smaller in her mind's eye; she saw Bobby disappearing into the mountains like a scholar in an old landscape painting, headed down a path to who knew where.

Drumming banging raining weeping.

New York was dry! The streets were dry, the buildings were dry, the sky was blue. Birds did not cower under plastic bags and overhangs, but swooped and chased each other up and down like the Hang Sen going crazy. In the middle part of the day, you could already feel the oven heat of July; Tina remembered this from her student days. Still, it was cool compared to Hong Kong, and of course Americans did not know what humidity was. Tina remembered, too, from her student days how, other than Wall Street, she had never thought New York impressive, especially Midtown was not impressive. She could never understand why the buildings were so short when the people were so tall. Buildings should be big like mountains, Tina thought, people should be tiny next to them, the way they were in Chinese landscape paintings.

Anyway, Midtown today was blue sky everywhere, a blue you did not see in Hong Kong anymore—too much pollution. And she liked it, this blue; it went with her new running shoes.

Tina would not normally wear running shoes with a Chanel suit, even a knockoff. However, she was jet-lagged, and who was there to see anything here? No one. The sneakers had blue lights that hadn't started blinking until after she left the store, Johnson said maybe they hadn't blinked when she bought them because of the store carpet. Too thick, he said, not enough *bah! bah! bah!*, and maybe he was right. She hadn't realized they would go *bi-bi-bi-bi!* like a string of firecrackers with a mute button. Now she glimpsed their reflection in windows and doors as she passed— better to look at than the bags under her eyes.

Johnson had stopped at an ice cream place and was enjoying a double scoop of green tea ice cream as they walked.

"Why did you get that? You can eat that in Hong Kong," she said.

"Just want to compare," he said. "See which one is better, ice cream here or in Hong Kong."

He licked. With his head tilted for drip control, his whole face seemed shifted to one side.

"The taste is the same," he announced finally, straightening his head. "Only one is Chinese, and one is American. You know what the real difference is between this ice cream place and Hong Kong?"

"What?"

"No red bean flavor here," he said. "Also no honeydew. No red bean, I can understand. But no honeydew, that's a surprise."

Next Johnson spotted a bubble tea shop.

"You sure you don't want one?" he asked.

"I can't eat."

"I make a prediction. They have honeydew flavor."

She waited for him outside, admiring her sneakers in the glass door. He emerged with a cappuccino bubble tea.

"Didn't they have honeydew?"

"Yes, but I'm not in the mood. Hey, you know, that's a Taiwanese shop. The owner is from Taipei. His assistant behind the counter is also from Taipei, but not originally. You know where he is from before Taipei?"

Tina waited.

"Brazil. South America. His English is funny. Instead of a Chinese accent, he has something else."

"Thank god, Bobby is not in South America."

"New Jersey is bad enough," agreed Johnson.

"Are we near Bobby's apartment?"

Tina had thought herself too tired to walk at all, but now she found herself strolling up Madison Avenue, window shopping.

"Mr. Koo! Mrs. Koo! Good morning! How're things in China?"

Of course Norman the doorman remembered them, how could he forget? He touched his ruddy fingers to his ruddy temples, as if pointing to his memory. But no, he hadn't seen Bobby in a while. Although yes, her unit was under agreement.

"Snapped up by somebody like you, from Hong Kong," he said. "His name is even very similar, if I recall correctly. A Mr. Hsu."

Tina and Johnson gazed past Norman, into the warm-lit lobby with its gilt mirror and striped satin chairs; and a little later, from across the street, they gazed up at Bobby's window.

"We don't have to sell." Johnson's hand was suddenly in Tina's. "Even if we don't use it so often, it will appreciate anyway. Every day we make money."

Tina nodded; Johnson's hand was somehow drier here than it was in Hong Kong, as if tied into the weather.

The closing was the next day, in the afternoon—four o'clock New York time, five in the morning their time. The office building was old; the elevator was slow. Still Tina was shocked, when its doors opened, by the office. The vertical blinds were missing slats, a matted gray path snaked through the carpet, and the receptionist barely looked up. Instead of a smile, she offered them a clear view of her white roots; she looked like a skunk with a desk job. Happily, the lawyer was friendlier. Len, he said his name was. With a rumpled jacket, a rumpled shirt, and rumpled skin, he could have just gone through a special rumpling machine. Still, he spoke normally enough, and the conference room had a view—no water, no mountains, no sky, but you could see very well into the building next door. On the conference room table, the forms were in piles, with a pen next to each pile.

"Folks should be along shortly," said Len, straightening a pen.

And that moment, just as predicted, an ox entered the room—Bobby's lawyer. Some sort of athlete, it seemed; in the back he had buttocks like honeydews, Chinese people did not get like that. And behind the ox, thankfully—Bobby! It was Bobby! Only with a blond crew cut and a dog in a bag, so like Betty's dog that for a moment Tina thought it was indeed Betty's dog.

"Bobby!"

Bobby froze. Only her thumb moved, calming her squirming puppy. "Ma? Da?" Compared to her platinum hair, Bobby's eyebrows looked strangely black. She was wearing a short green T-shirt and pants so low that her hip bones showed.

"Bobby!" Tina wanted to grasp Bobby's hand, but her daughter's eyebrows were knit with fury, and her mouth hung open like the dog's.

"What are you doing here?" she demanded.

"We're here to buy your apartment," said Johnson.

"What?"

"You people know each other?" The ox extended his stubby

hand toward Johnson; veins crisscrossed its top. "Hi, I'm Greg, by the way."

"Nice to meet you, Greg," said Johnson, shaking his hand and handing him a business card. "I am Johnson Koo, here to do some business for Mr. Hsu."

"What?" exclaimed Bobby.

"On his behalf," continued Johnson calmly. "This is Mrs. Koo, also here to help Mr. Hsu."

"What?"

The dog yapped.

"We have his power of attorney," said Johnson.

"You mean you bought this apartment with Uncle Arnie as a front?"

"Shall we sit down?" suggested Len.

No one sat, though outside, on the window ledge, several pigeons roosted calmly. Tina watched the people in the next building hold a meeting; someone was pointing at a whiteboard.

"This is what you call deceit," said Bobby. "This is—"

"I'm sorry?" Johnson cupped his ear.

"You understand me perfectly well, Dad." Bobby had the same defiance on her face as she'd had as a child—a stubbornness that came from her father. But what Johnson knew how to hide and use, Bobby spilled out. "Don't give me that your-English-is-too-la-di-da-for-me look, you—"

"La-di-what?" Johnson winked at Tina.

The dog yapped, pawing the bag.

"We just come to see how you're doing," said Tina. "See if you lost weight, have to eat some more, what happened to your hair?"

"Is that your dog?" said Johnson.

"We want to know where you are," said Tina. "If you are alive or not."

"It looks just like Betty's dog," said Johnson.

"I am getting a migraine," said Bobby. Strangely, she put her fingers to her temples the same way her doorman had.

"Maybe you did not drink enough," said Tina. "How about we go out for some tea? Can I make that suggestion?"

Bobby put her hand in her bag. "No nipping," she said.

"No nipping is right," said Tina. "We came all the way from Hong Kong to see you."

"That's crazy," said Bobby.

"You turned your cell phone off."

"It's still crazy."

"Okay, we are crazy. Let's go out have some tea. Come on."

"What about the closing?"

"Forget about the closing," said Johnson. "Tell you what. That is still your apartment. Free and clear, all renovated. We give back to you."

"But—"

"Not so far from New Jersey, you can just consider the apartment is your vacation house. Even if you don't use it so often, it will appreciate. Every day you make money."

"But—"

"Or you can rent it out. The income is yours, every penny after tax." Johnson picked up the contract nearest him and ripped it in two. "Time for tea."

A pen rolled out of position; paper fluttered onto the table and carpet.

"Anyway, I can't go," said Bobby. "Unless you happen to know a place that allows dogs."

"Forget it! Leave the dog here," said Johnson.

"How can I—"

"Let me ask you, Len," said Johnson. "How about instead of legal work, you take care of this dog? Just for short time. You can charge anything you like."

"That's very generous, Mr. Koo, but—"

"You bill, your assistant do all the work. That's a good deal." Taking the bag from Bobby, Johnson turned his attention to Greg. "We pay your bill, too."

"Now just one moment, Mr. Koo." Greg put his hand up commandingly, only to have Johnson hang the bag on it as if it were a hook.

"Babysit a couple of hours, send the bill to me," said Johnson. "Otherwise we will not leave, just stay here forever, getting louder and louder."

"I'm so sorry about this," said Bobby.

The lawyers looked at each other. The dog started climbing out; Greg pushed it back in and swung the bag a little.

Johnson ushered Bobby to the elevator.

"You have a headache," said Tina as they waited.

"I do."

"You cut your hair."

Bobby looked out the window.

"I like it. Blond."

"Good."

"Cool in the summer."

"It is."

"Convenient."

Even staring straight ahead, Bobby was vibrant—beautiful and smart, Tina's number-one child. How many herbs Tina took when she was pregnant! Though probably Bobby would have been just as smart anyway. Tina sighed now and looked out the window, too—the same meeting as before, the same whiteboard. Probably they were saying the same things.

"We were just worried about you, you know," she said.

The elevator dinged and opened.

"How do you like my sneakers?"

Bobby looked down.

"I didn't know they would blink when I got them." Tina and Bobby stepped into the elevator. Thanks to Bobby's fashion pants, Tina could see that her daughter had a tattoo on her *peepee*—some sort of dragon, with words coming out its mouth. She squinted and read, she thought, *Live free or die.* "Johnson said it was because the carpet was too thick, so I didn't *bam-bam-bam* enough. What do you think?"

"They're you." As if sensing Tina's gaze, Bobby hoisted her pants up a little.

"Betty has the same dog as you, did you know that?" Tina said. "They are practically twins."

"Well, that's no coincidence," said Bobby.

"What do you mean?"

The elevator descended, descended.

"Betty sent me the dog."

"What do you mean, Betty sent you the dog?"

"She called up some sort of special personal shopper. It was a present."

"She never told us."

"It was sweet. However, I don't exactly have the wherewithal for a dog."

"Now you'll have to go see her dog," said Tina. "Get the dogs together."

"That's an idea, but Zeke and I don't exactly have the wherewithal . . ."

"When Betty's baby comes, we'll send you a ticket," said Tina. "You know, we worry worry worry about you. Talk about a headache."

"I'm sorry," said Bobby. "I just—"

The door opened onto the sharp daylight of the lobby.

"Forget about tea, let's get some food," said Johnson.

"Isn't it kind of early?" said Tina.

"If you are hungry, it is not early. It is late! Let's find some Chinese food. See how it compares to Hong Kong."

"It's not going to be as good as the food in Hong Kong," said Bobby.

"Try anyway!" said Johnson.

The restaurant boasted a wall-size illuminated photo of the Hong Kong harbor at night. This cast its image such that the Star ferry seemed to plow across their tablecloth; Bobby and her parents laughed and looked. Hong Kong side, they said. The Bank of China. Jardine House. Must have taken the picture from Tsim Sha Tsui. If only the food were not so much like the photo!—Hong Kong but not Hong Kong. They had noticed that the fish in the tanks were not like the fish in Hong Kong, jumping out of the water; and sure enough, this fish tasted half dead, as if it had been eating hamburgers. The lobster, too, was strangely chewy, and who had ever seen such shrimpy shrimps? Plus it wasn't only the seafood you didn't really want to eat. An egg white dish that in Hong Kong would have been soft as a cloud was here more like a doormat. You had to chew chew chew before you could swallow one bite. Still, they ate, Tina listening like a psychiatrist as Bobby explained about the group house she and Zeke shared with two other couples. A great thing this was, she said, since Zeke was on the road all the time and they didn't want his thirteen-year-old son coming home to an empty house. Which Orion otherwise would, as Bobby now had a job as a department secretary at a university. Full benefits and it pays the bills, she said, plus she could take night courses for free, provided she could get away from Orion who, well, was still adjusting to not living on a bus the way he used to, that being life as a musician's kid. Orion insisted that he liked Bobby, but he also cut holes in her clothes. Every day she found another jacket ruined, another shirt.

Tina nodded, nodded, nodded. "But you like living with that drummer? That boy?"

"I like having a family," she said.

Tina made herself nod some more.

Happily, Bobby was at least thinking she might eventually want to go back to school.

"Not in anthro," she said. "I'm done with anthro. And right now I'm taking a Russian lit class, but what I'm really thinking about is political philosophy. There's someone in my department who's asking stuff like, What is government even for, anyway? And, Do people need to agree to be governed? I thought I might sit in on his course as a start."

Tina nodded.

"Then who knows, maybe I'll get a PhD and go into academia," said Bobby.

Tina nodded.

"Zeke says I'm a 'why' person, I should have 'why' work."

Tina nodded, nodded.

"That's a good question, Why," she said finally. "A very good question. In fact, now that we're talking about it, maybe I am a 'why' person, too. Because all I can think in these days is, Why why why why."

Bobby looked straight at her, her dark eyebrows somehow a lot darker than they were before. "I'm sorry," she said.

"You know, a lot of professors have to live in the middle of nowhere," said Tina. "Kansas. Or what is that called, that state, they have that very nice horse race—"

"Kentucky."

"Kentucky. They have to do everything the dean tell them. A

lot of them cannot afford new clothes. I don't know why they are so smart but decide to be slaves."

"Why? Because they would rather think what they want than buy what they want," said Bobby.

Tina said nothing. The dishes were cleared; the table filled up again with skyscrapers.

"So tell me," Tina said finally. "Is Zeke going to support you through grad school?"

"We'll support you!" put in Johnson, checking messages on his phone. "Anything you want to do, you tell us!"

Bobby played with her teacup.

"And who cooks, let me ask you. Does Zeke cook when he is home?" asked Tina.

"He makes a mean guacamole," said Bobby.

"Does he clean?"

"Zeke?"

"Do you have a maid?"

"Mom, this is America."

"No maid?" Johnson laid his phone down on a cargo ship in shock.

"So who is the maid?" asked Tina. And, "Do you like drumming?"

"Zeke isn't just a regular drummer, you know," said Bobby. "He does drum circles and stuff like that—if you know what a drum circle is?"

Tina did not want to know.

"It's a lot of people, all drumming on these Jim Bay drums. You should try it. It helps people get in touch with themselves—their real selves. He even uses them to help cancer patients. And guess where he's bringing them next."

"Where?"

"Hong Kong."

"Hong Kong?" said Tina.

"It's going to be great. People have so much bottled up— and they're organizing for an extra huge July protest before the Article 23 vote, you know."

"And Zeke is bringing drums?"

Bobby nodded.

"And you are going, too?"

"Of course. It was my idea."

"You're coming to Hong Kong?!" Johnson exclaimed.

Tina couldn't bring herself to ask if Bobby was planning to see them there or not.

"You know what I think?" she said finally. "I think no politics, make money is okay. I think we can all live very nicely in Hong Kong."

"Well, a lot of people don't want to live nicely. A lot of people want to live free. It's not even that they don't want to bow to Beijing—it's that they can't. They really can't. Can't you see?"

Tina contemplated the skyscrapers on the tablecloth. Outside the restaurant, it was still a beautiful afternoon, she knew, but somehow she wished it would rain.

"Actually, no," she said finally.

Bobby's eyebrows went up a little.

"Actually, I don't understand too well what you are talking about," said Tina.

"Of course, you understand!" said Johnson. "Your English is perfect!"

But Bobby spun her teacup around. "Thanks for at least saying that," she said.

Over orange slices, Tina and Johnson tried to convince Bobby to leave this Zeke and Orion. Of course, if she married Zeke, she would be a U.S. citizen. They could see that. But was it worth it? And Zeke should take care of his own son, they said, not dump him on her.

Bobby ate one slice of orange after another. "Well, I'm not going to promise anything," she said. "But to tell you the truth, I think Orion agrees with you."

"We all agree!" Johnson beamed.

"I'm not doing anything until after the protest. And I'm not saying I'm going to leave after that, either. I'm just saying I think that's what Orion thinks."

Tina waited.

"And let me just say it's hard to do what you have to," Bobby went on. "Even if you know what you have to do, it's still hard."

Tina nodded. "But of course, if there's one thing you know how to do, it is leave," she pointed out. "It's your specialty."

Bobby cocked her shorn head, listening.

"Just ask your mother."

For a moment, Bobby looked as though she was going to cry, and out on the street, she grasped Tina's hand. How different her hand was now than when she was little—how long her fingers. Tina did miss Bobby's little damp hand; her little girl had not walked anywhere, but always skipped. Still they strolled happily now, a mother and a daughter, until a taxi, spewing exhaust, pulled over a block ahead of them to let a passenger out.

"Do you want this one?" asked Bobby, and when they said no no no, look at that muffler, she abruptly hugged them. "Well, I'll take it, then," she said. "Have a good trip back!"

"Wait, your cell number!" they cried, sprinting after her.

"I don't have a cell!" she yelled back. "Thanks for dinner!"

"And the dog! Don't forget your dog! Your dog!"

But Bobby was waving, and the door was slamming. Tina ran—pretty fast, in her new sneakers; her pocketbook jounced. Still the taxi chugged noisily away, disappearing into a cloud of smoke. Tina panted. "The dog!" she shouted, "The dog!" even as the car receded—a yellow dot, then a yellow speck, then nothing. Johnson caught up to her and took her hand; buildings rose all around them, a lot taller than she had thought them before—indeed, quite tall for American buildings. Too tall.

"The dog," she panted once more. "The dog. The dog."

But there was no hope. Bobby was gone; and the dog, the poor dog, was on its own.

Mr. Crime and Punishment
and War and Peace

Roger Rabid, we called him. Jabbertalky. Evermore. But mostly we called him Gunner—Gunner Summers. I mean, it wasn't just our brilliant Mainland immigrant Arabella Li who called him that. It was pretty much all his fellow 1Ls—the immigrants from Azerbaijan and Poland and Brazil, and the students who were born here but who had been brought up to be respectful of others, too—meaning the kids of cops and farmers and teachers. We analyzed Gunner en masse: it was his upbringing, his genes, his ego. It was his insecurity—related, perhaps, to the fact that this was not exactly Harvard Law School we were attending. I was not of the persuasion that it was Gunner's looks as well that gave him the idea he was entitled to more airtime than other human beings, but others maintained there was a chart somewhere showing correlation if not causation: rugby build plus blond locks put you at risk, especially if you played tennis, sailed, and had really wanted to take Swahili but in the end had been forced to admit it wasn't as useful as French. In truth, there weren't a lot of people like Gunner in our ranks—people born with silver spoons in their mouths and their hands in the air. This was a fourth-tier school. But he inspired an expansion of our vocabularies anyway. By the end of the first month, everyone in our section could not only define but spell *logorrheic. Pleonastic. Periphrastic.* Indeed, you might have been forgiven for thinking we were strangely supersize contestants, preparing for the Scripps Spelling Bee.

As for the sesquipedalian adjectives, those were of course courtesy of Arabella, who everyone knew was smarter than Gunner and more prepared, too. For example, when in Property Law Professor Meister asked for examples of disabilities protected by the Americans with Disabilities Act, Gunner immediately supplied that significant myopia constituted "a physical or mental impairment that substantially limits one or more major life activities." And such was the spell of his utter self-confidence that even normally perspicacious Professor Meister agreed until Arabella lifted her elegant hand.

"What about *Sutton v. United Airlines* 1999?" she asked.

Meister raised an eyebrow.

"This was an employment discrimination case involving two myopic individuals who had applied to be airplane pilots, were rejected for failing the eyesight requirement, and subsequently sued United Airlines, alleging discrimination on the basis of disability," she said.

"And?" said Meister.

"Well, they were found by the Supreme Court not to be disabled for purposes of the law," said Arabella.

"Ah. Very good. That is indeed relevant." Meister flushed with embarrassment even as he grinned with delight. "Thank you. What a great example of how critical it can be to look up the leading interpretations of the statute," he said.

Gunner scowled.

But would Arabella ever wield the oomph she really should in society? Or out in the real world, would the Gunners somehow always triumph? She was, to begin with, most impressively unimposing. When the Red Cross came through asking for blood donations, she couldn't give; she didn't weigh enough. Rumor had it she was a size zero. Worse, she not only thought before she talked, she never seemed to forget that there were forty of us in the section, so that if everyone talked for five minutes straight, as Gunner was wont to do, classes would be two hundred minutes. Did this not spell defeat?

Of course, it bugged a lot of us, not just that Gunner was the ideal and knew it, but that he was the ideal to begin with. It bugged a lot of us that the professors wanted us to talk like him even if we were bound to get off topic and wind up having to finish covering the material on our own. And it bugged a lot of us that Arabella's being judged "too quiet" was potentially disastrous.

But this last injustice bugged me especially. Not that I was her boyfriend—she was practically engaged, of course. I was just your garden variety five-foot-nine friend also sort of named Li (meaning that my family spelled it with a double *e* but it was the same character in Chinese) who it just so happened could see how special she was. A lot of us Asian kids had the test scores and the work ethic, after all. She had something else. This clarity. This poise. This touch. Things I maybe noticed because I was what my parents had always called "the good-for-nothing artist type." I appreciated things like Arabella's style—how she could argue without hammering, for example, something our Constitutional Law professor was always trying to teach us. Professor Radin would never have singled out anyone in public, but when she talked about how it really was possible, even at our level, to be deft, we knew she was inspired by the example of Arabella—that Arabella had sparked a flicker of hope in her for us all. Arabella was, what's more, the only member of our class who could ever admit she didn't know something. And she was kind. When people were at one another's throats, she sang

funny songs like "So sue him, sue him, what can you do him?"
Once she drove three hours to get a depressed classmate's cat
from her house and smuggled the animal into her friend's
apartment; the friend found her cat under her covers, purring.

I don't mean that Arabella was an angel. For one thing, she
disliked Gunner as much as anyone; whenever his name came
up, she would move her mouth fast and wink. For another, she
sometimes signed up for two slots on the treadmill at the gym
when you were only allowed to sign up for one. Like she'd use
her initials in the right order for one slot and reverse them for
the other. "AL" then "LA." It was such a pathetic ruse, you had to
think she was going to get caught, especially as she did it all the
time. But this was Arabella: though everyone at the gym knew,
no one wanted to bust her.

One more imperfection. She was, it must be said, a tad
unliterary. I once told her that *Crime and Punishment* was my
favorite book, to which she answered that today someone would
no doubt help poor Dostoyevsky, and that if talking weren't
enough, he would probably be put on something nice. Also, she
said she didn't like the word *punishment,* as she strongly believed
rehabilitation to be the appropriate point of all sentences, especially incarceration. It's true that, when I pointed out that *Crime
and Rehabilitation* lacked a certain je ne sais quoi, she conceded
I was probably right. But she maintained that she didn't like the
title anyway and thought Dostoyevsky should have gone back to
the drawing board and come up with something different.

"Like *War and Peace?*" I said.

To which she replied that I could make fun of her but honestly? That was a great title, and while the historical record could
not, of course, prove this conclusively, it did lend support to her
contention.

If I had had her in the Russian lit class I TA'ed back in college, in short, she might not have gotten an A.

To return to her cardinal flaw, though—her failure, according to the professors, to be more Gunner-like—she said it was a species of Western hegemony that people like her and me were always being pushed to do something fundamentally at odds with our culture. It stressed her out, she said. It stressed us all out. She said that as a rule she just listened to her body and talked as much as felt comfortable, and that if her breath shortened up, suggesting a certain pulmonary preset, then she stopped. And if that kept her from getting a good grade, while people like Gunner were physiologically equipped with some manner of embarrassment override, well, so be it. She didn't need to finish first in our class. She was only in law school, she said, to learn to help ordinary people with their ordinary problems anyway.

And that was the truth. She really did just want to help people with their immigration problems. She did not want one of those fancy paneled offices with the in-house cappuccino and the million-dollar view. She wanted the kind of office you saw in 1940s movies, with worn wooden floors and frosted-glass doors. She wanted to tilt her head and give a kindly look to clueless people sitting on the edge of their chairs; she wanted to ask them, "So what brings you here?" People like her family, who had fled to America after Tiananmen, only to be told to go back when her parents misspelled their street name. In the end they had thankfully gotten their asylum anyway. But the mess left a mark on her. She wanted to get people like them out of hot water. She wanted to straighten out their green cards and help them get their hearings. She wanted to fight their deportation orders and see them become citizens.

Other people wanted her to be a judge. In fact, in my heart of hearts, I wanted to see her on the Supreme Court. The first Asian American on the Supreme Court! Or didn't she want to work for the ACLU? I asked her once. Of course, to even begin to think about it, you had to have a minimum of six years of litigation experience—that's what it said on their website. And to get litigation experience, you had to get a public defender or prosecutor job. Or if you had loans and needed to make more money—as she did, I assumed?—she nodded—you needed to do the litigation track at a top-notch firm, from where you could go to a U.S. attorney's office or DOJ, the whole sleep-no-more slog.

"Sell my soul, you mean," she said, but I could tell she was thinking about it. The ACLU.

"No, no," I said. "You wouldn't have to sell your soul." Never mind that all I knew about a life in law came from Scott Turow novels; still, I sagaciously went on. "You'd just have to talk enough in class for Professor Radin to stop describing you as quiet. You'd have to channel your inner Gunner and, you know. Gun a little."

She looked at me and crossed her eyes.

"Have you always fastened on the utterly quixotic?" she asked. Then she uncrossed her eyes and smiled and said, "Actually, Eric says the same thing. About talking more, I mean."

As Eric was her boyfriend, this was and wasn't what I wanted to hear.

But the next day she began to try, and that was what I wanted to see.

Not being a big-name law school, we were not exactly overrun with visits by Am Law 100 firms; it was mostly regional firms that came to recruit. A smattering of powerhouses did come through, though—typically because someone had some connection to the university—and every once in a while, a student subsequently landed a big-deal summer associate job. Once in the known history of the school, too, it had happened that, after the big-deal summer associate job, a person from our school went on to land a permanent position at the firm—becoming an honest-to-god big-deal associate. Granted, that was a decade ago, but still. Why shouldn't the second person be Arabella?

She scoffed. But when the class rankings came out, and there she and Gunner were—she at number one and he at number two—she did begin to sort of wonder if maybe, when the time came, she should interview—?

"Yes!" I all but yelled at her. "Yes! You have to do it! You do! You have to do it for all of us!"

"Whoever 'us' is, I think you should do it for yourselves," she said, stiffening. "Starting with you."

In the end, though, she agreed that I was no lawyer. As for why, then, I was in law school? I didn't really have to tell her. For while she herself wasn't in law school because of her parents, she *was* here at Podunk Law because they wanted her nearby; she knew how Chinese parents could be. But never mind. When an on-campus interview sign-up sheet was posted, she held her nose and did it. She signed up.

It started out that three Big Law firms were coming. But first there was a hurricane, and Westfall and Howe canceled. Then Berger, Berkman and Leebron canceled, too, also because of the storm. That left Thompson, Pierce and Shore, who was scheduled to come a week later than the other firms. I helped Arabella prepare, combing the internet for advice, and finding that most of it fell into three categories. The first was normative: Be positive! Be assertive! Be confident! The second was gnomic: Show that you are agreeable, but show that you are no pushover. Show that you are unique, but show that you fit in. Show that you have questions, but show that you do your homework.

Arabella rolled her eyes but listened carefully.

The third, toughest, category was spatial. Take up room with your arms, went this advice—especially if you are a woman. Take up room with your voice. Take up room with your manner. Take up room in your chair.

Take up room in your chair? Arabella tried manspreading her legs; it hurt her hips, she said. As for thrusting her chin out and squaring her chest, she simply could not do these things with a straight face. But she could, she figured, wear her roommate's size four jacket and, under it, a vest for bulk. And after a few tries, she found that pretending she was Gunner helped with her manner. Suddenly she could respond at length even to lamer-than-lame prompts like Tell us about yourself, and Do you have any weaknesses?

She answered, answered, answered. I nodded.

"Anything else we should know about you?" I asked finally.

"I broke up with Eric," she said.

"Ah." I jotted that down on my clipboard.

"Also," she said, "since I know we don't have a lot of time, I'd just like to make sure you realize I'm available for dinner after the interview."

"Six o'clock?" I said.

"If that's how business is done in your firm."

"It is," I said. "I mean, I hope it isn't. But it is. It is."

"Good," she said.

As for what she was supposed to do if the interviewer threw his clipboard up into the air for joy, I decided not to test her.

Instead I just said, "You're going to be great, Arabella."

"Thank you for your time," she said. And, "You are the most generous person I have ever known."

The day of the interview, I did one more thing. I greased the seat of Gunner's bicycle with Vaseline and, for good measure, his handlebar grips, too. Not so much that he would be in an accident, but enough that he'd have to spend twenty minutes in the men's room trying to get the grease off before he could shake any hands. And then, of course, there would still be the issue of his crotch. Were anyone's interview chances ever scotched because he had grease in his crotch? Of course not. Still, I hoped that it would disconcert and distract him. As for whether this was my finest moment as a human being—not exactly. Still, I did it. Then I waited.

Arabella's interview, she reported, went well enough. No surprises—for which she had to thank me, she said. I really had prepared her beautifully. However, she did think her interviewer—the "Shore" in Thompson, Pierce and Shore—a bit inscrutable.

"Or maybe I should say guarded," she said. "He looked like he had the nuclear codes and thought I might ask for them."

"Hmm."

"He did smile at the end, at least."

"That's good."

"I guess his firm does some Mainland business—import-export, mostly, but also some auto factory acquisitions—in all of which, he thought my Chinese would be a plus."

"Great!"

"Until he discovered my parents were dissidents, that is."

"Oh, no."

"Then he asked me how tall I was."

"Did you tell him?"

"Yes. Also I said that if he was wondering, I weigh ninety-one pounds."

"You didn't."

"You're right, I didn't. But I almost did."

We laughed. I had picked a local hippie restaurant with every variation of tofu and brown rice possible, and with four kinds of kale smoothies. We tried all four. Then we tried three of the Buddha bowls, and then an udon-miso thing, and all the world glowed with warmth and antioxidants until I told her about the grease.

Though his aunt turned out to be married to the very Shore who had interviewed Arabella, Gunner did not get a summer associate position—which so crushed him that he missed the whole next week of class. Some people said he was dropping out, others that he was transferring to business school, and still others that he was thinking of becoming a tennis pro. Who knew what was true? What was clearer was that classes were not the same without him. We missed having someone to irritate us, and the professors—the poor professors—were suffering. Indeed, they were getting so discouraged, having to cold-call people for every single question, that after a while we started to put our hands up more, just to help them out. They were nice people who deserved better jobs, after all. We felt sorry for them. So sorry, in fact, that a bunch of us tried gunning—including me—which wasted a lot of time, to be honest. But it was fun and did make the professors perk up.

As for Arabella, she, too, got a thumbs-down from Thompson, Pierce and Shore. Still, she was glad she had interviewed, she said, because it helped her figure a few things out. For example, it helped her figure out that she should try and transfer to a higher-ranked school. She was going to apply and see what happened, she said, and if she got in, bring it up with her parents.

"I am also going to start lifting weights," she said. "I am too small."

"Isn't that selling your soul?" I said.

"No," she said. "It's strength training."

Meanwhile I got thrown out of school altogether. Arabella had called me a reprobate and a miscreant for the Vaseline business, but she hadn't reported me. It was Gunner who eventually figured out who had smeared him, so to speak, and though I apologized and had his suit cleaned twice, he nonetheless filed an official complaint—hearing which, my parents were predictably upset.

But Arabella observed, "I don't think you're even sorry."

"About Gunner?" I said. "Because I am. I am very sorry about Gunner."

"About school," she said.

"Well, about school, let's just say I'd rather be punished than rehabilitated," I said. "I'm not about law."

"No, you are about crime and punishment and war and peace," she agreed.

"And justice for the people I love," I added—which was kind of an overly venturesome thing to say, really. I didn't think before I said it; in fact, you could say I was just gunning. But she turned and gave me a kiss, and when I plunged on and said I was going to try and find a job near whatever school she ended up at, she looked serious.

"Rich Lee," she said thoughtfully. "Mr. Crime and Punishment and War and Peace." And then, deft as ever, she didn't tell me not to.

Amaryllis

Oh! To be a real person with a husband, and a household, and squealing dependents. Or at least to be involved in a sordid affair—in a narrative of some sort, in the sending up of shoots and buds. Instead, Amaryllis Chen de Castro, age forty—Paralysis, she called herself—was mired in an e-affair that had died down several times, only to resurrect itself like a computer virus.

if i had it to do all over again, well, you can guess

What a far cry, that, from a real relationship, with careers to juggle, and family issues to work out—homework crises and internet rules and laundry.

i had a pebble in my shoe today which of course i felt with every step and should have taken out but it reminded me of you somehow—believe me i knew how silly this was, and yet

She replied:

You indeed should have taken it out. Please don't be ridiculous.

And one day, finally:

You can write these things but you know I am flesh and blood. I need someone to cook with and eat with and do the dishes with. Someone to complain when I produce horror for dinner.

He responded:

if only i could be that someone! a great true regret

And for a few days afterward she received sentence fragments:

a great regret

if only

what horror could you ever be capable of

Blather. And yet as the fragments continued, she began to feel, despite herself, touched. The man was a corporate treasurer. But that reckless candor—she recognized that from any number of poets. This was not poetry! The impulse, though. She knew it, that's all. She typed:

I would be happy to be friends. But please do not write again until you have returned to your senses, by which I mean standard grammar, including standard punctuation. I love you.

Why did she write that? She hated him. He was a strange man, she knew it the moment they met—at a holiday party, this was, in the lobby of the building where he worked, beside a photo series her agency had put up. The art was, in truth, awful. But the Chinese had bought up the building—having bought up a lot of Midtown, it seemed, even the Waldorf Astoria—and her bosses knew what they wanted. No matter that the Koos were from Hong Kong—they understood Mainlanders, and Amaryllis understood the Koos. So there it was. As others gamely mingled, Amaryllis and this man—his name was Nathaniel—manacled themselves together, making their way, frame by frame, through the work. It was a bit like placing the series all over again, except that she did not have to point out how well the colors would complement the couches.

Instead, she and he simply looked at the pictures. Heroically scaled, obsessively wrought, all in sepia, the photos featured strange inventor figures in otherworldly settings, with elaborate inscrutable inventions. Leonardo gone Rube Goldberg, he said. She laughed. They talked. Alternate realms, the painting aspirations of his youth; her disastrous visit to the artist's studio, including how she had knocked Leonardo off a ladder. Even as the crowd thinned and the help removed the ice reindeer, they talked. People saw them. He put his hands in and out of his pockets; he played with his wedding ring. She could hear her friend Tara Hsu as if through an aural implant: *There is something the matter with his life.*

Still, from the lobby, he and Amaryllis went for a drink. And by the end of the evening, lo: there perched the wedding ring atop the wet orifice of a wine bottle. What's more, she was coming to see something about him—how he gripped things. Not unlike the inventors in the lobby, he had narrow channels of intense interest. His life was someone else's life, though, an institution-size edifice risen up, as if of its own stony will, out of the generations. Family Bibles, family portraits, family summerhouses. Kids. Absurd as it sounded, he was building a summerhouse of his own now—a laughable stab at freedom. There would be a boys' dorm and a girls' dorm, he said. For those who did not care for dorm life, there would be tents.

Amaryllis shook her head. Her life was the opposite, a careening thing, her father having thrown over his Caribbean Sephardic roots for a Chinese immigrant's daughter, only to have the Chinese immigrant's daughter say things like *No one can live alone* and *What society doesn't have rules?* To which Gideon would say, *Fuck convention. Your mother behaves as if loneliness is not the human condition, which, believe me, it is.* Did all people lose their sense of humor after a stroke? Amaryllis wondered. Nathaniel shook his head. Not all. But some did, yes. And: it must be as if your father has turned into someone else. It is, she said, noting that what hair this Nathaniel had was half gray. Was that not slightly horrifying? "I'm glad I met you," he said, showing his well-cared-for teeth. He had brown eyes and laugh lines. It was a wonderful moment. In their maturity they agreed not to get together again. Why, though, had they exchanged email addresses? And why had they gone on to write to each other, as they had, for the better part of a year? Never even discussing having coffee, say—just writing.

They were a case.

Now he did not reply and did not reply. She trained herself not to look for his name in the Sent By column. She deleted his old messages and threw herself into looking after her friend Tara's grandfather while Tara went off to save orphans in Zambia. That was a long story, about the orphans, whom Tara had gotten interested in back when she, too, worked for the Koos. Back then, though quite a bit younger than Amaryllis, she had been just as stuck. Until she discovered Zambian *chitenge* dresses such as the one she was wearing now, with huge gold circles on a vibrant turquoise background. And after that, talk about event, action, narrative! Tara bit her lip, getting lipstick on her teeth, as she showed Amaryllis pictures of the kids. A little girl who never smiled—sullenness, it seemed, being a sign of malnutrition. A little boy whose hair was turning rust-colored—also a sign of malnutrition. It went without saying that no one was teaching them to read, unless it was in English and so that they could read the Bible.

"I'm not going to Zambia forever," Tara said. "Only for four or five months. If that's okay?"

"Of course," answered Amaryllis.

"It turns out China is buying them up even worse than they're buying up the U.S., did you realize that? Like the copper mines. They own a lot of the copper mines. Meaning that at one point the managers even fired on the workers with guns, only to have the government basically slap them on the wrist. Because they need the investment. So, I don't know. I guess I'm thinking maybe there's some way to use my Chinese over there. I mean, eventually. Do you think? If I go back to school? And in the meantime, you know, the poor orphans. Maybe I can help them first?"

"Yes! Go! Help! Learn! Stay as long as you need to!" Amaryllis said—words she knew Tara needed to hear, as her younger brother resented her do-gooding, and did not like her anti-China talk, either. Andy was, after all, a successful U.S. real estate broker, thanks to their mother, Lingli, who had sold the family tea shop and moved back to China with their ne'er-do-well father. With her Chinese connections, Lingli had thought she could maybe feed Chinese investors to Andy, and she did—so many of them, in fact, that he was now supporting them all, ungrateful Tara included.

As for Tara's job, that was to keep an eye on their grandfather Ed, who had refused to move with Lingli and Duncan. Meaning that in order to go to Zambia, Tara needed Amaryllis to look in on him every now and then, a task for which Amaryllis was well positioned. The subway from Flushing into Midtown was convenient to her office and—half-half though she was—Amaryllis was Tara's only friend whose family had come, like hers, from outside Shanghai. Of course, in one way it was strange that such a fact should still figure in Amaryllis's modern American life. But in another—it was a claim of relationship. She had so few. She yearned, in truth, for more.

Tara, in contrast, did not care about getting married. That was a dead idea, at odds with the patently polygamous nature of human nature, she said. Of course, she might think differently when she was Amaryllis's venerable age. But for now she was twenty-five and planning while in Zambia to take up residence in a guest house. She winked.

As for what Amaryllis had to wink about, well, she said, there was this corporate treasurer. "He sleeps in his suit," she said. "If he gets a new one, I may not recognize him."

Tara guffawed, showing her dimples. She was larger than Amaryllis by quite a bit, and her laugh was proportionally louder. But anyway—Tara's grandfather Ed. Yeye, Tara called him.

"He's going to want you to give him a bath," she warned. "Just say no."

"No baths," promised Amaryllis.

"And he goes to get groceries in Manhattan Chinatown on Wednesdays, don't ask me why, we're just glad he still knows when it's Wednesday. So if you go and don't see him, that's where he is."

"How old is he?"

"How old is he. Eighty-nine, we think? Though he seems a lot younger. He's more agile than I am. His doctor is always asking what he eats."

"Is he difficult?"

"Difficult? No. But he can be stubborn. And mischievous.

Like sometimes he forgets his English for real but sometimes he forgets it on purpose. He once planted his hearing aids in a pot of daffodils."

Amaryllis laughed. "He sounds amazing."

"He is amazing, as are you. You are the only person I know who would do this."

"Oh," said Amaryllis, "don't say that."

Tara's grandfather was no help to a woman trying to make a life of her life. But there he was in it. He did not look like a person who might ask someone to give him a bath. He was spidery thin and pale, with the long trickling beard and 3-D white eyebrows of a sage. His face was kite-shaped; his skin, thin and spotted, was tenuously adhered. His lips were dry, his teeth mostly there—accordioned in places, and stained, and showing some waist near the gum, but there. He sported a tweed cap with its brim flipped up, even indoors; with this went a flannel shirt, a sweater vest, and aqua training pants with intermittent hems. His hands shook. And yet Tara was right about his agility. He negotiated his cluttered apartment with grace, apparently thanks to the *tai qi* he did in the park every morning. Amaryllis did not call him *Yeye*, as he was not her grandfather. Neither could she pronounce his name in Chinese. So instead she called him Uncle Ed, uncle being what Chinese people called older men at all close to them. Amaryllis might be, as a California boyfriend so sweetly put it, barely Chinese, but even she knew that much.

Though Tara had brought Amaryllis to the apartment and introduced her, Amaryllis began the first couple of visits with an inane "Hi, remember me? I'm that friend of Tara's, Amaryllis"— trying to ease the awkwardness of barging in on him. Tara had said that her grandfather would probably not hear the door if

Amaryllis rang, that she should just use her key and let herself
in. But how weird to simply show up and begin filling the air.
I think this fish has gone bad. Does your radiator always clank?
I see there are no more lightbulbs. She wished she could speak
Chinese; she thought that would make him feel more comfortable. Though maybe she was the uncomfortable one? Both visits he had half-watched a Chinese program on his enormous
flat-screen TV, barely reacting as she puttered around, cleaning
out his birdcage, and picking up as best she could. One whole
room of his apartment was jammed with furniture and boxes,
everything thrown in an enormous pile, willy-nilly; it looked as
if there had been a fight, or as if he had been unable to pay his
moving bill—something.

The third visit Amaryllis began to notice, first that he took
his hat off when she came in, and then that he lifted his left
ear—his good ear?—when she spoke. Maybe he liked being
spoken to, even if he didn't quite understand her? In the park,
Amaryllis had seen how mothers talked to their babies as if the
babies could understand; the babies kicked and talked back. Of
course, Uncle Ed was no baby. Still, she imagined him taking a
similar simple pleasure in her talking and so was startled to find
his gaze, by the fourth or fifth visit, alive with an ironic bemuse-
ment more grandfatherly than infantile. His dimples showed; so
that was where Tara's dimples came from. Would her mother's
grandfather, had she ever met him, ever have looked at her this
way? She knew little about her great-grandfather but had the
impression that he would have more likely looked straight past
her to his male progeny—her great-grandfather having been a
financial mogul of sorts, who had kept a low profile but was
drowned by Red Guards during the Cultural Revolution all the
same.

Her sixth visit she knocked on the door instead of letting
herself in with the key. She was afraid for a moment that Uncle

Ed had not heard her. But the door opened, and this time, when she introduced herself, he smiled.

"You told me many time," he said.

He was talking! Softly, and straight down into his chest, but he was talking!

"I wasn't sure you understood," she said, speaking slowly and loudly.

"You talk so fast." He mimicked her, opening and shutting his mouth.

"You do this." Amaryllis mumbled into her shirt.

He lifted his chin, his beard rising free of his sweater vest. "Tara is a good girl," he continued mildly.

"She is," she agreed.

"You are a good girl, too. Chinese girl, I can see it."

Hapa, actually, she wanted to say. Though she had the straight black hair, nobody called her a Chinese girl. People, in fact, did not generally call her anything, though they sometimes asked, *What are you?* Drunken men, especially. That wasn't the only reason she had ended up single. There was also a failure of the stars to line up. A failure to realize how much harder it was to meet people once she'd graduated from college. But maybe it was her father in her, too—her *Fuck convention* father—thanks to whom she was moved to say things like *What am I? I'm a person with no patience for idiots like you.* It was one of the things Amaryllis had liked about Nathaniel, that he had not set himself up for such an answer.

"My grandparents on my mother's side were Chinese," she said. "From northern Zhejiang Province, right near Shanghai." She tried to pronounce *Zhejiang* correctly.

"I can see it," he said. "Zhejiang people are capable."

He understood her! Her grandmother Opal would have been proud.

"They are not lazy, like Jiangsu people," he went on. "Jiangsu people have too much land. In Zhejiang, there is no land. Everyone has to work hard, even the rich people have to work hard."

"Was your family from there?" She did not dare try and say *Jiangsu*.

"Our hometown is in Jiangsu Province," he said. "Yes. But we were not rich. No."

Amaryllis was hoping he would say more, but instead he sank into his armchair, put on his hat, and went to sleep. By his shoulder, his bird chirped.

The seventh visit she came early in the morning to watch his *tai qi* group, which turned out to be one of several groups of white-haired Chinese in the pocket park. One was a dance club with a cassette recorder. Another did tricks involving two sticks with a string between them and a kind of drum—how they made it jump and spin! The groups were not large— three, five, eight people—but they occupied every corner, as well as the paved antechamber to the park, which was really part of the street. Amaryllis, wearing high heels, felt strange. No one, though, looked at her strangely. Even Uncle Ed, after waving, looked past her. His group was beginning their routine— slow, even, hypnotic movements that made the old people seem younger, Amaryllis thought. Or, no, not so much younger as of indeterminate age—somewhere between life and death, she wanted to say. Or, no, that was wrong, too. They were simply, wholly alive. And yet as the brilliant morning light shot through to them, exploding past the yellow leaves of the sycamores, the group—more women than men—did seem to step and lunge in a sphere removed from ordinary reality. They did deep, deep knee bends—Uncle Ed's deeper than almost anyone's. Their legs stretched long; their shadows longer. Forward and back they moved, unperturbed by the bolting squirrels and loudly crunching leaves. A funnel of birds pooled suddenly around them on the cracked asphalt and then just as suddenly spiraled away, flapping. Still the group gazed calmly at their slowly moving hands. Uncle Ed's moved as steadily as anyone's—no sign of their shake. What did it mean, that unison, that focus? That planetary attunement. She could hear her mother's voice: *No one can live alone.* As it was cool, the group was wearing its team uniform, the padded vest, often with stretch pants. Only Uncle Ed wore a hat. Most wore sneakers, though one person wore plastic sandals with socks.

It surprised Amaryllis that the old people did not do more together after *tai qi.* She gathered that some did go to a senior center, where in a fluorescent-lit room they took classes and played mahjong until three o'clock, when several had to pick up their grandchildren. Others hung around the park. But Uncle Ed preferred to sit home and watch TV. He hadn't always been this way; according to Tara, he used to be lively and social. Then suddenly the senior center was too hot. The park was too cold. Tara wrote in an email how she would almost have thought he was pulling in and hunkering down, preparing to die, except for the *tai qi* and the grocery shopping. And look how he still cooked for himself.

Wednesdays. "Why do you go to Manhattan to shop?" asked Amaryllis. "Isn't it more convenient to shop here?"

"Cheaper," he answered.

"Are you sure?"

"Cheaper."

Tara had warned Amaryllis that on the trip home his backpack could be heavy, especially if he had bought rice or soy sauce. And indeed, some weeks Amaryllis worried it would topple him right over. But even more worrisome was his apparently new tendency to become disoriented. One week he got lost between the subway station and his apartment. It was just lucky that Amaryllis had happened to visit that day, after work; she found him in the park, cold and confused. The next week he was fine. But the week after that he lost his way again, and this time he did not end up in the park but wandered the busy streets—traipsing around and around with his backpack. By the time Amaryllis spotted him crossing the plaza of the new library, his whole body was shaking. Why hadn't he at least gone inside? His feet and shoulders were blistered and raw. He was so tired, he half fell into his apartment and, though he had accepted her offer to make him some tea, fell asleep before the water boiled.

She offered to take him shopping. She offered to pay for a cab.

Stubborn. Just as Tara had said—not difficult, but stubborn.

She began waiting for him in Flushing, meeting his subway car.

In truth, she worried about the Manhattan part of his trip too but wasn't sure what to do about it. Should she tail him there and back in some stealthy way? She decided no, there being no indication yet that he became confused on that end. Maybe his blood sugar levels were higher early in the day, or maybe he knew Manhattan Chinatown better; Tara's family had moved him to Flushing only a few years ago. Not that he had lived so long in Manhattan Chinatown, either. In fact, they'd only moved him there, at his insistence, when their grandmother Marge died; before that, they'd all lived in the suburbs. But in any case, meeting him on the Flushing end was tricky enough. Appointments had to be scheduled accordingly; colleagues made comments. Happily, the Koos had said nothing so far. Still, Amaryllis felt annoyed at Tara, at Uncle Ed, at herself, even as she found that she had begun to like the ritual of leaving the office. She liked needing to leave the way so many of her co-workers did—all the time, it seemed—to bring their kids to the doctor, to pick up a birthday cake, something. She liked the number-seven train and the people on it; she liked waiting at the platform, on the wooden bench facing the ticket booth. The Flushing stop was the last stop of the line. Why did she like even that?

Though he wore no watch, Uncle Ed usually arrived close enough to three-thirty that she fretted if he was late. Not just because she would be late getting back to the office, though that was certainly an issue. More, she worried that something had happened. She worried that he had tripped, that he had gotten mugged, that he had decided he didn't like Flushing and was staying in Manhattan. But finally, always, he materialized here, in the subway station, before her. Then she nodded coolly and fought with him over whether she could take his backpack for him. More and more often now, she won, which she enjoyed, although once or twice, as he handed it over, he called her Tara. He also once asked her, as they crossed the platform, what had happened to Tara. Was she married? No, no, said Amaryllis. Tara's away. In Zambia. In Africa. But he persisted. Who did she marry? And, Did she marry Chinese? They took the escalator up, the skylight growing bigger and bigger overhead. On the way to his apartment, they were going to stop under the bridge to get some of those four-for-a-dollar pork buns they both liked.

Dear Tara, I love your grandfather but have to say that I wonder if he doesn't need professional help. The wandering, as I've told you. Today he put his groceries out for the pigeons. He seems more and more confused. Did I tell you he sometimes thinks you're married?

Married?! Oh no! Can you manage?

I'm not sure. What if something happens?

OK. I'll tell my parents. Maybe my dad should move back to the States. And I'll make Andy check in when he gets back to town. In 10 days, I think? Is that soon enough? In the meanwhile, thanks again for doing this!!! I honestly did not realize Yeye was so out of it.

Amaryllis began eating with him every day. Not all three meals but she did do breakfast and supper. And how happy this made him! He took off his hat. He smiled. He laughed, showing the white spots on his tongue. His dimples appeared. Did he ever brush his teeth? She brought him strawberry-flavored toothpaste to try. "Strange," he said. She brought him cereals—Raisin Bran, Cheerios, Lucky Charms. He loved peanut butter and honey sandwiches, especially with banana. She was surprised. He loved Oreos. Rice Krispies treats. Yogurt-covered raisins. He began to clean up after his bird, who seemed happier, too. Chirpier.

They talked more.

"You don't speak Chinese," he said.

"No," she said. "I don't."

"It's a pity."

"Yes," she said. "It is."

"I had the same problem with my sons. Even Arnie does business in China, he still can only speak a few words. Duncan married a Chinese, so he can speak more. Tara, too. But Andy. Andy does not know one word."

"Well, my mother was born here. Like Tara's dad. And on top of it, my father was Caribbean Jewish American." She stopped herself from trying to explain how some Sephardic Jews had migrated to the Netherlands after the Inquisition, and from there to the Dutch Caribbean and America. None of that seemed to matter anyway since her father's stroke.

"You are not really Chinese, and yet we get along very well."

"It just so happens."

"Chinese, not Chinese, make no difference."

"Oh, I don't know," she said.

He told her about his life. "I remember when the Japanese came. The Japanese came and boom! Bombs. Once I saw a girl blown up. There was blood everywhere, but her book bag was clean. It was lying right in the road, right there in the middle. So I put it on a rock, and the next day it was gone. My mother said, Why didn't you take the bag? She thought I could trade it for something. But I told her I couldn't, no. It made her cry. She said that the way I thought, we were going to starve. But I couldn't take that bag."

And:

"My nephew, his wife, his child all died of TB. Actually TB is more common in the South than the North, where they live. But they had bad luck. My brother, too, and his wife—all their luck, very bad."

And:

"I used to go to the senior center. I even had a girlfriend. Cantonese. She liked to sing karaoke—she would hold the microphone and sing some Cantonese opera. Nice and fat. If we went out to eat, there was always someone nosy to follow us— a lightbulb. But we knew how to escape. Now who knows who is hanging around there, where they come from. Fuzhou, Wenzhou. The older ones don't speak Mandarin, the younger ones speak, but who can stand listening to them? The way they think. Money, money, money. My wife was like that. Marge. Now she is dead. And my girlfriend, she is dead, too. All my friends, dead dead dead. I am the only one left. I don't know why. There is no reason."

Dear Tara, I am embarrassed to say that I am wondering how much of your grandfather's problem was just depression.

> Now that I'm spending more time with him, he talks and
> talks. His whole affect has changed. His birds too, I swear.
> Truth to tell, I feel a certain lightness myself.

She waited to hear back from Tara, but Tara did not write. Maybe
the internet was down at the hostel, or the closest internet café
had closed—who knew. That iffy electricity. She received instead
an email from Nathaniel.

> Forgive me the lapse in our communication. It is inexcusable,
> I know. I imagined that I was doing us both a favor. But
> now I see I was misguided. Forgive me! You will note my
> observance of standard grammatical conventions. They are
> as per your request but do feel strange.

Three days later he wrote again:

> I see that you do not reply. And frankly, now that I think about
> it, why should you? Why not repay silence with silence? And
> why feel things for which we cannot make a place in our
> lives? That is another question. My guess is that you cannot
> see the point. Correct? Whereas I am acquainted with what
> ice we can become, if we don't take care. And how little is
> captured by the social forms we have—I know that too. How
> much lies beyond them, like the rain beyond the confines of
> a cistern. So there it is, an old man's wisdom. Make that an
> older man's wisdom. ☺ Which came to me with difficulty,
> and which I express here in the most poetic sentence I have
> penned this decade. You need not reply.

To this she wrote:

> You are right. I don't have time for relationships that go
> nowhere. As if we are going somewhere, you will say. And

yet I feel a pressure you don't remember. I can't afford to be wasting my time.

Time! What do you know about time?

You don't remember. Though since you mention ice, I will say that even now in the twilight of my youth I can already feel how I might become brittle, if I'm not careful. If I don't hurry. How I might become obscurely sensitive. Proud. Do you know what I mean? How I might become one of those people who care more about not appearing desperate than almost anything.

You need not become anything. Shall I say what I feel? What font should I use?

No font.

You know.

Some things are better left untyped ☺.

Untyped it remains, then. But there it is.

He wrote again a few hours later:

there it is there it is there it is

What was it? It was nothing. It was something. It was nothing. That day she brought flowers to Uncle Ed and found the energy to clean out the main room of his apartment. She washed the windows, the curtains billowing; for an early winter day, it was surprisingly like spring. She made him his favorite dinner—tuna noodle casserole—and brought up the subject of bathing. He headed for the bathroom with lightness in his step, and an air of expectancy.

"My wife," he said as he got in the water.

"Careful," she said.

"My wife," he said, "used to give me a bath. When she was alive."

He looked as though he were going to cry, even as he beamed with pleasure. Amaryllis could not believe how old and small his body was, how shriveled and bony and veiny. Here and there a strand of hair sprouted, each one an event. His ribs stuck out as if they had outgrown him. And yet he was happy. He was happy to have water poured down his back, and happy to have what hair he had, washed. She soaped, rinsed. His scalp flaked. She soaped and rinsed again. His beard dripped. She was surprised how hot he liked the water and how pink he turned, especially against the green tile. And she was surprised, too, that he seemed to have an erection when he got out of the water. It was so low she could barely tell if that was what it was. A kind of pudginess. He did not seem to notice. Still she smiled and chased after him with a towel as he padded, dripping, into the living room.

Tara's brother Andy appeared. His lips were thin and pale, his black hair cropped. Though all of twenty-three, he wore cuff links and a monogrammed shirt and a tie with a tiny knot. Amaryllis knew his type from work; she could picture how in meetings he leaned back in his chair tapping his pen on its arm, then abruptly rocked forward, his mind made up. In college, she happened to know, he had switched majors four times. Now he exuded decisiveness. There being no conference table in the apartment, he seated himself at the kitchen table, reaching between his legs to pull his chair forward. Then he nod-

ded politely as she explained to him some of what had gone
on. She left out the bath. He tapped his pen on the Formica. To
his credit, he did at least listen. And he asked real questions,
pointed questions, trying to get a handle on things. She tried
to smile at Uncle Ed as she answered—including him, even as
he watched TV. Slumped as he was, his torso looked short, and
his knees sharp. Also his slippers seemed big, as if his feet had
shrunk. He was wearing his hat.

Andy sat forward, frowning.

"Okay. His cognitive status." He tapped his pen on the table
again. "We need to assess that. And after that, a strategy. We're
going to need a strategy." He tapped once more, tightening his
mouth. Then, to her surprise, he laid his pen on the table, put
his head in his hands, and ran his fingers through his dark hair,
his wedding ring shining.

"I think he can live on his own a while longer," said Amaryllis. "He just needs someone to look in on him every day. Not two
or three times a week—every day. Which I can't do. But he's not
that bad, really. I almost wish I hadn't said anything to Tara."

"You almost wish . . ." Andy raised his head.

"I didn't mean to worry her."

Andy stared. "Well, you did worry her." His eyes were beady
and intense. "In fact, you worried everyone. I had to drop everything in the middle of a fifty-million-dollar deal to come figure out what to do. Do you realize? I'm supporting my whole
family."

"That's tough, but I really can't do this forever."

"You know, we'd be happy to pay you."

She drew in a shocked breath. "Thanks, but I'm not for
hire," she said.

"I see. You have better things to do."

She wasn't entirely sure there was an edge to that. Still,
she did think she felt something hard and cold pressed against

a place she could not quite protect. And so with dignity, she hoped, she said, "It simply isn't possible."

The TV droned. Uncle Ed had fallen asleep, his mouth open. Amaryllis watched his chest to be sure he was breathing.

The radiator clanked.

If at that point Andy had broken the silence to say, *You know, we appreciate your generosity,* she might well still have answered, *I've come to love your grandfather and I'd love to go on doing what I can.* She might have even gone on to say, *Fuck convention.* Or, no, maybe not that. She never said *fuck* anything. But *No one can survive alone.* She might have said that.

Instead, clanking. Until finally Andy said, "You have a life."

"He's your grandfather, not mine," she countered— surprising herself with the readiness with which she spoke.

More clanking. Andy pressed his fingers to his eyelids. "I'm sorry, I'm just tired," he said. "As in very tired."

"You're under a lot of pressure."

"Who knows how long this China spending spree is going to last, right? And then I turn into a pumpkin. You know, another Asian guy no one can quite see as a major player, it's hard to say why. Something about his social skills, yada yada."

"You don't need this."

He paused, then said, "I don't. But you're right. This is not your problem."

"He's an extraordinary man, your grandfather."

"He deserves so much more than any of us can give him. Having lives of our own, you know. I have really got to do something about my hours. But now, Tara. Tara needs to go save Africa."

"She wants to help, that's all. She wants to do something meaningful with her life, and she's starting with these orphans."

"Orphans." He buried his hands in his hair again. "Little black orphans."

"That's no way to talk, Andy."

"You know what she is? She's a white savior who isn't even white. And you know what the Blacks over there think of her? I'll tell you what they think of her."

"Don't," she said immediately. "Please don't."

And with that she stood up, gave her key to Andy, and bent to give Uncle Ed a quick kiss on his hat. The tweed was rough; he did not wake. She let herself out the door.

The air in the hallway was stuffy and hot, the air outside biting and cold.

That Andy! She would file the full report with Tara. Yes.

At home, though, she did not write to Tara right away. Instead she read through her more recent correspondence with Nathaniel. She opened her Trash, too, and rescued what messages she found there—read them and backed them up. Then she clicked on New Messages and wrote, and thought, and wrote some more. About Uncle Ed, about Tara, about Andy. About what happened.

> How easily I could have said, I've come to love your grandfather. And I almost did, you know. Other things too. But I didn't, because of Andy. Because I just knew what he was thinking. I did.

There it was.

> I guess you'd have to say I've developed sensitivities after all. And poor Uncle Ed! He must be so confused and sad. Bereft. If he even realizes what's happened. Did I tell you he loves peanut butter with honey? I am going to go visit again and bring him a Fluffernutter. In the meantime, I write to you—return to you too, and to this. Our rain catcher,

you could say. Which I can just see in a sepia print, with
Leonardo. Can't you? He would have to be holding the thing
up in a torrential rain, so all would be water and mist except
Leonardo himself. Leonardo would be strangely lit, as if
from within—as if by this sheer weird joy.

Rothko, Rothko

She was working in an old garage with a wooden door. There would have been reasonable air flow had the garage door been open, but as it was, the ventilation consisted of a side door, a window the size of a road atlas, and a noncommittal box fan. It was dark inside, too, lit by what appeared to be a forty-watt bulb; the bulb hung head-down in a yellow cage. No wonder that she was wearing a camper's headlamp, so that the first thing I saw when I came in the door was an elastic band reading, in stretched-wide lime-green letters, REI.

"Knock, knock," I said.

She didn't turn around.

But there she was. A slight woman, maybe in her late thirties? Even on a stepstool she appeared smaller than my wife, Arabella, whom a significant subset of men were moved to call "half-pint." Did that make this woman a quarter-pint? I knew she was supposed to be some kind of genius, but what with her black hair, flat face and flat nose, she mostly brought to mind a flat tire. Ming Ding, my student Achilles had said her name was—either that, or Ding Ming, he wasn't sure which. The Chinese name thing was as confusing for him as for me because

he was, like me, second generation, only born in Africa; he was
deeply grateful, he once said, that his parents had at least given
him an English name. Achilles Chen. But, whatever. I knew this
was the woman I sought because of the painting she was working on, which was the reason Achilles had sent me her way—
a painting that did look for all the world very like a Rothko. One
of the dark ones, from late in his life when he'd been reading too
much Nietzsche. It was taller than she by a good bit and about
five times as wide.

Ming, as I later learned I should call her, had a dozen repro-
duction Rothkos taped to the cinder block beside her. These
ranged from postcards and magazine pictures to a poster I
could have sworn to be the same one my college roommate had
hung up on his dorm room ceiling to hide the glow-in-the-dark
stars his ex-girlfriend had stuck up there with Gorilla Glue. But
Ming's creation was not a copy of any of the reproductions. It
was, rather, its own thing—two vertical black rectangles all but
obliterating a dark purplish background. The rectangles, paradoxically, were not the light-absorbing black holes you might
expect. Quite the contrary, they boasted an unaccountable
luminosity—not gleaming, exactly, but emanating somehow.
And they evinced a strange lightness, too, as if they had somehow been suspended an atom or two in front of the canvas. I
seemed to recall from my art history phase—short-lived as it
was—that Rothko had always asked for the gallery lights to be
turned down low, and now I thought I got why: it encouraged
this viewer, at least, to sense more than to look—to feel and
attend more than to analyze. Were the rectangles inviting or
foreboding? Tombstones or doors? Never mind. I could feel
those sorts of ideas float clean away, irrelevant and crass. This
was something from another sphere.

Of course, the thing was a fake. It was worth nothing, and at
some level, it was nothing.

At the same time, there it was, my response to the nothing. Was that something? I was a man with pressures—a man with papers to grade and students to see. A man with projects. My to-do list had a kind of auto-renew feature. And yet, and yet.

It was a mystery.

Ming was wearing pants that might have been a perfect fit had she been twice her size. The points of her shoulders stood up, knobby, from her tank top; her collarbones stuck out, and her cheekbones, too. Her hair was wispy. She had no discernible muscle tone. She could really use, I thought, some Soylent. But for all the vitality her body lacked, there was vitality in her brush—a house painter's brush, it appeared, and quite an unwieldy thing relative to her hand. How did she get it to move so quickly and surely?

I pulled a stool up in front of the fan. The air pressed weakly against my back as I began to make out how she used her whole body, a loose wrist, and only the very tips of her bristles. Her paint—a blue-green mixture in an old Revere Ware pot—was so astonishingly diluted, it looked like Easter egg dye. As for what it actually was, who knew? On a cheap white plastic end table such as might normally hold guacamole and chips, she had set up an electric burner with a double boiler, around which sat many things you'd expect—bowls, pots, brushes, spoons, tubes of oil paint, jars of pigment, and jars of something called mineral spirit acrylics. On the floor there were also several gallons of turpentine, a box of rags—some of which appeared to have begun life as spaceship-themed pajamas—a camo-printed thermos, and a jug of water. But in addition, there was a jug labeled PHENOL FORMALDEHYDE, two rolled-up Chinese scrolls, a bottle of vinegar, a crate of eggs in cartons, and a large variety of baggies, twist-tied shut.

I squinted at a label. "Does that say 'dammar resin'?"

She did not react right away. But finally she nodded.

"And—'hide glue'?"

"Yes."

I nodded as though that made perfect sense when in fact I had no idea what these things were. Meanwhile, so diaphanous was the wash she was now adding that I probably would not have been able to make it out were it not wet. When she finally turned to me, her headlamp was blinding. I put up a hand; she switched it off.

"How much?" she said.

"Four hundred, maybe?" I said.

"My friend Bei got nine thousand dollars for one same like this." She turned the fan so that its breeze blew on the painting rather than on me, then contemplated her work. "Actually, same but not as good."

A simple statement of fact. I might have been surprised except that I had heard something similar from Achilles—about Bei Shantian, who was a legend, and about how much he used to get for his Rothkos, for his Pollocks, for a Diebenkorn—as well as about how Ming was at least as good a painter, maybe better.

"Bei uses tea," she went on.

"To make it look old?"

She nodded, disgusted. "Like someone sell something on the Dirt Market."

"In Beijing?"

She nodded.

"A common 'antiques' dealer, you mean."

She nodded again. "And his paint." She grimaced.

"He doesn't use hide glue like you? Or eggs?"

"He does not really follow Rothko."

"Ah."

"Only I follow how Rothko do. Many layers, all different kind."

"Ah."

"In between, phenol—" She gestured.

"Phenol formaldehyde?"

"Yes. Very important."

"Ah," I said again. "Bei had a New York gallery connection," I went on. "If his gallery is still buying, maybe you can sell to them. But even he probably didn't start at nine thousand, you know. His prices probably went up slowly."

"They like him." Ming studied the canvas. "So they pay more."

"He had a track record."

"Track?" She cocked her head.

"Track record," I repeated. "They knew he could make money for them. That people would buy his work. He was, you know, established." Would the word "established" help or confuse her?

Anyway, she was nodding. "I get," she said. "Track record. He had track record."

"In any event, that gallery had to close," I said.

She didn't reply.

"Because of the lawsuit. Which maybe you've heard about?" Certainly, as a painter in this world, she had heard that the chairman of Cabot's had bought one of Bei Shantian's pieces, discovered it to be fake, and sued the gallery for three times what he'd paid? "It was all over the news. The gallery lost."

She had heard.

"So the question is, Who is buying now, right?" I said. "If anyone."

"If anyone," she agreed. "If there is a new gallery kind of like take over."

"Same game, another name, you mean?" I said. "I doubt it." And, indeed, I actually hoped this was not the case. If nothing else, to pay an artist nine thousand dollars for work you then sold for upward of $8 million! It was too much.

But Ming seemed disappointed.

"Same game, another name," she repeated—intrigued by the rhyme and placing a kind of wistful hope, it almost seemed, in it. For was it not a phenomenon, if there was a phrase for it? "Same game, another name."

I thought. "I don't think it's likely. But let's say that there is such a gallery somewhere, taking over from the old one. How good a friend of yours is Bei? Could he maybe tell the new gallery that he painted this?"

I motioned at the canvas even as I kicked myself. Had I really just suggested that a forger forge his forgery? And how was I going to make any money this way?

Ming thought. "Then we can split. Fifty-fifty."

"Fifty percent of his fee would probably be more than I can pay," I said.

"Okay. I ask."

"If it works, good luck," I said gamely. "If not, let me know."

"Okay."

"Or maybe I can do a little better," I said.

"How much?"

"I don't know. I have to email some people."

"Okay."

"Can I call you? Text you? Email you?"

She shook her head.

"All right." I didn't ask why not, as I could see there was no point. "I'll check in again if I find anything out. Also to see if you've heard anything from Bei."

"Okay," she said.

She asked then if I would help her turn the canvas.

"Turn it?"

She wanted it rotated it ninety degrees clockwise, so we did that. The canvas now hung sideways.

"Do you do that every layer?" I asked.

She nodded.

"But then sometimes it will be upside down."

"Of course. It is upside down now."

It was?

As she prepared to apply a layer of something else, I stepped back out into the September sun—as blinding as Ming's head-lamp, after the dim light. It was cooler outside than in the garage.

Home was a futon-furnished living room, an eat-in kitchen, and what Arabella called my "sanctum sanctorum." This was actually a hallway with a backless stool on one wall and a fold-down shelf on the other, just big enough for a laptop. It was good for my posture. However, it was less than ideal for what Arabella called my "novel," though I myself could not bring myself to dignify what I was working on with that word, much less the other word she liked to use, "opus." My opus. Was she proving herself a stalwart believer in my talent when she used terms like these, or was she inadvertently demonstrating that she had no idea what an imaginative feat a novel was really? Maybe, I thought sometimes, she was trying to conjure a book into being, as if that were the first step to my becoming the rebel artist she had thought she had rebelliously married.

Our apartment had no view, which was not to say it had no windows. We actually had two. One opened onto an alleyway; the other opened onto an air shaft. It was okay. We wouldn't have wanted a view onto the street anyway, studded as it was with drug dealers and their ever-changing sidekicks—their renewables, as Arabella called them. At the same time, this was not our dream apartment. When Arabella and I were getting along, it was cozy. When we were not, it was something else.

" 'Let me know'? 'I'll check in again'?" She was making avocado toast with poached eggs and sriracha sauce for us—a treat and normally a happy occasion. Jabbing a knife now into an avocado pit, though, Arabella brandished it in the air. "What is this, Rich?"

Of course, "this" was an attempt to augment my salary as an adjunct instructor. If upon graduating from law school, Arabella had gone into corporate law, we would be all set. But she had stuck to immigration law, to my hearty applause, just as I had gone and gotten my MFA, to hers. As a result, four years later, what we heard was not the sound of each other's clapping. What we heard, night and day, was our parents, miraculously united by an evident truth: we were crazy. The many corollaries of this they did not, we tried to emphasize, need to articulate. Still they did, starting with, Even idealists need to eat. This was actually only half true: Arabella, conveniently, could live on air. I, less conveniently, needed five scoops of Soylent meal replacement a day at a minimum and, heaven forgive me, preferred food.

"It's the chewing," I found myself explaining a year or so ago. I was trying not to sound defensive. "I like to chew. I guess because I grew up that way. You know. Chewing."

Arabella crossed her eyes then and laughed understandingly, her eyes sweet and soft. "You are nothing if not atavistic," she said, good-naturedly agreeing to allow us one real meal every other day. The exceptions would be birthdays and holidays, when we'd have a real meal regardless.

But now she seemed to be developing a set to her mouth. I hadn't known that could happen to someone thirty-two, much less an Asian someone. But since the election, her phone rang even more constantly, if that was possible, with frantic relatives.

Removal proceedings were ordered for the flimsiest of reasons; cases took years to come to trial. All of which meant we were never going to have a baby, she said, but I thought there was still time. Because wasn't there?

"And what are you going to do with this thing, pray tell?" she went on, continuing to brandish the avocado pit.

"It's not a thing. It's a painting, like the ones Achilles says a gallery in New York used to sell for millions of dollars—that's how good these fakes are. Especially the ones by this Bei guy who isn't even as good as she is."

"And how does Achilles know, may I ask?"

"His dad is some sort of operator, I'm not sure from where. Singapore, maybe? Macau? And before that, Africa. The gallery apparently even sold a 'Rothko' to the chairman of Christie's."

"Really?" Arabella put on the water for the eggs. "How'd they manage that?"

"Beats me, but it was a colossal mistake. Because the guy figured it out, sued, and shut that gallery down. Though there may be some regrouping going on even as we speak—or so Ming hopes."

"Same scam, different management, you mean?"

"Exactly. Same game, different name."

If some part of Arabella wanted to smile at my more elegant formulation, it didn't show. Instead there was the set of her mouth again.

"I mean, I myself doubt any of the big galleries is going to try this again," I went on. "But anyway, this guy Bei has gone back to the Mainland."

"Leaving an opening for Ming? Is that what you mean?"

"Not like the old one. But—"

"But what? Assuming she really can paint as well as you think she can—a big assumption—how could you possibly fence this thing? What are you going to do about provenance papers? And why has Achilles's father even involved you in this?"

"He's just trying to help. He knows we need money, and he apparently thinks I know a little about art. Which I really don't anymore, if I ever did, but whatever."

"And let me guess. In exchange for this 'help,' you're going to be asked to give Achilles an A."

"They know I'm not the type, Arabella. Plus, it's not clear there's even any money in this."

"Not without the father's help arranging for papers and maybe another gallery, you mean. As they'll no doubt let drop now that they've gotten you interested in helping this poor woman. They've probably figured out that mere monetary gain is motivation but not motivation enough for someone like you—that to overcome your moral scruples, you'll need to feel you're doing good as well. So they've assembled some special bait—bait that involves both."

"I'm not going to be giving Achilles any A's, Arabella."

She laughed a short laugh that went with the set of her mouth. Though the water was hot now, she did not crack the eggs and pour them into ramekins, readying them for poaching the way she normally did. Instead she shut the heat back off. "All I can say is, one false step, and you're going to end up in jail, Rich. Where, by the way, you will get to chew to your heart's content."

"No Soylent there?"

"No."

"Well, scratch one disincentive anyway," I said. "But in any case, I'm not looking to Achilles's father to arrange a dealer. I have my own in mind."

"You know another dealer?"

"Yes."

"You're kidding."

"Through a former student," I supplied. "Lower profile—there won't be any multimillion-dollar sales. But Ming doesn't need that, and neither do we."

"Your students are amazing," said Arabella.

And of course, this was true, though it was also just what happened when you were the lone Asian American teaching literature and writing in an obscure branch of a city university. "Amazing" students found you, some of them amazingly rich. They took all your courses; they took you to lunch; you had to include a no-presents policy in your syllabus. It was a very different crowd than the one Arabella served. She was, heaven help her, trying to drum up more employment-based work, for institutions that paid, and soon. For now, though, she did deportation defense for the desperate, while I taught the sort who, for all their educational lacunae, could nonetheless spell "Lamborghini."

"So are you going to lie to this dealer?" she asked.

"No. I am just not going to volunteer where the thing came from, should they happen not to ask."

"Any reputable dealer is going to ask, Rich. Especially after the Cabot's suit."

I shrugged. The toast popped up. She ignored it.

"And who exactly is this peerless entity?"

"Johnson and Tina Koo. You know, that Hong Kong couple I see every now and then. The ones with the daughter."

"That student of yours who disappeared, you mean—Bobby? Wasn't that her name?"

"Very good. Bobby Koo. The one who was into samizdat lit. And just to be clear, I wasn't really her teacher per se. I was just her TA in a summer school class. As you probably remember."

"I didn't realize her parents were art dealers."

"They have their fingers in a lot of things. I think this is for fun. And my sense is they might not resell the thing, by the way, if they buy it. They might just hang it in one of their lobbies. Or give it to a school and take a deduction."

"Which the school is going to fork over, no questions asked?"

"Or maybe they'll just keep it for themselves. Bask in the envy of their friends."

"A deduction can be worth millions, you know."

I sighed. "While I, their middleman, am only going to make thousands."

"And the poor painter makes hundreds."

"Would it make you feel better if she makes thousands, too?"

Arabella hesitated—meaning that, yes, it would make her feel better. Categorically opposed as she was to the whole idea, though, she could not admit it.

"Okay. You've convinced me," I said. "I'll split the take with her, fifty-fifty."

"Rich. Why are you talking this way?"

"I'm talking this way because I don't actually think this will ever be resold as a Rothko," I said. "And I'm talking this way because you aren't the only one wondering how we're ever going to be able to afford a baby."

"Well, thank you for that, at least."

"Oh, come on. You know it's true, Arabella. I'm talking this way because the Koos will do their thing whether or not I supply them with a picture. And I'm talking this way because . . ." I hesitated. "Because I don't actually think Ming's a crook."

"Oh really."

"I actually think she's an artist."

"And you think this because?"

"Because I saw some scrolls on the floor," I said.

"Because you saw some scrolls on the floor." Arabella crossed her eyes. "It's a good thing you dropped out of law school."

"I'm not presenting that as evidence," I said. "It just contributes to this sense I have of her. Why I say I think she's an artist."

"Ah."

"There is also the way she talks. The way she thinks."

"The way she thinks."

"She's a purist. Like, she copies everything she knows of Rothko's methods even if it's fiendishly complicated and even if Bei didn't. Even if no one will ever know."

"Rich. There are pastry chefs in Shanghai who are like that. Baristas."

And of course, she was right. Never mind if the objects of their obsessions were European, as they frequently were. These acolytes sought out masters. They practiced indefatigably. They carried on great traditions with fanatic fidelity.

Still I insisted, "There's something about her."

"Why are you defending her?" demanded Arabella and, when I didn't answer, went on, "Could it be because you see yourself in her? The genuine article somehow fallen between the cracks?"

"She is way more of the genuine article than anyone I've ever known, Arabella, much less me."

"You're being modest."

"I'm being honest."

"And what would Rothko say if he were alive? Does that matter?"

"He'd probably feel ripped off," I allowed. "Though maybe he would have hired her as a studio assistant."

"This is illegal, Rich. It is dodgy, discreditable, and probably felonious."

"What if I tell Ming not to sign the thing?"

"It is painting with the intent to deceive," she said. "It is artistic malfeasance."

"It is copying out of love and homage and selling the result to someone who understands completely what it is but may choose to misrepresent it," I argued. "I think that makes her an accessory to a potential misrepresentation, and me an accessory to an accessory to a potential misrepresentation."

"I take back everything I ever said about you and law school. You're a natural born hairsplitter."

"How about if I specify that the Koos not sell or donate it? How about if I make them promise to hang it in an atrium or a house?"

"It would still be pretty rich, Rich," she said—one of our standard jokes.

"And what if Ming's money is going home to China, to pay for her mother's medical expenses? Does that change things?"

"Is it?"

"That's what Achilles says."

Arabella looked down at the cutting board, where the sliced avocado lay arrayed like a sacrifice-in-progress to a cruel vegetarian god.

"Make your own avocado toast," she said.

Then she repaired to the living room to take one of her thousands of phone calls. She refrained from slamming the door; she was not the door-slamming type. But she did shut it unequivocally in my face.

As I had told Arabella, the Koos were not gallery owners. They were collectors who also did some friends-and-family dealing in what they called Reasonable Art. My guess was that they were happy enough not to ask questions, lest they get answers; and as I had suggested to Arabella, they had lobbies to fill. Atriums. Boardrooms they would otherwise decorate with Monet-lite aquatints. Why not give them something brooding and profound to hang instead—something that might inspire reflection?

Something that might even awaken some latent spirituality—that might stir their depths, that might remind them of the finitude of human life and the vanity of human striving? What was the matter with that?

I pondered these questions in an idle kind of way as I went about my teaching. I did not, that's to say, visit Ming again. Instead I assigned, I discussed, I introduced. I enlightened and reviewed. I explained. Occasionally, I inspired. And of course, I graded, graded, graded. I tried, in my grading, to be fair. And early in the semester, especially, I did not sort the papers in any particular way but just graded the pile as it arrived, starting at the top and reading through to the bitter bottom. As the semester wore on, though, I did sometimes save what I expected to be the best essays for last. My guesswork wasn't always right. Sometimes essays I expected to be awful were great, and vice versa. In general, though, this approach got me through my grind. Indeed, as mid-September turned into late September turned into mid-October, it so improved my productivity that I often had a clear two hours a day for my own work. I still shied clear of using the word "novel" for my project. But I could see that my whatever-it-was was putting on heft. It had its own momentum; indeed, it was positively alive—more alive than I was. Did it emanate the haloed gravitas of Ming's canvas? No. But there was something there. Characters coming to life. Characters taking over. Characters sabotaging my plans. I had read that that could happen—even that that was supposed to happen. But it had never happened to me. I was excited.

And so it was that one gray day, I reached the end of my pile with especially keen anticipation and began an essay by Mary Ann Evans Wang. Mary Ann Evans was one of my favorite students and very much after my own heart: she had come to America intending to pursue finance but had fallen in love with literature and, despite parental pressure of the sort that some Asian parents had raised to a high art, had bravely declared herself an English major. She was always asking for extra reading recommendations and was full of interesting questions. Like, who was Jane Austen's father, that he had so many books? And what happened to Jane Austen's brother? And why did we feel sorry for Jane Austen when she didn't have to work and could stay home and write? My student's original name was Huiyang Wang, but after she read *Middlemarch*—and, two-year marathon that it was for her, she did read the whole thing—she changed her name to Mary Ann Evans.

"Why Mary Ann Evans?" I asked. "Why not George Eliot?"

"Because George Eliot is like a coat she has to wear when she goes out," she said. "I think when she is inside by herself, with her pen and paper, she is just Mary Ann Evans. I think Mary Ann Evans is still a girl with some things she like to write down. A girl who has more and more ideas every day. A girl who has to learn a lot of languages so she can discover a lot of things."

A wonderful student. But her essay, entitled "Social and Spiritual Energy in *Middlemarch*," began:

> It is insufficient to say that *Middlemarch* explores the ways in which social and spiritual energy can be frustrated. *Middlemarch* explores the ways in which social and spiritual energies ("ideals," if you will) are completely laid waist. One need only look to Lydgate to see an example of idealism completely and utterly destroyed, if not demolished, by his environment. At the start of the novel, we are introduced to the "young, poor and ambitious" Doctor Lydgate, who has great plans to build a hospital.

I sighed and turned to my computer. And there, sure enough, I found an almost identical opening passage on www.StraightA. com. It was with a heavy heart that I marked nothing on her paper but wrote that I wanted to see her during office hours.

She bounced into my office in high spirits. She loved costumes: one week she might be a study in flounces, the next she might appear in a suit. Today her hair was plaited into twin heavy pigtails. Having recently discovered the university natural history museum, she had a giant blue Morpho butterfly clip tucked behind one ear like a flower; she looked like a hostess in a bug house.

I asked her to sit down.

"Do you remember what we said about plagiarism?" I said. "Do you remember how serious a matter we said it was here in America?"

"I remember."

"Then how can you have turned this in?" I typed the first few sentences of her piece into an antiplagiarism program, which promptly brought up the original with the source sentences highlighted.

Her face filled with confusion. "I used Turn-It-In.com," she said. "Before I turned it in. And it said my score was okay."

"What do you mean, your score was okay?"

"In China, my teachers said you are okay if your score is thirty percent. And my piece was only fifteen percent."

"Fifteen percent? In America, we allow a score of zero percent. An essay like this has to be your original work, period." I sounded like Arabella, I knew, but I had no choice. It was my job.

"The article said so many interesting things," she said. "It had so many thoughts better than my thoughts. And the writer writes so much better than I can do. My writing is so poor."

"Your writing is improving all the time."

"I think it is—how do you say?—plateau. I work very hard but always I get a B+, never an A. So I do not see how I can improve any more, writing my own words. It is just as you always say. The English tests in China give too many points for complex grammar and complex vocabulary. Now it is hard for the students to write another way. We had too much training. But I think if I write some other words, I will learn how the words should sound. I think I will learn to write in a simple way, for communication. And I think someday I will write a beautiful article like that."

"That is all great and you can learn by imitation, but you cannot turn it in," I said. "It's cheating, as I think you know. I am going to have to give you an F for this."

"But my parents!" She began to cry, her butterfly bobbing. "My parents saved for twenty years so I could go to school in America! Every time I got a B+ they say, You see! How can a Chinese get an A on an English paper? A Chinese could never succeed as an English major! They say, You think you can go to graduate school in America with a B+? You think anyone is going to hire you in China with a B+? Now we are going to die poor and despised."

I tried to explain that she still shouldn't have plagiarized and that this was just one paper. No one was going to die despised. "Look," I said finally. "I have to report this to Academic Affairs. I have no choice. But I will ask them if you can rewrite it, okay?"

Should I have said that? I could hear Arabella's answer, but it was too late. Mary Ann Evans was already nodding.

"I don't know what they'll say, but I'll ask," I said. "Then I'll email you and tell you their answer."

She tried to nod some more but was still crying. Her butterfly clip fell to the floor; I picked it up for her. She grabbed it and fled.

A half hour later I was still composing my email to Academic Affairs when Achilles appeared in my doorway, his teeth perfect as the kernels of a blue-ribbon ear of corn. He carried a sleek designer backpack.

"Ming wants to see you," he said, his free hand on the doorframe.

"When?"

"Right away."

I did not ask why or how he knew. Instead I just said, after a moment, "All right."

He winked.

"Bei say no," said Ming without turning.

"Is Bei here?"

"Just come for some visit."

"I thought he had to stay out of the country to escape prosecution."

She shrugged.

I watched her apply what I took to be a first coat of paint to a bare canvas. The double boiler was in use, and a digital thermometer; there was a bowl of maroon-colored something in the top half of the boiler. The air smelled funky. "Is that the hide glue?"

"Rabbit skin." She added some water from the thermos to the mixture.

"Ah. And Bei said no because?"

"There is too much trouble," said Ming, stirring. "He say yes, there is a new gallery. But even the new gallery say he should wait. Not paint for a while."

"Ah."

"Especially Rothko. No Rothko."

"Because of the lawsuit, you mean."

She nodded, bringing the bowl over to the canvas. "Also," she said, starting to paint, "he do not like my painting."

"What do you mean, he doesn't like it?"

"Maybe he think I will compete with him."

"He doesn't like it because it is too good, you mean."

"Today we split fifty-fifty, but maybe tomorrow the gallery find out."

"And then what? Is that what you think he thinks?"

She nodded.

"I'm so sorry."

"Of course, if I make some happy with him, maybe he change his mind."

It took me a moment to understand her; I tried to contain my shock. "But you didn't? I hope?"

"I am too old," she said matter-of-factly, still painting. "Too old, too dry."

I cleared my throat. She was thin. However, she was not old. Nor—though I knew I shouldn't be thinking this—did she appear dry. Far from it.

"I don't think these paintings should be sold for millions of dollars anyway," I said, sticking to business. "Or even thousands. Because, you know. They're not really Rothkos."

"Rothko is the master," she agreed. "We are all just improve a little."

"But something—I can't help but feel they're worth something."

Her brush stopped. "My mother, she is sick. If I do not give her money, she cannot pay the doctor. And in China, if you do not give the doctor money, they will not operate. Bei say even he do not agree to fifty-fifty, still he will give me some money to help. He say I do not have to paint anything."

"You mean, he said he would help you for nothing?"

"He is from my hometown," she explained. "His mother

know my mother. In fact, before his mother die, they work in the same factory. A lot of chemical there. Many people got sick. His mother, my mother. Other people, too."

I nodded. As it happened, I, too, had lost Chinese relatives to cancers caused by chemicals—three of them, in fact. I remembered the look on my mother's face every time she heard about another sick sibling. And I remembered how unable to sit still with her grief she was—how my father had made her retire so she would not work herself to death. *You know what China is?* he said. *China is a black hole.*

It was generous of Bei not to close his heart.

"But maybe he also just doesn't want you to paint," I said. "And that's how much it's worth to him. That he would pay you to stop."

"Correct."

"So will you take the money and stop?"

"I will take the money, yes. But stop? No."

"Will that work?"

She shrugged.

"Is it enough money?"

"No."

"But it is still some help."

"Yes."

I stood. "Let me talk to my people and get back to you." I tried to speak coolly, as if some channel of understanding had not widened between us—as if there were not even more water flowing through it, shining. But of course, there was.

Bobby Koo was one of my earliest students. Back when she left Wall Street, she'd taken a department secretary job of all things—to pay the bills while she sorted things out, she said, and in the meantime she could take classes for free. And this was how it was that I found myself her TA in a Russian lit summer school class between my junior and senior year. As for whether we became friends, as a detective later told the Koos, the truth was that she was more like an older sister than a pal. She liked me because I let her write about Václav Havel's "The Power of the Powerless" when that wasn't Russian, and because she knew that I was as unlike my parents as she was unlike hers. So we were fellow renegades; but that, really, was all.

In short, it was only out of dogged desperation that the Koos still called me whenever they were in New York—hoping against hope that Bobby would someday get back in touch with me, and that I would let them know. Or did I know something that I myself did not know I knew? It was sad. Even all these years after her disappearance, they would sometimes look at me as though they believed that somewhere in my depths I had something for them—some piece of information, some explanation—though more and more, I think, they invited me because, having known Bobby, I helped keep her memory alive.

At any rate, I had become, thanks to the ritual, a kind of extended family—as happy and used to having a meal on them as they were happy and used to treating me, especially since I enabled them to order lots of different things: Tina was such an inveterate sampler of dishes. Today, for example, she took a nibble of everything, then delicately passed the rest of each morsel to Johnson; he dutifully dispensed with it. As that still left most of each dish untouched, however, it fell to me to scarf down as much as possible so it wouldn't go to waste. I did this now most obligingly.

Tina, though, frowned. "This place used to be very good," she said. "But now, a new chef."

Johnson agreed vigorously. "Restaurant business very hard," he said. "I always say it. The chefs have too much power." Though I thought the food delicious, he seemed to think the restaurant finished. "If I was the owner, I would have given the old chef anything he want. Anything, so long as he will stay. Anything."

No one mentioned Bobby and what they would have given to get her to stay. Still, to change the subject, I asked them whether they thought the upcoming July protest would be smaller than in other years. They said they hoped so. I asked how bad they thought the typhoon season was going to be. They said not too bad. I asked if they thought it a bad thing that Xi Jinping had no term limits anymore. They said they had no opinion. Finally, I described Ming and her work. Were they perhaps—

"Yes!" Johnson said, brightening. "We are interested!"

"Of course," I said, "it's not really a Rothko. It's—"

"I know just what it is!" he roared.

Tina had reservations. "I just have one question," she said, her chopsticks poised midair. She cocked her wrist as if about to launch a dart at a dartboard. "What color is it?"

I explained. The deep purple background, the black rectangles, the way they floated. I did not say anything about tombstones. She in turn described a lobby she had in mind. It was in Nevada, its theme was bubbles, and it was about floating, too.

"Not everything is bubbles," she said. "But bubbles pull it all together."

"So you want me to ask Ming if she can do something more . . . bubbly?" I said.

Tina nodded.

"More . . . Vegas?"

She nodded again.

"We always like the artists who think in a more flexible way," said Johnson. "More creative. Willing to try something new."

"Of course," I said. "You like the innovative ones."

Now Johnson was nodding, too.

"I'll get back to you," I said.

He gave me a double thumbs-up. "Send us an email," he said as Tina mirrored him. And at the sight of all those thumbs, I, of course, gave a double thumbs-up back. That made six thumbs in the air, a sight that somehow made me most miserably happy.

The good news was that Ming's new piece was much further along. Also, because she was using more red, the background was almost lively. However, this particular red was distinctly evocative of bloodshed and hellfire. I sighed.

"I talked to the potential buyers," I said.

She separated eggs until she had a bowl full of yolks.

"They are interested," I said.

She added linseed oil. Vinegar.

"Egg tempera?" I asked.

If she was surprised that I knew this, she didn't show it. "Tempera grassa," she said.

"Ah. In any case, they would like something a little brighter," I went on. "Cheerier. More positive. You know how some Rothkos are gold and pink and blue? More like that." I could not produce the words "bubbly" or "Vegas." "They're from Hong Kong," I finished lamely. "Their name is Koo."

Ming added some black pigment. "How big?" she asked.

"I'll find out," I said. "Can I call you?"

"No."

"You're not legal," I guessed.

"Correct."

"If you can't sell some paintings, you will not be able to stay here. And if you can't stay here, you will not be able to make the money you need to save your mother."

"Correct."

I hesitated a moment; I didn't want to change the subject.

And yet, "I brought you a present," I said, pulling a sleek white package out of a rumpled brown grocery bag.

"What is it?"

"It's called Soylent. You mix it with water, then you drink it. You can drink it instead of eating. It's good for you."

"Medicine?"

"No, it's not medicine," I said. "It's food."

"American food has no taste," she said, starting to paint.

"This may be tasteless, but it's good for you," I said. "It's nutritionally complete, and it's convenient. Of course, you might miss chewing."

I couldn't tell if she understood me or not.

"Anyway, I'll leave it for you." I stood up. "Maybe you can try it over rice. You can add soy sauce."

"Okay," she said.

"I mean, I know that sounds odd. To add soy to something that's soy-based. But you can't taste the soy in it. Because, as you said, it's American food and has no taste."

"Okay."

I watched her paint for a while. When she was finally finished, I cleared my throat. "I have a question."

She looked at me; I put my hand up—the headlamp. She switched it off.

"Do you like Rothko?" I asked.

She laughed loudly, surprising me. Then letting her arm fall, she contemplated the bag of Soylent. It gleamed like something left behind by an extraterrestrial.

"Yes, I like him," she said. "In his heart, Rothko is a Chinese painter."

"Interesting."

"His brushstrokes are not so good. But out of very little, he can make a lot."

"I see."

"Also, everything have something else inside. You cannot see it, but it is there."

"You cannot say what exactly is true, you mean. Even 'that square is blue' is complicated. You cannot quite say that."

"Correct. Also, he want you come inside the painting. Not just stand outside. He want you come in."

"And that is Chinese."

"Correct. Like a painting of a Chinese mountain, you can see the path you should walk there. The painter do not want you just stand there and look, then say something."

I considered. "Do you think Rothko would change the colors for a commission? Use happier colors?"

"No."

"And you? Are you willing to?"

"I cannot afford more paint," she said diplomatically. "I have these colors. That's all."

"How about if I bring you some more pigment?" I said. "Or more of those Golden mineral spirit acrylics? How about that? If I bring some, will you try them? In some new colors? Would you like that?"

She contemplated her work. "Okay. But not to make some happy mood."

"I'll bring some real food, too—Chinese food. I'll bring Chinese food."

She looked at me suspiciously. "These colors," she said, "are my heart."

"I see," I said. "Do you mean the black? Or the red? Or the purple?"

"All of them."

"One on top of the other," I said. "You can't see them, but they are all there inside."

"Correct."

"Is that what makes you a better painter than Bei?"

"I am not better than Bei," she said. "But Bei can paint all the painters. I can only paint Rothko." She thought. "Rothko, Rothko," she said. "That is me."

I emailed Johnson and Tina.

> **Ming said maybe. I think it depends on what color you want. If you give me an idea—maybe a paint sample?—I can run it over to her and see what she says.**

For four days, they did not reply. But finally, they wrote:

> **Next month we will see the interior designer. Then we can send sample, OK? The theme is still bubble, but maybe she will like to add some neon to the piece. Or some words. Have you ever heard of an artist, her name is called Jenny Holster? Her work have some strange words coming out all the time? The designer thinks maybe we can put some words like that on those big patches of Rothko.**

> **You mean you might want multimedia?**

> **It is not definite. But maybe we can ask your artist if she can do it? Then if she say yes, you can write the words. Since you are a writer. Of course, we will pay you, too.**

Music to my ears. Still I wrote:

> **You do not have to pay me. Just let me know what you decide.**

I added a smiley face.

.   .   .

Mary Ann Evans was suspended. I petitioned the academic review board, but they were adamant.

"This is such a problem," said the head of the board, adding in a low voice, "Honestly? Honestly, we are seeing a lot of this. Is it everyone? No. It's not everyone. But if we don't crack down, we are going to lose our accreditation, and we'll deserve to. We've sold our souls for their tuition dollars. We have to set an example."

I could see his point. But did he have to set it with Mary Ann Evans? And would I have reported her had I known this would happen? I had many reactions—one inside the other, as Ming would say. As for how much I could do about the situation, that was exactly nothing, especially as all of Mary Ann Evans's accounts were immediately cut off. I could not even email her.

A few days passed. Then I found out through other members of the class that it might be possible to send her a note. So I wrote:

Dear Mary Ann Evans,

I can't tell you how sorry I am that all this has happened. As you are probably aware, an instructor in my position has no choice but to report cases like yours. Still, you should know that you were one of the most wonderful students I have ever had. I know everyone will tell you that you should have stuck to finance but that's wrong. You were right to follow your heart. And a B+ isn't a bad grade either, by the way, whatever people say. The mania over A's is just that—a mania. What counts is whether you've actually learned a few things and have made true progress, which you have. I hope that you will continue to read and study in any way you can— maybe in China, where there are some great English departments

*these days. And though this may be dreaming, I hope you will do so
well at it that you will one day be able to support your parents using
your knowledge of English literature—that you will be able to make
up for the tremendous loss this development must represent. Please
do be in touch if there's any way I can be of help. I would be happy
to explain what happened to anyone who might ask, for example—
that you made a mistake, that's all. Just let me know.*

Your fan,
Rich Lee

Though I did not expect an answer, I was still disappointed
not to receive one. Instead, during office hours the next week,
I found Achilles waiting to see me. He sat down without being
asked.

"I heard what happened with Huiyang," he said.

"I am not at liberty to discuss it."

"She always had such interesting things to say."

I nodded.

"I am not so interesting."

"You have interesting things to say, too."

"I think, not so interesting. That is why I only get a B." He
pulled out his last paper.

"You can bring that grade up," I said. "Do you know about
the Writing Center? They can help you with your English and
also make sure that you know when to footnote. Because that's
really important here in America—to know how to support your
argument with evidence."

"Can they teach me how to be original?"

I answered carefully. "They can teach you to recognize your
originality—to distinguish between thoughts that are your own
and thoughts you've absorbed from others, for example."

He looked down with what appeared genuine dismay; he

had surprisingly long eyelashes. "You know, my father does not believe in literature," he said.

"It's hard to explain its value," I said. "People either get it or don't, it seems."

"He doesn't get it. And he doesn't see why I should take literature classes if all I'm going to do is get B's. He says they should be easier than computer science classes, not harder. Bring up my GPA."

"All the more reason to go to the Writing Center," I said. "If you bring up your writing, you can get better grades. And then you will be happy, and he will be happy, and I will be happy. Because you will have actually learned something."

Achilles nodded. "I will go," he promised. "Scout honor."

"Scout's. Scout's honor."

"Scout's honor. But let me ask you one question."

I braced myself.

"It is not my own question." He shifted in his seat with uncharacteristic embarrassment. "My father asked me to ask you."

"Okay."

"He asked me to ask if you could tell me one original thing to put in my next essay."

"Achilles. Do you really have to ask me that? What am I going to say?"

"I told my father you would say no. I told him it was no use to ask you, Americans are like robots. They say the same things over and over. I also told him I could ask you about an A, but you are not going to answer."

I did not answer.

"I told him Americans are stubborn."

"Correct," I said. "Although it's not just Americans who can be stubborn." I refrained from bringing up Ming, clearly as I could hear her words even as he and I talked: *These colors are my heart.* And, *I can only paint Rothko.* And, *Rothko, Rothko. That is me.*

Achilles grimaced. "I told him."

"And what did he say?"

"He said you would never see that woman painter again."

I froze.

"And you don't have to worry about her mother, either," he went on.

"She has no sick mother," I guessed. "Is that what you're going to say? That she made it all up?"

"Her mother died yesterday," he said.

Why did I stop at the paint store? Why did I spend an entire week's rent on pigments and paints, none of which said "bubble" or "Las Vegas"? Why did I stop in Chinatown, too, and pick up more food than Ming could eat in a month? And why did I stop at a cash machine, and take out $600, bringing our account balance to zero? I rushed around, procuring these things, then drove foot-to-the-floor to Ming's studio.

She was gone. Indeed, every trace of her—the light, the stool, the table, the double boiler, everything—was gone. It was hard to tell in the dark, but it seemed that there wasn't even any paint on the floor. And how cold the floor was; the cold came up through the soles of my shoes. I forded a river of weeds to the house next door; all the curtains were drawn. No one answered the doorbell. There was a spiderweb in the corner of the doorway, with an enormous dead spider in its middle—floating midair, it seemed. Still I rang and rang and rang.

Arabella, when I got back home, said it was just as well.

"I don't mean to sound hard-hearted," she said. "But people disappear every day. And you were going to end up in jail."

Nonetheless, I mourned. "She was so talented. And for her to disappear right after Mary Ann Evans—for them both to go, one, two." I could barely shake my head, I was so upset.

"Do you mean that it's worse when they're talented and sincere? That because they can paint and read, their disappearance is worse than that of my clients?"

"Yes!" I said.

I expected Arabella to take my head off in fine adjectival fashion, but she refrained.

"And you don't ever know, do you, if they were even telling you the truth about everything," I said, after a moment. "Your clients, I mean."

"No," she agreed. "It's just like with your painter. Was her mother really sick? And did she really die? Or did Achilles's father just pull the plug on the deal when he realized that Achilles was not going to be receiving any A's?"

"Or both."

"Or both."

"And was Ming a better painter than Bei? Or did I just think that because Achilles had planted that idea and the lighting was bad?"

Arabella looked sympathetic. "The story was consistent, at least. That makes it more credible. And some of the details. I have never heard such details."

"Mary Ann Evans Wang explaining her name choice, you mean."

"Exactly."

" 'I think when she is inside by herself, with her pen and paper, she is just Mary Ann Evans. I think she is still a girl with some things she like to write down. A girl who has more and more ideas every day.' "

"The cheaters don't make up things like that."

"And what was it Ming said? 'Everything have something else inside. You cannot see it, but it is there.'" I thought. "I'll always remember they said those things."

"They're like presents."

"Yes. But what did I give them?"

"Maybe they will remember that they themselves had something else inside, and once, at least, someone saw that. 'An American teacher, his name is Rich Lee.'"

"Though maybe Mary Ann Evans will mostly remember that I never gave her an A, and Ming that I offered her four hundred dollars and some Soylent."

"You're American, that's all," said Arabella. "They know what that means."

"That we are like robots?"

She laughed thoughtfully—the way she used to laugh sometimes when we were in law school. "That we can miss the forest for the trees. Even if we weren't born here."

I thought about that. "And what's going to happen to them?" I said. "Do we know?"

"We have to move on, Rich." And there it was again—the set of her mouth that was Arabella now. "We have no choice."

"It's like human trafficking and political corruption, you mean," I said. "Late-stage capitalism. Patriarchy. Electoral reform. Bermuda triangles into which your happy life could disappear without a trace."

"It's too much vicarious trauma. As it is, I don't know how much longer I can hold out."

"And I know. You're thirty-two."

She didn't answer.

"I'm sorry. That came out wrong. We have to change something. We do. We will." I gave her a hug. "We really will," I promised again. "But you know, they were keepers of a flame."

She softened enough to say, after a moment, "Like you."

"Except that their winds are higher," I said. "A lot higher. I'll admire them forever."

"Well, maybe they'll keep you going," she said. "Maybe one day you'll put them in your opus."

I laughed, but as we ate some of the Chinese food, I chewed hard. We put the rest of the food in the freezer. She took four phone calls and answered eleven texts. Then I gave her the $600 I'd taken out, which she said she'd deposit back into our account. As for the pigments and paint, she said she'd take care of returning those, too, if I had saved the receipt—which, of course, I had. Our parents, we agreed, would be proud.

No More Maybe

Since my mother-in-law came to visit America, she is quite busy. First, she has to eat many blueberries. Because in China they are expensive! Here they are comparatively cheap. Then she has to breathe the clean air. My husband Wuji and I have lived here for five years, so we are used to the air. But my mother-in-law has to take many fast walks, breathing, breathing. Trying to clean out her lungs, she says, trying to get all the healthy oxygen inside her. She also has to look at the sky.

"*So blue!*" she says during the daytime. "*I have not seen such a blue since I was a child.*"

At nighttime, she says, "*Look at the stars. Look! Look!*"

She has to post pictures of the stars on WeChat for her friends. And she has to take some English-language classes. Because these classes are expensive in China! she says. Here they are free.

She thinks this is very strange.

"*Why are they free?*" she says. She says, "*America is a capitalist country. What about so-called* market force?" "Market force" sticks out of her Chinese like a rock in a path. "*And what about so-called* invisible hands?" she goes on, and there it is—another rock.

"Invisible hand," my father-in-law says. Because he is the professor in the family, and the one who knows everything.

In fact, my mother-in-law only just learned about the invisible hand two days ago. Even yesterday she called Adam Smith "Alan Smith." But in China, she was a volleyball coach. She has a lot of self-confidence. She talks with her chin in the air. Even though she is retired, she uses only the top half of her bifocals. It is as if she is still watching some game, looking for weakness on the other side of the net. And sure enough, look: already she has found something fake about America. America calls itself capitalist, but no one should be fooled. It is China that is capitalist.

"You know what free classes are?" she says. *"Free classes are socialism!"*

If my father-in-law likes to make points, my mother-in-law likes to score points.

Now my father-in-law hides his face in his rice bowl. Only his chopsticks move. It is as if he is trying to scratch a small, small message inside the bowl. One line. Two lines. Still scratching. We think maybe he cannot explain the free English lessons either, or maybe he just needs time to prepare his explanation. He was an outstanding thinker when he was young. But since he retired, he has crazy wild hair like that conductor Seiji Ozawa, and his thinking is crazy wild, too.

We talk to help him. Try to make him comfortable, try to smooth things over.

"America is very strange," I say.

"It is not socialism," Wuji says. *"It is capitalism with American characteristics."*

"It is politically correct capitalism," I say.

Because this is what we know how to do. We know how to say something true enough to hide a bigger truth. We know how to hide people's weakness, how to protect them.

Of course, when he was young, my father-in-law also protected people. Every day there was a new kind of craziness, every day a new kind of corruption. He had a lot to manage. Still, no matter how bad the situation got, he protected us and a lot of other people, too. It was a big talent he had, a real strength. We all remember it and appreciate what he did. But now that he is older, he sometimes scatters seed for the chickens, as they say. He stirs things up, instead of calming things down. Maybe this is what couples do when they do not have sex. That is what Wuji says.

Wuji is full of such theories these days because I am too pregnant for sex.

Now my father-in-law's chopsticks stop scratching. He lowers his bowl.

"Maybe the government watches to see who comes to the English lessons," he says. "Maybe that is why they are free."

"That is crazy!" my mother-in-law says. "Watching everyone is a lot of work. Do you think American people will do that kind of work? Only Chinese people will do it. American people are lazy."

"Maybe it is a trap," my father-in-law says.

"What is there to trap?" my mother-in-law says. "Who wants to know if I am taking English lessons? No one. I am nobody. No one is interested."

"Everyone knows the government here spies on people, just like in China," my father-in-law says. "Look at that Oliver Stone movie, what was it called?"

We would tell him the answer if we could remember. But actually, he is quicker than we are.

"Snowden," he says. If he is amazed himself that he remembers, he does not show it. "They spy here, too. They do."

He reaches for some steamed fish from the dish in the middle of the table. My mother-in-law takes her glasses off, as if the score is tied and she is ready to fight the other coach. So now poor Wuji has to say something. He is kind of like the ump.

"Yes, *they spy in America*," he says. "*But it is not just like China. Here there are many more laws to protect the common citizen.*"

Wuji is careful because even an ump must know how to handle my father-in-law. He knows he must first agree with his father and only afterward disagree.

Still my father-in-law argues. "*Every government is the same,*" he says. "*What if that person is so-called illegal immigrant, right? You go to the free English classes. Or you pick someone up there. Then what? Then they catch you.*"

And suddenly we think, maybe my father-in-law is right. We should be careful. Because sometimes I meet my mother-in-law at the library, and while my father- and mother-in-law are here on tourist visas, Wuji and I have just fallen out of status. Meaning that if we don't leave we will soon be illegal immigrants.

As for how we fell out of status, that was all because Wuji applied for a green card. He applied for a green card because his school said they would sponsor him and because they said the work visa rules could change anytime. Especially these days the U.S.-China relationship is so bad, they said. You never know what will happen. So okay, he applied. But on the application form, he wrote that he has no middle name, that he has just one name, Wuji. *Why did you do that?* I asked him. *On your J-1 visa application you wrote that your first name is Wu, and your middle name is Ji.* But he said he forgot that he wrote that before, and anyway no one ever calls him just Wu. His name is Wuji.

As a result, the immigration people said his application was incomplete, also that he tried to so-called defraud them. So now he has to hire a lawyer, her name is Arabella Li. She says she can help; she speaks Chinese; we like her very much. But still, we see the stories on the internet. People are being stopped! People on buses. People in hospitals. My father-in-law says we should not talk too much to outside people, but of course we do not talk too much to them anyway, because this is a city. People do not talk here, they honk. *Honk, honk, honk! You are in my way!* they say. If they talk, they yell. *What the fuck are you doing? Don't you speak English?* But these days, we talk even less. In fact, we are starting to think maybe my mother-in-law should not go to that English-language class when she says to my father-in-law, *"If you think you can stop me from studying English, you can't! This is America! You can't!"*

Her eyes glare so hard at him that he ducks back quick into his rice bowl. Not as though he is backing down—more as though he has thought of something else and has some more scratching to do.

So that is score one point for my mother-in-law.

Actually, English has no use for her. But my mother-in-law has always wished she could speak English like my father-in-law. It was just her bad luck that she took the college entrance exam in 1977—the first time you could take it after the Cultural Revolution. She is still talking about how fierce the competition was, and how two generations both had to take the examination together, all the teachers and all the students, side by side. She says today she would probably get a top score and go to a top college like my father-in-law, because he was smart but also just lucky that he did so well. And he agrees. Some people did well who were not so smart, he says, and some people did not do well, though they were very smart. He agrees that today my mother-in-law would probably be outstanding, especially since if you don't like your score you can always try again. So she would probably try eight, nine, ten times! Until she succeeded. She is that way.

In other words, she is not like Wuji or me, who were not outstanding and did not work so hard either. We went to third-tier colleges and wished we had scored higher, of course, but did not care so much. Wuji says maybe this was because there was some money in his father's family, and even I knew ever since high school that Wuji and I would get married. So both of us knew we would not have to work crazy hard just to live. Also, his parents are kind of like a fire generation. After a fire generation, it is only natural to have a water generation.

Actually, my mother-in-law could relax a little, too. But she was always crazy worried when she was growing up, and now she says, since my father-in-law's English is declining, maybe she can catch him. She says maybe if her English goes up while his goes down, they can meet at kind of like an intersection.

"And then what?" I ask.

"Then I will wave and say hi," she says. *"Then I will say,* How are you, Professor? I can speak English, too."

It is absurd, but it is also sad; I feel sorry for my mother-in-law. It is as if she were born inside a box, so that she can never really stand up straight. My mother always says I have pity for people I should not pity, and she is probably right. I am too soft. After all, my mother cannot really stand up straight, either, and at least my mother-in-law has plenty to eat. My mother does not have plenty to eat. Still, when my father-in-law looks up from his rice, ready to fight with my mother-in-law again, I quickly say, *"The baby is kicking!"*

He laughs a little then, as if to say, *You Chinese girls are so obvious.* And, *Why does everyone manage me?* But he lets go, too. He does not say anything because the baby is why they came. They came because Wuji and I are having a baby, and because they could afford to come. They are not like my mother, who was okay when my father was alive but now can only Skype. Besides, no one wants to upset the baby—and if I am upset, the baby will be upset. That is how Chinese people think. One thing always affects something else.

So for now we have peace. I reach down and tell the baby, *Shh, shh.* He kicks hard on one side, a real boy. Everyone is so happy I am having a boy. And on the other side, there is his round head. It is soft-hard, kind of like a volleyball.

The English teacher recommends an English-learning app but my father-in-law says, *"Do not install it!"* Though my mother-in-law can only say a few words so far, already he has had enough of her learning English to compete with him. Also he thinks the U.S. government can trace us through the app. But one day while she is taking a nap, he picks up her phone, and there it is. A little orange square on the screen.

"Did you help her?" my father-in-law asks.

I nod because, in fact, he already knows the answer. My mother-in-law cannot upload, download anything, after all, and Wuji would not dare defy his father. So I have no choice. But I nod very gently, with both hands on top of my belly.

"No one can stop her anyway," he says then. Meaning, *At least you answered honestly and did not insult my intelligence.*

I nod again. *"She will never stop,"* I say. I say this simply, as if dropping a stone in a pond.

"That is true," he says then, and his manner is simple, too. It is as if he is just happy to have this little conversation—to have someone agree with him, the way everyone used to do. He sips some tea.

Often still I drive my mother-in-law to the beautiful library, with the glass walls and the café and the green grass all around it.

There is so much grass all around it! In China, one day you see *chai* written on the old buildings, and the next day they are sure enough destroyed. And the day after that, a glass tower springs up like bamboo. But none of the towers have grass; they are all squeezed together as if they have been built on a subway at rush hour. Here there is more elbow room. Here there is grass. And here there are all kinds of people, including Black people and a lot of people you cannot say what color they are, you can only say they like books. My mother-in-law does not mind them. Every day she finds a DVD to check out, so she can practice her English some more after class. Then I pick her up so she can cook for me.

Actually, I help a lot when she cooks for me—especially, I help with the shopping and the chopping. But she does the planning and the cooking, because my baby will be born in two months now, and she wants me to eat all kinds of special food. On the outside, my mother-in-law is a modern sportswoman. Inside, though, she is a traditional type. So she gives me American prenatal vitamins and calcium and DHA, but also steamed egg porridge with rice, and millet porridge, too. A glass of milk, red dates, fruit, and nuts every day; tofu and bean sprouts every other day. And a lot of soups: pork rib soup with lotus seeds or Chinese yam; hen soup with mushrooms and more red dates; soybean and pork trotter soup; and even swallow's-nest soup, which is very expensive. Because I am in my seventh month and my body has heated up, and because she has an app that says it's okay, I am also allowed to have some cooling foods I could not have before. For example, I can have some of her blueberries with a little ice cream. In China, there are pregnant women who eat a lot of blueberries, they think it will make their baby's eyes shiny and round. But my mother-in-law says that is illogical thinking and will only let me have a few.

Very important, too, everyone wants me to rest. *"Take it easy,"* they all say. *"Go slow, go slow."* And, *"Rest, rest."* As if anyone can rest when my mother-in-law is cooking and learning English.

Although my father-in-law is not as busy as my mother-in-law, he feels he has to keep up with her. Of course, he used to be very active, too. Wuji says his father used to have so many ideas, he had to keep a piece of paper next to his bed at night to write them all down; only then could he go back to sleep. And now he still keeps a piece of paper next to his bed. But in the morning, it is almost always blank. If he writes something, he says he cannot read it, the writing is too unclear. When he watches my mother-in-law's DVDs, too, he nods as if he still understands everything, but then he complains. Why does she have to bring so many DVDs home? And why a new one every night, each one with faster English than the last? Another day, he complains she is so active, she moves her legs even in her sleep.

"As if she is going somewhere!" he says.

Still, to keep up with her, my father-in-law moves things around. For example, he does not think the feng shui of our apartment is very good. So he moves a bookcase to the entrance. The bookcase is not that tall, only chest high. But never mind, it is a help, he says—a small wall inside the front door will block evil spirits from entering. Then he sees that our bookshelves are not well organized. So one by one, he takes our books and puts them in order. Now we cannot find anything and have to walk around the bookcase to go out.

And today he wants to clean everything, too.

"No need to clean anything!" we say. *"Everything is clean already!"*

All the same, he cleans the fridge. Then he cleans the stove.

Then he cleans the microwave. Then he fixes the bicycles: he oils Wuji's bike chain; he adjusts our brakes; he repairs my bike basket. Actually, there was nothing wrong with my bike basket. Now it is pushed so far to the back, I cannot clip my light onto it. But no one can ask him to put it back to where it was before, or he will say, *"Don't tell me what to do."* We have to do it quietly, by ourselves.

We are just glad when he is finished.

One night in bed, Wuji says, *"I told them they can stay as long as they like."*

"How could you promise that?" I say. *"We do not even know if we can stay here. What if you don't get a green card? What if we get deported instead?"*

"That lawyer Arabella *will arrange everything. You'll see."*

"And how could you promise without talking to me? That's another thing," I say. *"Is that respectful communication? Is that how a husband ought to behave? Does no one consider my feelings? Does my opinion not count at all?"*

Before I was pregnant, I did not talk this way. But it is as if my belly is pressing down on my nerves; the bigger my belly, the more I say. Of course, Wuji is sorry. But do I remember? he asks. Before we got married I agreed that his parents could come live with us when they got old. Also, he agreed that my mother could come. Remember? Because thanks to the one-child policy, we were both only children. Our parents were our responsibility. We had no choice. Yes, he should still have told me he was going to raise the topic. But he didn't have that opportunity, he says. Because he was trying to calm his parents down.

"Again," I say, though inside I am happy at least he remembers his promise about my mother.

"Yes, again," he says. *"That is my life's real job. And now I have to calm you down, too. My poor pregnant wife."*

He puts his hands on my moving belly. The baby kicks him. *"Hey! So strong!"* he laughs. And then I say, *"I understand,"* because I do really feel sorry for him, that he has so many people to calm down. My mother always believed I would end up a servant to everyone. *Soft and capable, the worst combination,* she used to say. *You will serve everyone, and no one will serve you.* Was that true? Maybe it is a mistake to tell Wuji he is right. Maybe it is a mistake to admit my pregnancy is making me talk crazy. Maybe it is a mistake to say I do not want to make trouble for him. But still I say, *"Poor Wuji."* Maybe because inside I think this is the best way for my child.

"If they move in with us, maybe they can help us buy a bigger place," he says. *"There is that advantage to."*

"That is true," I say. *"Assuming that we can stay. There is indeed that advantage."*

"Plus, even if we buy a place together, they might not move in right away," Wuji says. *"Maybe they won't, right? We don't know."*

"Maybe," I agree. *"You're right. There's a lot we don't know."*

"Maybe they won't really like it here," Wuji goes on. *"Maybe they'll miss China and want to go back. Or maybe they'll go back and forth. A lot of people do that—go back and forth."*

"Maybe they will, too," I say. *"You're right. A lot of people do do that."*

"Plus, maybe my father will be fine, right? We don't know. Maybe my mother will be able to handle him herself."

"Maybe," I say. *"And maybe she will indeed be able to handle him. You're right. It's hard to say. Maybe everything will work out."*

Maybe.

In China, I had a clothes store. Not a very big store—in fact, quite a small store. Still, my friends would make clothes, and I would sell them, and we always made a little money. Because I figured everything out so well, my friends said. Because I made everything so smooth. But actually, their designs were outstanding, too. They were especially good at coats thanks to a friend who taught them everything, her name was Tricia. We were all so sad when she got sick. Of course, she was a master designer, and my friends were only students. Still, their work was always improving.

Then Wuji went to America for his doctorate, and I went with him, and now my store is like a beautiful picture I saw on Taobao a long time ago. At first, my friends said they would send me clothes so I could still have a store.

"Okay, I try. Maybe Americans will like the clothes," I said.

But later I said, *"I think maybe the Americans do not like them."*

And now I say, *"For some reason, the Americans just do not like our clothes."*

No more maybe, in other words. Because that is just what happens. One day it is maybe, and then you just know.

My father-in-law says maybe he will wash Wuji's car.

Of course, he knows Wuji bought a silver-colored car. In fact, he has been in Wuji's silver car several times. Once he tested the air conditioning. Once he told Wuji he was surprised there was no screen to show you how far away you were from the car behind you. Because all the children of his friends who had cars had that kind of screen, he said. Very useful. Of course, he understands that, in terms of technology, the United States is often quite backward. He knows that in the United States many people still use cash, for example. Still, he was surprised.

Wuji agreed then that the United States is backward. But in this case, his car had no screen, he said, because his car was a used car.

"Ah," his father said.

"My car is an old model. Too old to have that kind of screen," Wuji said.

"Ah," his father said again. Then he said, *"It is because you are only a lecturer. It is because you are not a professor."*

"Yes," Wuji said. *"A lecturer's salary is quite low."*

He was calm because, in fact, he already knew what his father thought. Also, in his heart he would like to be a professor like his father, too.

Still, my mother-in-law said, *"Wuji is just as successful as the other sons! He got his PhD in America! And at least he is not a volleyball coach, right?"*

"Wuji jumps like an elephant," my father-in-law said. *"He is so slow he has to wave the flies away; he cannot swat them. How could he have become a volleyball coach?"*

If Wuji was not the ump in the family, maybe he would feel bad. But instead he calmly said, *"I am not a coach and I am not a professor. I cannot jump, and truly, I am slow. But I am going to be a father."*

And my father-in-law agreed then that Wuji had accomplished at least one important thing. Because a child born in America is a U.S. citizen. And a U.S. citizen can do anything!

Of course, that was assuming the baby is indeed born here.

Now my father-in-law says he has washed Wuji's car. But when we go out to the parking lot to admire it, Wuji's car does not look clean and shiny.

"Beautiful!" we say, though we can see that it is not only just as old as before but still quite dirty.

Then my mother-in-law whispers, *"Look!"*

And that is when we see that the silver car across from Wuji's car is all nice and clean. Should we say, *Wuji's car is a* Nissan, *that car is a* Toyota?

Not even my mother-in-law will try to score that point.

For two days, we say nothing. I knit some baby clothes, I help cook. I eat and eat. My mother-in-law has found a special oatmeal place near our house and is interested in the grain, which is milled very fine. It is not like regular oatmeal, she says. It seems more like millet to her. She serves it to me with soy sauce and sesame oil.

"Good for the baby," she says.

Meanwhile the shiny car does not move. Every time we go out, it is still there in the parking lot. Clean.

The third day my father-in-law washes Wuji's car.

We go outside again.

"Beautiful!" we say as if we have never said that before. We stand on the cracked asphalt.

My father-in-law makes a kind of flower blossom with his lips. Then suddenly his eyes light up and he says, *"Is there another silver car I can clean tomorrow?"*

We laugh and laugh and laugh. We laugh because it is funny. We laugh because we are relieved. And we laugh because we want to cry. Because there he is—the professor he was before his hair got so long. The professor who knew how to handle every kind of situation. The professor who made jokes and did not argue all day with his wife.

So what to do now about the first clean car? Should we write a note and put it on the windshield? And if we do, what should the note say?

"It should say, We are so sorry we cleaned the wrong car, but we are from China," my father-in-law suggests. *"It should say,* We older people especially only recognize a few brands of cars. For example, BMW."

We laugh.

My father-in-law says, *"Or else we can write,* Those Japanese cars, you know, they all look the same."

We laugh again.

But Wuji thinks it would be a mistake to write anything.

"You are right, we can write a note," he says. *"That is one approach. But American people don't like people to touch their things. If they find a dent or a scratch or anything wrong, they will complain. If they can, they will even sue you. And then maybe the immigration authorities will find out. So I recommend we not write anything."*

Everyone is quiet. Will my father-in-law feel Wuji is telling him what to do?

"Don't tell me what to do," he says.

But in the end, he follows Wuji's recommendation and does not write anything.

The next day the doorbell rings. Outside there is a short Black man with a cardboard box. We cannot see him too well because of the bookcase and also the screen door. But we can see that, actually, he is not really Black. Actually, he is a tan color, kind of like a piece of leather. He is wearing blue jeans and a T-shirt, and he is very similar in size to my father-in-law, except for his chest and shoulders and arms. My father-in-law is quite thin. This man's muscles bulge out. He is wearing gold earrings, too, kind of like the Buddha, only with both in one ear, instead of one in each ear.

"Hi, my name is Jeff," he says through the screen. "I heard you cleaned my car."

He looks friendly. Still, my father-in-law stands between the bookcase and the door as if this Jeff is an evil spirit the bookcase might not be strong enough to block. My father-in-law is holding on hard to the apartment doorknob. He leaves the screen door shut.

"We did not clean anything," he says, speaking slowly and clearly.

Jeff raises his eyebrows up so high, three creases appear on his forehead. The rolls of skin between them look like dragons.

"But our neighbors said they saw you out with a bucket and a sponge," he says. "I just wanted to say thank you."

Out of all this, my mother-in-law understands only the "thank you." But just as she has been practicing in English class, she cries, "You're welcome!" in response—spiking the words like a volleyball across the room. They are loud and clear; her pronunciation is perfect, she could be the voice on the Learn English app.

Does Jeff feel encouraged by her words? Anyway, he starts again.

"I just wanted to say thank you," he repeats. "I brought you a present."

We think maybe my father-in-law needs more time to prepare, but we cannot help him.

And sure enough, he says then, slow but clear, "Is that really your car?"

Maybe he is just surprised—a Black man with a newer car than Wuji's. And who knows? Maybe this Black man has a screen to show him what is behind his car when he is backing up.

But Jeff thinks something else. "Did I steal it? Is that what you mean?" he says.

"If you find something wrong, we did not do it," my father-in-law says firmly.

"There's nothing wrong," Jeff says.

"We did not wash your car," my father-in-law says. His hand is still holding the doorknob. "You have no proof."

"Is that so." Jeff gives my father-in-law a funny look. Then finally he says, "You know what I am going to do? I am going to leave this cake here anyway."

He opens the screen door.

"Stop!" my father-in-law says.

But one foot is already inside the apartment. Jeff holds the screen door still with his shoulder. Then he opens the lid of the cake box. He props the box on top of his knee as he writes something quick in the icing with his finger. Then he closes the box and licks his fingertip.

"Here." He hands the box to my father-in-law.

My father-in-law does not move.

"Take it," Jeff says.

Still my father-in-law does not move.

"I said, take it," Jeff says. "Take it."

"Take it," Wuji says from behind the bookcase, in Chinese.

"Don't tell me what to do," my father-in-law says. But finally he takes the box.

Jeff leaves, muttering something we cannot hear.

We lock the knob lock and the bolt lock behind him, then put on the chain lock, too.

At dinner, we can see that, though the cake originally said THANK YOU! on it in fancy blue letters, on top of that is now something else.

" 'Fucking A's,' " my father-in-law reads. " 'Fucking A's.' " He frowns.

"I think it means 'Fucking Asians,' " Wuji says.

My father-in-law looks blank.

"The Blacks do not like us," Wuji explains. *"Because we are too smart."*

"Also, we do not spend money like crazy," my mother-in-law says.

"They are afraid China is going to surpass America," I say.

" 'Fucking Asians,' " my father-in-law says. Then suddenly

he says, *"I saw that there were two cars. But I thought Wuji's car must be the new car."*

He says, *"I was confused."*

He says, *"A lot of English I do not understand anymore."*

Then he stops. And of course, my mother-in-law should be happy. Finally she and my father-in-law have met at an intersection. Finally she can wave and say, "Hi! How are you, Professor? I can speak English, too!" But instead she is looking down through the bottom of her bifocals. Instead, she is batting back tears.

No one moves. Only the baby is turning over and over, as if he is in a washing machine.

After a while, Wuji says, *"We should give the cake back."*

"We should serve the cake into that man's windshield!" my mother-in-law says. She holds her hands as if she is ready to toss the cake in the air and punch it.

"Good idea!" Wuji says.

On the way out of the apartment, he carries the cake up high, as if he is in a parade.

"Make sure you hit the Toyota*!"* my father-in-law jokes. *"Make sure you don't hit the* Nissan*!"*

Everyone laughs.

But Jeff's car is not there. So when we come back in, we still have the cake.

"Maybe we should scrape off the frosting and see how it looks," I say.

"Good idea," Wuji says.

We scrape off the words, and sure enough, the cake looks better. My mother-in-law says, *"Let's have it with blueberries!"* And in the end, even I get three berries.

Then we turn on the DVD player. The DVD today is *The Sound of Music.*

My father-in-law nods. He has seen this movie before, after all, and knows the whole story. He is prepared to explain everything. Of course, in fact, we have all seen the movie. In fact, we all know about the children and Maria, and about the brave father who manages the situation so well.

Still I say, "The Sound of Music!" as if it is something new. My father-in-law smiles.

Am I being too obvious? Am I insulting his intelligence?

"You will be a good mother," he says. "You will manage things very well for your child." He stops. "Then one day your child will manage you."

And now it is my turn to cry. I cry because he is right. I cry because I am sorry. And I cry because there he is, one more time, underneath the crazy wild hair. The professor who knows everything—the professor we will all miss.

Detective Dog

"No politics, just make money," Betty's mother, Tina, liked to say. And when it came to China: "See nothing, hear nothing, say nothing. Do you hear me?"

"I hear nothing," Betty had wanted to say sometimes. Or, well, many times, really. But instead she said nothing and, as directed, made a lot of money. After all, she was the good daughter.

And that was how it was that when umbrellas took over Hong Kong, she had a nice place in Vancouver. And that was how it was, too, that when racism took over Vancouver, she could up and move to New York. It was convenient to be rich, you had to say. In New York, she didn't even have to buy an apartment. She and her husband and two boys just moved into her sister's old place, which they liked so much that they bought the apartment next door, and then the apartment on the other side, too. They figured they'd turn the extra kitchens into bathrooms.

"Buy another one!" bellowed her father Johnson over Face-Time. "Buy the whole floor!" Johnson, who had always loved acquisition, had recently started a file called "Ghost Towns of the World." One of these days, Betty's husband Quentin said, Johnson was going to buy them all up. Corner the market.

"Every time he says, 'Too many people in China,' I can hear his pitch," said Quentin with a hint of awe in his voice; he did think Johnson a genius. "*Now anyone who don't like where they live can move somewhere else. No problem.* It's a hit."

Betty laughed. "Well, maybe out there somewhere there's a ghost town for us, too."

"Maybe." Quentin seemed to be considering this seriously.

But never mind. "Three apartments for four people is enough," Betty told Johnson now, smiling but firm. "We are not buying any more." And when he continued arguing, she shrank him down from full screen to half.

In Vancouver, people had complained about her. *The Chinese are taking over,* they said, *the Chinese are buying up everything.* That's when they weren't yelling, *Go back to where you came from!* Betty tried to reason with them. If she were the sort of Chinese who wanted to buy in Vancouver but not live in Vancouver, if she were the sort of Chinese responsible for Vancouver's empty houses and empty apartments, how could she be standing right there for them to yell at, right? And she was not an invader, by the way, she was a parent. She was a Hong Kong parent worried that her older boy would go out protesting on the street with a yellow umbrella. And then what? Then he would get tear-gassed, that's what. And by the way, tear gas wasn't so great for the baby they'd adopted during the 2012 unrest, either.

But a Chinese was a Chinese was a Chinese to them.

"When people want to yell, all they can hear is what they want to yell," Tina liked to say.

Which was why after five years Betty and her family finally moved from Vancouver to New York, where all anybody said was *We are so happy you are willing to chip in for the new elevator,* and *Did you know we will soon need a new roof?*

"Yes," she said. "Yes, yes." And, "Anything else?"

Now in the gilt lobby mirror by the striped chairs, she looked happier to herself. A little plump, it was true; she did not like her chin joining up with her neck as if they just needed to be together. But she liked her short-short hair and her cheery cashmere hoodies, and look how she could just push her over-size sunglasses up onto her head—no tear-gas-puffy eyes to hide. When the Hong Kong police stormed the universities, she and Quentin and the boys sat on their lilac leather couch and watched on their computers, lined up like ladies in a hair salon. One, two, three, four. Even when COVID came, at least they worried about sickness and death but not jail.

Of course, Theo, now sixteen, was upset all the time. All his old Hong Kong friends were involved in the protests; sometimes he thought he spotted them on his screen, although it was hard to say for sure because they'd grown up and because everyone was wearing gas masks. Really, it was crazy to take screenshots and zoom in the way he did—running his fingers through the long hair on top of his head and scratching the short hair on the sides. Is that Victor? Is that Pak? Don't you think that's Pak? he would say. Or, That must be Wing-man, I recognize that scar.

As for whether Theo would have stayed so riled up were ambulance sirens not going and going was hard to say. It shook Betty up, too, heaven knew, that even nine-year-old Robert knew "ventilator" was spelled with an "-or." She was just glad he wasn't sure how to spell "morgue," although, imaginative and intense as he was, he was writing a story with dancing morgues in it for the mystery unit in his English class. It was a murder mystery, he told her, in his quiet, unnerving way; he was not like the other boys at all. The last story he wrote was about mind-reading hats that looked like regular fur hats but then stole your thoughts right through your scalp. How they did it was the mystery.

Betty herself almost never told stories, but having read a book about how Western creativity grew up like a flower out of the soil of curiosity, she was trying to at least ask a lot of questions. And not just any questions but the right questions, meaning, not questions like What do you mean you were out all night? Where were you?—the sort of questions she was prone to ask Theo. She asked Robert questions that showed interest. Like, Do the morgues ever stop dancing? Playfulness, too—she had underlined that in her book. She tried to ask questions that showed playfulness.

"Do the morgues ever stop dancing?" she asked now.

"Yes, and when they stop dancing, all the people are going to come out, alive again," Robert said. He had had a perfect bowl cut before he started trimming his hair himself. Now he looked as if he'd been transitioning into Mark Zuckerberg, only to change his mind halfway.

"And then what?" Betty asked. She relied a little heavily on *And then what,* she knew, but she couldn't think of anything else to ask. "Will they breathe okay?"

"Yes, but they'll be a little dizzy," he said.

"Interesting." Another thing she said too much, but oh well. "And what will the people say?"

"They'll say, It's great to be alive, what happened to my phone?" he said. "But I'm not sure what the morgues will say back." He touched his tongue to his nose; he had a tongue like a dog's.

"How about 'We're not responsible for personal effects'?" she said—thinking that he would not know what that meant. But who knew where he'd picked it up, he did know, Robert being an avid chaser of what he called true facts. He retracted his tongue and laughed as he wrote—by hand, as he liked to, with a pencil:

"It's great to be alive, what happened to my phone?"

"We're not responsible for personal effects."

"What kind of a morgue are you? Didn't your mother teach you anything?"

"No, we're the worst of the worst. Because of the virus, they had to scrape the bottom of the barrel."

Betty laughed. "Great! Done!" she said.

"I still have to figure out what the mystery is."

"The mystery is how all of this could be happening," she said.

Robert's handwriting had deteriorated since he had come to the U.S., but if Betty had ever had the energy to nag him about it, she did not anymore. Remote learning! Robert's school theoretically went from 8:25 to 2:25 but that included ninety minutes of independent learning, thirty minutes for lunch, and thirty minutes for recess. Why did the kids get a break when it was the parents who needed a break? And how could the teachers still be complaining about how much they worked? Why did they not even make the kids show their faces on Zoom? How could it be okay for them to just show their names? Right now, for example, Theo was playing *Liberate Hong Kong* on his computer while in trigonometry class. How could that be okay?

"You realize that plays about morgues are not normal, right?" said Theo, looking up from his game.

"So? It's not normal to be jamming virtual surveillance cameras as if you're a real protester either," Robert said.

"I am so a real protester."

"The kind who shouts *ga yau* from the couch, you mean."

"If I were there, I'd be on the streets," said Theo.

"Not now during COVID, you wouldn't."

"Even now, I'd be there. I'd be at the malls. And as soon

as things started up again, I'd be throwing petrol bombs, don't worry."

"You can tell we're not really brothers," Robert observed to the air. "I would never say something violent like that."

"Adopted brothers are still brothers." Quentin's nostrils flared when he was being serious, and today this did make the boys settle down. When Theo started up *Animal Crossing*, with its desert islands full of protest banners and target images of Carrie Lam, Quentin was even able to say, "Aren't you supposed to be in class?"

Theo switched sullenly back to full screen.

But what Robert had said was true. He wasn't violent like his older brother. He didn't say the sorts of things that made Betty and Quentin thank the Lord they were safely on the other side of the world, far away from what their friends in Hong Kong called "protest trouble." *This generation, they are like firecrackers, one explodes, and the whole string goes,* they said in WeChat posts. And, *Do they realize they are not dealing with a paper tiger? This is a real tiger, with teeth. They are going to get themselves killed.* There were friends who approved of the protests. *I give my kids food every day to take with them to share. Bottled water is also important, and when they come home, I wash their clothes right away to get the smell out.* But others wished they had gotten their kids interested in sports. *Better for their health, better for their college applications, better for everything,* they wrote. *However, you need to be athletic.*

"You know what your grandmother always says," Betty told Theo. "No politics, just make money. That's good advice."

But where she had listened, Theo did not. Theo was her biological child, but his outrage reminded her of her older sister, Bobby—Bobby, who had, unbelievably, tried to send them a letter last week. After all these years! Betty was shocked. And who sent real letters anymore, much less a letter via a personal family messenger? Only Bobby would somehow enlist Uncle Arnie through his Shanghai factory, as if they were all in a spy movie. She had apparently even instructed Uncle Arnie to hide the letter in his shoe, which he did not do in the end because he was afraid airport security would make him take his shoes off. Instead, he tore it up and flushed it down a toilet—because he knew it was trouble, he told Betty later, and because he didn't want to upset Tina and Johnson. As for why he had even told Betty that there was letter if he'd torn it up, he said it was because he was too honest, but Betty knew the truth: there was something in the letter that he couldn't keep inside. He swore he hadn't read the thing before tearing it up, but of course he had, Betty knew. He had! And where was Bobby? she demanded. Her parents had been dying to know for years, the whole family had. Uncle Arnie insisted he didn't know. The letter and some instructions had been left for him in a plain envelope, he said, and there had been no clue even on the security cameras of who had snuck it into the factory.

"Anyway, 'no politics, just make money.' Isn't that what your mother always says?" he finished.

Meaning, the letter had to do with politics. If Betty ever wrote a mystery, it would be about a world without politics and what a mystery it was that we had to have them when everyone hated them.

Meanwhile, it was amazing how many things her mother's words could mean. To Theo, for example, they meant that she and Quentin were going to hell.

"Is that how you want to live your life?" he yelled. "Is that your motto? Just make money?"

"All it means is, that is the way to be safe," Betty said. "It is like 'The tallest tree catches all the wind.' That does not mean a short tree is a good tree. It means that a tall tree pays a price for sticking up, that's all."

She did not know how to tell Theo that when a son yelled at a mother, the mother cried for a week. She kept that inside, though she knew Robert knew anyway. Never mind that he was the adopted child—Robert would shoot her that quick look of his, like a flash of light in the dark that could only be a signal. He understood her while all Theo understood was his opinion of the family.

"I hate you," he would say, for example. "I hate your values and your way of life, and I do not respect you. What have you ever done but look the other way no matter what was going on? Did you ever tell the truth? Did you ever speak up? No matter who was being killed and who was being jailed? You know what the word is for people like you? The word is 'complicit.' I bet you don't care about the Uighurs either."

So he ranted—ranted and ranted—as if he had not been the first to complain when Betty said that because of COVID, there would be no maid and no cook. Even though there was pretty good takeout in New York and she knew how to make a few dishes herself, he objected. And now every day Theo brought up colleges farther away than the colleges they'd talked about before. Colleges in Alaska. Scotland. New Zealand. He wasn't applying until the fall, but still they discussed the possibilities constantly.

"How about a semester in Antarctica?" Quentin suggested at dinner. "There must be semesters abroad in Antarctica."

Betty glared. Robert cleared the table. Quentin winked but kept going.

"You can study penguins," he said, showing Theo an article on his phone. "Did you know they poop out so much laughing gas that their researchers go cuckoo?"

"They do?" said Robert. "Let me see, that's so cool."

Theo, though, stood up without a single bite of the Oreo mousse cake Betty had made from a recipe he'd found and especially asked for her to try.

COVID. COVID was making people crazy.

Should they buy one more apartment after all? For the sake of family sanity? Quentin and Betty talked it over. But just when they decided yes, Theo needed more space, more independence, more something, he got the hang of online poker. Betty had heard about online poker from her friend Susu, whose son had learned to do this and made a lot of money, which you wouldn't think would upset Susu but did. Because once her son made a lot of money, she lost control of him, she said; she just hoped he wasn't doing drugs. Hearing which, Betty had shaken her head in sympathy—and later, when she told Quentin the story, she had said how glad she was that Theo was no good at math.

"Although sometimes a quick calculation can mean millions," Quentin pointed out.

"But still," she said. "Poor Susu."

"Poor Susu is right," said Quentin then.

And now it seemed that Theo was better at math than they thought.

"I underestimated myself," he said. "I guess I did need to work harder." And: "All I needed was to put more time into it."

Time that he had now, thanks to COVID.

It was hard to know whether to cheer or to worry when he won a hundred dollars. Then he won a thousand dollars. Then he lost five hundred dollars.

"Thank god he got a lesson," Quentin said. "In Macau, at least you have to book a hotel room to gamble. On the computer you can gamble with no overhead."

"No disincentive," said Betty.

Then Theo won five thousand dollars. Then he won ten thousand dollars. Then he won another ten thousand dollars.

"Beginner's luck," he said modestly. And to be sure that he didn't gamble away all he'd won in that little run of luck, he bought a car.

"A car?" said Betty. "How did you buy a car?"

"With cash, that's how," said Robert, when Theo didn't answer.

He'd chosen a little red Miata with a pop-off roof; it got great mileage. Susu said it was an excellent deal, too, a real COVID deal, as she knew because her son had cosigned the papers—which he could do because he was old enough, and which he had thought was okay because, unlike most city kids, Theo had gotten his license so he could go see friends in the suburbs.

"At least it's not drugs," said Susu.

As for whether Betty and Quentin preferred Theo rich or angry, they could not agree.

"It is as if his heart is hidden. Disappeared under a blanket where no one can see it," said Betty, adding, "I think he just wants to get away from us."

"Away from us?" said Quentin, astounded.

"Susu says this is what sixteen-year-olds are like, especially in the U.S. They are separating. It's their psychological stage."

Quentin shook his head. "And when do they stop?"

"I don't know."

His question hung in the air like the kind of smog that used to drift down from the Mainland and choke them. They tried to sleep.

They did not think Theo would use his car to leave them. There he was, though, two days later, packing up.

"Where are you going?" asked Betty.

"You cannot use our charge cards," warned Quentin.

But having his own money as he did, Theo just knit his eyebrows and kept packing. One duffel bag, two, three. Children his age did not believe in suitcases.

And the next morning, he really was gone.

"He made his bed," said Quentin quietly.

Of course, they were shaken up anyway. But the bed! They hadn't even known Theo knew how to make his bed.

"Complicit," he had called them. Complicit. And what was that he liked to yell?

Betty remembered. "I think it was 'Do you ever tell the truth?'"

"What truth?" Quentin said.

Betty kept it inside that she kept a lot of things inside.

Instead, she asked Theo's bed, Where are you, Theo? She asked the kitchen counter and the apartment buzzer, too. Where are you? Where are you? She did not tell any of her friends what had happened. Neither did she post anything about it on WeChat. She told his school he was sick. A fever and cough, she said, no loss of taste but they were having him tested for COVID. And yes, yes, of course, confining him to his room. The school was mostly interested in the confinement part of the story.

Besides that she and Quentin simply watched their chats and email, hoping. Theo would be back soon, they agreed. And just about any place was safer than New York. So that was good. If only they were among the friends on his Find My Friends app.

"He went to visit someone," they told Robert.

"But he was supposed to stay home," said Robert. "Everyone is."

"You're right," said Betty. "He was." And, "I hope he brought enough masks. I hope he is being careful. I hope he is using hand san."

She hoped, too, that Robert would know enough not to ask who Theo was going to visit. And, thankfully, he did know.

Instead, he said, "I'm sick of COVID. I want to play soccer. I want to see my friends." And, "I want a new dog."

"Is there something the matter with Bongbong?" Betty asked.

"I want an upgrade."

"An upgrade?" said Quentin.

"I don't want another of the same kind of dog. I want, like, an original dog."

He said this because Bongbong was not their first dog. Bongbong was a replacement dog they'd gotten after Yappy died, you might even say a carbon copy of Yappy, whom everyone in the family had liked. But of course, "everyone" had not included Robert, who hadn't been born yet, much less adopted. Betty could see his point in a way. Still. An upgrade?

What a way to think.

When Robert had wanted to be paid for making his bed, they had paid him. Because the maid used to get paid, he had argued, and that was true. It seemed fair. Then he had wanted to be paid for getting out of bed in preparation for making it. To which Quentin said okay without even asking Betty. Now Robert wanted to be paid for brushing his teeth.

"Does your price include flossing?" Quentin asked.

Meanwhile, Tina and Johnson were so upset when they heard about Theo that Betty did not even tell them about Bobby's torn-up letter, much less that Bobby had once told Betty she had written a last letter, as had many of the Hong Kong dissidents, just in case something happened to her. The letters declared that they were protesters and had not committed suicide—that being what they'd felt they had to write, given how many more people had been detained than were in jail. Given, that is, how many people had disappeared.

And later Betty thought she should have told them that on FaceTime—she should have! But at the time she didn't see how she could; they were so busy reassuring her that Theo wasn't going to disappear like Bobby. He wasn't, they said. He couldn't. Although—five days? She should hire a private detective right away, the way they should have with Bobby.

"Before she got too far away." Even after all these years there was a catch in Tina's voice.

"One thing good is that it is very difficult to transport a Miata to Hong Kong. So Theo probably didn't go there," said Johnson.

"If you don't want to call the detective, we can call for you," Tina said.

"In fact, we call right now," said Johnson.

It was everything Betty could do to divert them to the subject of Robert's demanding to be paid for everything. Finally, though, Tina said, "You know who gets paid for everything?"

"Who?" said Betty.

"American children," she said. "And let me tell you, if you let Robert become too American, you will regret it."

"Do you think so?" said Betty.

"You will! Your mother is right!" Johnson thundered. "Become American citizen is great. Hold American passport is great. But do not let Robert get American ideas. You know what they are, those American ideas?"

Betty waited.

"Twentieth century," he said. "They are one hundred percent twentieth century."

As for whether she should have told her parents that what Robert wanted money for was to support Black people, why would she do that? Knowing that they would have said, Black people! Only Americans are so concerned about Black people!

But this was what happened when you sent children to school in New York—they joined the People of Color club. No politics! Tina would have said, and Betty herself wanted to tell him, We are not people of color, Robert. We are rich.

But unfortunately, he was the president of the club. And thanks to COVID, the kids had nothing else to do but to Zoom and discuss whether or not they were racist. Robert said he was elected president because, being of Chinese origin, he was the most racist, as everyone agreed. The Chinese are the worst! they said.

Listening to which, Betty was happy for Robert that he had found a kind of acceptance Theo never had at his age. Still, like Susu, she wished they could have all just stayed in Hong Kong. In Hong Kong, there was no People of Color club because they were all the same color, and if you said bad things about white people, it wasn't racism, it was resistance, unless you said it to their face. Then it was speaking truth to power.

Now Quentin mused, "If I pay Robert five dollars to get up, and five dollars to brush his teeth, at least he will have some pocket money and not take up poker." He did not want Robert to catch the poker bug from Theo.

But Betty did not like Quentin's approach.

"In my opinion, it will make him as money-crazy as the rest of the family, including you," she said. "Please, please do not pay him anymore." But what is a mother but someone who cannot stop anyone?

Before Theo left, they had mostly noticed the ambulance sirens at night. Now that there was less yelling, though, the sirens seemed to go on all day as well. How long was this going to last, this New York "on pause"? And why was wearing a mask such a big deal in America? In Hong Kong, no one complained about their glasses fogging up. They just wore their masks, and not in such a way that their noses stuck out. Of course, as Quentin pointed out, their noses were smaller, and flatter noses fit under the masks better, too. Still.

Betty wrote to Robert's teacher, **Could you give him some extra work? Because your homework about the Canarsee tribe of the Delaware nation only took him a half hour to complete. That was better than the gravity assignment that took fifteen minutes, but nevermind. Please—we parents are going crazy.**

Of course, she knew Miss Strange was just going to write what she always wrote to what everyone knew she called "pushy Asian parents," namely, **The curriculum is age appropriate.** And so she did, though this time she added that there would be **NO CHANGE** to the no-grades-this-semester policy no matter how much extra work the kids did. Which Betty couldn't really blame her for saying, since some of the Asian parents really were complaining. What's more, as Miss Strange herself complained, it had been everything she could do to shift her entire class online, parents had no idea how stressful it was, especially since she had three children, four dogs, no husband, and a phobia about technology, which was why she went into teaching to begin with. However, she said finally, just this one time she would provide an extra-credit assignment for interested students.

Thank you, thank you, Betty typed. For she really was grateful.

If only the extra-credit assignment was not to tell a family mystery to a pet.

"It doesn't have to be a real pet," said Robert. "It can be an imaginary pet." And, "Miss Strange said parents could help."

"Parents could help"—Betty sighed. It was revenge. It was the revenge of Miss Strange.

"How about a story about your grandpa," Quentin said.

"How about a story about Yeye and Bongbong meeting in heaven? Yeye could feed him people food, and Bongbong could ask why he never got to eat food like that on earth."

"That's not a mystery," said Robert.

"It's a mystery to Bongbong," said Quentin, at whose feet Bongbong was even now sitting obediently, looking hopefully up at a cookie. His white tail thumped as if it had a special chip in it.

"And I don't want to use Bongbong anyway," said Robert. "Bongbong is a lapdog. I'm going to use an upgraded dog."

"Like?" said Betty.

"Like a German shepherd seeing-eye dog," said Robert.

"Do you know what a seeing-eye dog is?"

"It's a dog with superpowers." And true-fact finder that he was, he spoke with an air of authority.

"Well, a seeing-eye German shepherd would make the story more interesting," Betty conceded. It was going to be a long homework session, she could see.

Quentin left the room—having work to do, he said. How was it that he was now the boss of the business that she had founded over his strenuous objection? His bottom left an imprint on the leather stool seat, which was lilac to match the couch; the decorator did that.

"What's the dog's name going to be?" she asked, trying to be playful.

"His first name is Detective."

"And his last name?"

"Dog."

"So—Detective Dog?"

"Yes. His name is Detective Dog, and he is interested in missing people." Robert raised a big round magnifying glass to his eye—one of Quentin's, which he kept on the kitchen counter in case he ever wanted to do a crossword puzzle.

Betty stayed calm. "Theo isn't missing," she said. "Theo is coming back."

"From his friend's house," said Robert.

"Yes."

Robert gave her his quick look. Then he squinted through the magnifying glass, which fit neatly under the part of his hair he'd cut off.

"I want you to tell me a mystery so I can solve it," he said.

With Theo gone, it was as if she and Robert were on a desert island in that *Animal Crossing* game, except that instead of protest banners, they had sirens. He was so quiet and intense the whole apartment was quiet and intense.

"Is it my job to help you solve a mystery or my job to tell you one?" she asked.

"To tell me one."

"Are you sure that's what Miss Strange said?"

"Yes."

Betty sighed. "I don't know how good a mystery it will be, Detective. I'm not a storyteller like you."

"It doesn't have to be good," he said. And, "We can start today and finish tomorrow. I'll ask you questions."

"Well, okay." How could she say no? She thought, then began, "Once upon a time there was a number-one daughter who everyone agreed was the best daughter in the family."

Robert cocked his head. "What do you mean, the best daughter?"

"I mean that out of three sisters, she was the smartest. She got into all those top schools. Andover and MIT and Harvard Business School. In fact, everywhere she applied, she got in. She got an internship on Wall Street, and then she got a job on Wall Street. She was making a lot of money. But all of a sudden one day, she dropped out and ran off with a drummer."

"Why a drummer?"

"I don't know. All I know is that when her family later heard that she had left the drummer, they celebrated! They had a dinner for her, even though she could not come. But after that, she did not come back. In fact, she disappeared completely."

"Like Theo?"

Theo has not disappeared, she wanted to say.

But instead she said, "She went somewhere—no one knew where. For many years her parents cried. Then one day, guess what? I saw her again."

"Are you in the story?"

Quentin came back into the kitchen for a bag of chips. There was a lunchbox-size bag, but he took a large one—meaning, *don't bother me.*

"Are you in the story?" Detective Dog asked again when Quentin left.

"Yes, Detective," she admitted. "It was almost by mistake that I saw her a couple of years ago. We were about to move to New York, but we still had a business in Kunshan and sometimes stayed in Shanghai, as you probably remember. In the French Concession, where there are a lot of old European buildings, and restaurants and cafés and yoga studios. Do you remember?"

He nodded. "Shanghai was great."

Betty smiled. "It was. And, well, one day I went out to a café, and who did I see? She did not look the same as the last time I saw her. The last time I saw her she had blond hair and tattoos and a gas-mask pouch. Now she had plain hair and plain clothes, as if she were in disguise. We had some coffee. Of course, she was surprised to see me, too. I waited for her to tell me what she was up to. But she did not tell me right away. Instead, she raised an eyebrow and tilted her head. Meaning, there were cameras everywhere. I told her I needed to stop by my apartment, which

I did, so that I could 'forget' my phone there, and no one could trace me with it. Then I met her in a park. I was not surprised to hear that she was trying to evade the police. Because actually I had seen her once before, when she was involved in the protests in Hong Kong."

"You saw her before but didn't tell anyone?"

Betty looked away.

"Why?"

"Because I promised."

"So you knew other people she knew. Who would have wanted to know."

Betty hesitated but finally nodded.

"But you're telling me now."

"It's your homework," she said. Though what she really wanted to say was, Because you'll find out one day, I can see. Because you are like a mind-reading hat. And because I don't want you to leave one day, like Theo.

"And why didn't she want you to tell?"

"Because the Chinese government likes to know all your family members. So if it isn't enough to pressure you, they can pressure them."

"Meaning, it was her family you didn't tell."

She nodded.

"Who were your family, too."

She nodded.

"Meaning, she was your sister."

Somehow it was a shock to hear it aloud.

"Yes," she said bravely. "Who, you know, did not want to be in trouble anymore. Or at least that's what she told me. She said she had come to Shanghai to try and give up her dangerous work. In fact, she had been effective—very effective, I think. She was so smart. And for a while she had believed that things would work out—as a lot of people did. If nothing else, there were so many people involved in the protests. How could Beijing arrest so many people? They thought they couldn't be ignored.

"But in fact, they got shut down hard, and now all she could think about was 2047, when Hong Kong would be swallowed up by the Mainland forever. And the funny thing is that the way she said that, for the first time I also just wished the Hong Kong we grew up in was not gone. Of course, back when the Mainland first started to rise up, we were proud to see Chinese people stand up to the West. Talk about bullies! The West always had to humiliate everyone and, by the way, now that Hong Kong needs help, do you see them? But in the end, the Mainland turned on us, too—they attacked us the way they fired on their own people in Tiananmen. Of course, you were a baby, so you didn't know too much about what was happening."

"I am a dog," he reminded her.

"Oh, that's right. I mean, you were just a puppy," she said. Playful, the way she was supposed to be.

He gave a woof.

"You were only two and a half. But Theo never got over leaving his school and his friends, especially since he got bullied in Vancouver."

"That's why he became a bully."

"He's not a bully."

"And how was Shanghai going to help her give up her work?"

"I think we should take a break here." Betty glanced at the oven clock. "Time to start dinner. When is your assignment due?"

"Next week."

"So we don't have to do the whole mystery today."

He agreed.

And when Quentin reemerged, they made an American-style tuna noodle casserole with cream of mushroom soup. Then they played video games and looked for new recipes to try. Robert wanted to make peanut butter Snickers cheesecake whoopie pies, which Betty said they could if he would do a yoga video with her once a day without pay. He said he would.

"Of course, the real mystery is where Theo is," she told Quentin in bed that night.

"He'll come back."

"I don't know. He has all that money." She pulled the quilt up under her chin; though it was nowhere near summer, Quentin liked the AC up high sometimes—it reminded him of Hong Kong. "And now Robert's homework."

"Why don't you charge him for every five minutes of the story?"

"I can't charge him," said Betty. "I'm his mother."

"He'll forget about it." Quentin yawned.

But the next day Robert ate his cereal without a spoon, with his snout in his bowl.

"Detective Dog here, reporting for duty," he said. He licked his lips with his tongue.

"In this house dogs eat dog food," warned Betty. "Purina Puppy Chow."

"Not detective dogs," he said, crunching. "Detective dogs eat granola. So why did your sister move to Shanghai?"

Betty sighed, adding a scoop of vanilla ice cream to her decaf. She used to only allow herself this in the afternoon, but since Theo left, she had been allowing herself to have it in the morning, too.

Detective Dog raised his magnifying glass, which somehow seemed bigger today than it was yesterday. "Why didn't she just move to New York?"

Betty drank—slurped, really. "Because, Detective, even if way back when she had married the drummer and become a

U.S. citizen, which anyone else would have done, she could have had trouble getting an exit visa. And, anyway, she hadn't. She had to hide in China someplace. And so she thought she would hide with her boyfriend's family outside of Shanghai."

"She had a boyfriend?"

Betty drank, then answered, "He was also a dissident—played the guitar and apparently knew how to talk to journalists and get them to write things. I guess you could call him a kind of press agent. But his family was originally from this little village. And so the plan was to go live there for a while—to retire from protesting and live a simple life with chickens and a garden. Of course, a lot of the protesters were worried about getting arrested; they were worried they would be tried in a court on the Mainland. Some tried to escape by boat to Taiwan. But she thought that if she and her boyfriend just kept quiet, the government might realize they were done causing trouble. And then she thought she might be able to finally reconnect with our family. She said it was torture being separated, and that she had never thought we would be separated this long."

"And then what happened?"

"Well, the boyfriend's family had no money. So she decided to do some teaching, first in a little school, and then in an international school. English language and U.S. history, since she had, after all, studied in the U.S. And these were international kids who could use some history beyond, you know, George Washington and Abe Lincoln."

"And then?"

"Well, she had a spy in her class. The spy was up front about sharing things with her father. My father this, my father that, she would say—not to scare Bobby, exactly, so much as to put her on notice. Bobby just shrugged it off. She said there were informants in all the classes."

"So this was Aunt Bobby?"

Betty started a little but nodded. There it was. She had not meant to say Bobby's name, but she had.

"The missing one no one talks about?"

Betty nodded again.

"Can I have some milkshake?"

She pushed her coffee forward. It really was practically a milkshake, what with all the melted ice cream.

Detective Dog slurped. "And so, what about the spy?" he said.

"Well, one day, Bobby taught Thoreau's essay 'Civil Disobedience'—a famous essay about disobeying the law when your conscience won't let you just go along. She did not think this was so sensitive; after all, the point of the discussion was not whether the Chinese should disobey the law—she knew better than to encourage anything like that. The point was how important that idea was to Americans. And she was cautious. She did not use the words 'civil disobedience' in the file name, for example. She called it 'Thoreau.' Luckily, too, the spy happened to be absent the day she taught the essay. But then the spy came to office hours. And as Bobby explained the essay, the spy recorded her. With the result that she was invited to tea by the authorities." Betty paused.

"So what's the matter with that?"

"Tea is never just tea. It's intimidation. Which worried her enough that she asked me not to tell anyone. Though she wanted me to know."

"That?"

"That they might think she would never stop. That they might think she was the kind who would always stoke the fire under the cauldron. The kind who would not only make trouble but also spread trouble."

"And then?"

Betty got herself another scoop of ice cream.

"And then?" Detective Dog asked again.

"Well, and then I believe she was arrested. Every now and then I wrote to her boyfriend and asked if he had written any new songs. And if he said yes, I asked if they were happy songs or sad songs. But he always answered, Not too happy. Then he asked what you were up to."

"Changing the subject, you mean."

Betty drank.

"And what about the letter?"

She startled. Had Robert overheard her and Quentin talking? "I have not received a letter," she said.

"Interesting," he said.

She said it again. "I have not received a letter."

But there was his quick look, until finally she admitted, "There was a letter. But I did not receive it because it was torn up."

"Do you know what it said?"

As Detective Dog held the magnifying glass up to his face once again, Betty heard Theo. *Did you ever speak up? Do you ever tell the truth?* Outside, the sirens went on and on.

"In Shanghai, Bobby told me that she had once written a letter to say goodbye just in case, and that she had told her boyfriend to make sure we got it if the time came. A last letter, she called it."

"So was that the letter?"

"I don't know, Detective."

"Why was it torn up?"

A ghost town. She wished they could all move to a ghost town.

"I think because Uncle Arnie knew it would break our hearts," she said finally.

"Uncle Arnie was the messenger."

" 'The Chinese government likes to know all your family members,' " he said.

"Yes. And here you are safe. So it worked. But she loved true facts, you know. She spoke up. She wasn't like me."

"You speak up, too," said Robert.

But Betty shook her head no. "Not like Bobby. She was the best of us. And you," she said, "you, Detective Dog, are her son."

"Yes. Also he maybe knew in his heart that in our hearts we already knew."

"So why did he tell you he had it at all?"

The ambulances. The sirens. *Now you know why your grand-mother always says, No politics,* she wanted to say. Because that was the moral of the story. *No politics.*

Instead she said, "Because some things you cannot keep inside." She watched the strobe lights move along the tops of their windows.

They sped up then slowed then sped up again as Detective Dog pressed his nose to the magnifying glass.

"Why do you always call me Robert?" he asked, his nose flat and distorted. "Why do you never call me Bobby?"

If she weren't crying, she might have been able to answer.

"Is it because you promised my mother?" he asked. He was still holding up the glass; the sirens went and went.

"She was the best of us," Betty managed. "The smartest and the bravest."

"Was." Robert put down the magnifying glass, pulled at his shirt sleeve, and wiped his eyes on the stretched-out material.

"We don't actually know," she said. "We may never know." She tried to hug him but he struggled away.

"My name is not Detective Dog," he said, his nose in his shirt.

"No," she said. And, trying to be playful, she said, "To begin with you are a boy, not a dog."

"My name is Bobby Koo," he said.

"She was trying to protect you."

"Maybe Uncle Arnie will tell us where she is."

She tried again to hug him but hugged his shirt more than his small body. "And maybe Theo will come back," she said.

The sirens went and went.

THE RESISTERS

The time: not so long from now. The place: AutoAmerica, a country surveilled by one "Aunt Nettie," a Big Brother that is part artificial intelligence, part internet, and oddly human—even funny. The people: divided. The "angelfair" Netted have jobs and, what with the country half underwater, literally occupy the high ground. The Surplus live on swampland if they're lucky, on water if they're not. The story: To a Surplus couple—he once a professor, she still a lawyer—is born a girl, Gwen, with a golden arm. Her teens find her happily playing in an underground baseball league, but when AutoAmerica faces ChinRussia in the Olympics, Gwen finds herself in dangerous territory, playing ball with the Netted even as her mother battles this apartheid-like society in court. Provocative, moving, and yet paradoxically buoyant, The Resisters is the story of one family struggling to maintain their humanity in circumstances that threaten their every value.

Fiction

WORLD AND TOWN

Hattie Kong, a retired teacher and a descendant of Confucius, has decided that it's time to start over. She moves to the peaceful New England town of Riverlake, a place that once represented the rock-solid base of American life. Instead of quietude, Hattie discovers a town challenged by cell-phone towers, chain stores, and struggling farms. Soon Hattie is joined by an immigrant Cambodian family on the run and—quite unexpectedly—Carter Hatch, a love from her past. As each character seeks to make a new start on life, World and Town asks deep, absorbing questions about religion, love, home, and meaning.

Fiction

THE GIRL AT THE BAGGAGE CLAIM
Explaining the East-West Culture Gap

As East and West become more and more entwined, we also continue to baffle one another. What's more important—self-sacrifice or self-definition? Do we ultimately answer to something larger than ourselves—a family, a religion, a troop? Or is our mantra "To thine own self be true"? Gish Jen, drawing on a trove of personal accounts and cutting-edge research, shows how our worldviews are shaped by what cultural psychologists call "independent" and "interdependent" models of selfhood. Coloring what we perceive, remember, do, make, and tell, imbuing everything from our ideas about copying to our conceptions of human rights, these models help explain why the United States produced Apple while China created Alibaba—and what that might mean for our shared future. As engaging as it is fascinating, *The Girl at the Baggage Claim* is a book that profoundly transforms our understanding of ourselves and our time.

Social Science

ALSO AVAILABLE

The Love Wife
Mona in the Promised Land
Typical American
Who's Irish?

VINTAGE CONTEMPORARIES
Available wherever books are sold.
vintagebooks.com

Acknowledgments

Heartfelt thanks to the many readers whose experience, expertise, and discernment have enriched this manuscript, including Nancy Berliner, Margot Livesey, Mary Kay Magistad, Martha Minow, Jane Qiu, Louise Radin, Claire Thomas, and Ellen Winner. I am grateful, too, to Ann Close and LuAnn Walther, whose steady support has sustained me for decades now, as well as to Victoria Pearson, Dan Kirschen and Todd Portnowitz, whose indefatigable attention and faith have been critical. As for my children, Luke and Paloma, and my extraordinary husband, David, I can only say yet once again that in writing as in life, I owe you everything.